CHANGE PARTNERS

Change Partners

Cathryn Cooper

HEADLINE
Liaison

First published in 1997
by HEADLINE BOOK PUBLISHING

A HEADLINE LIAISON paperback

10 9 8 7 6 5 4 3 2 1

ISBN 0 7472 5401 X

Typeset at The Spartan Press Ltd,
Lymington, Hants

Printed and bound in Great Britain by
Mackays of Chatham PLC, Chatham, Kent

HEADLINE BOOK PUBLISHING
A division of Hodder Headline PLC
338 Euston Road
London NW1 3BH

Change Partners

Chapter 1

MICHAEL'S STORY

It was Michael who started it really. They were all at the country club and had just finished showering after a workout in the gym followed by a swim and a sauna. After washing away the sweat, they were mellow and glowing, their outer and inner selves resplendent with the illusion of renewed vigour.

Perhaps their nakedness had something to do with it, symbolising the putting aside of their inhibitions as well as their clothes. All the same, Michael initiated the telling of secrets with a simple enough question.

'How old were you the first time you had it, Jamie?'

Shaking his sandy-haired head, Jamie's smile turned to a chuckle. 'Young but virile. What's it to you?'

Michael's expression reflected the mood of the moment as he stretched his well-worked-out torso in the sequestered privacy of the men's changing room. They were all boys together, confident of their own sexual prowess, but still possessing an adolescent curiosity about that of others.

'Natural interest.' Michael shrugged cheerily. 'Anyway its all water under the bridge. We can all look back on our successes and failures now in the light of experience and, boy, have I had some experience!'

'Okay, okay. If you're the great super-stud, Mickey boy, then why so nosy about my first time?'

Michael got up from the bench, stretched, and turned his eyes to his biceps as he flexed his right arm, his muscles tensing and relaxing as he curled and uncurled his fingers. His penis quivered as he did so. After exercising and showering, Michael always did his cooling-down stretches naked. The others did their best to appear disinterested, yet it was hard not to admire his body and wonder just how many women had admired it too.

'I'm only asking out of interest,' Michael went on. 'Nothing wrong with comparing notes is there? Anyway, who's to say you can't teach me something?'

'Tell you mine any time,' said Thomas in that calm, low voice of his. Leaning his head back against the coolness of a metal locker, he closed his eyes and smiled. He had a white towel wrapped around his waist. His flesh looked a deeper brown against it than it actually was. He had a few dark brown moles scattered over his shoulders and down his back – like beauty spots. 'I can see it all now,' he said softly. 'Firm round bottoms, long, girlish legs.'

'And that was only the boys!' It was Michael who said that. Michael who was so sure of his looks, his masculinity, his sexual prowess. Michael, who was married to Josie, an artistic and charming wife; so gifted, so pleasant, and so long-suffering.

They laughed like men do when they're together on their own territory, where a sign on the outside of a door confirms the fact: Changing Room. Men Only.

Jamie, looking thoughtful, rolled his bulging shoulder muscles. As he did so, his chest hair – which was as much as Michael's and Thomas's combined – moved in shuddering waves. Like Thomas, he too was wearing a white towel around his thighs. But Jamie did not like Michael to outdo him. He flung it to one side and exposed the crinkly hair that clustered thickly in his groin. His cock was stiff, begging the others to look at it. They appeared not to, but that did not mean they had not noticed.

2

Jamie tried to look unconcerned. 'Interesting to think back,' he said casually. 'Interesting to wonder what we would have done if we'd had the experience then that we have now. Would we have married the women we did?'

A quick furtive look came to Michael's eyes, then was gone. A more gentle look came to Thomas's. Jamie saw them both, but did not comment. He smiled a satisfied smile beneath the partial camouflage of his sandy moustache. 'Tell me how old you were when you first used your weapon.' He directed his question at Michael.

Taken aback for the moment, Michael ran his fingers through his blue-black hair whilst he collected his thoughts. Then he fingered the well-defined and exceedingly tight muscles of his stomach.

'I was young,' he said rather carelessly. 'When I was younger, I'd already peered down a few knickers for a lollipop or the privilege of letting a girl see what I had down mine. You know, the usual stuff. As time went on, I also got to feeling their hairless little quims and squeezing their adolescent breasts. They're hard at that age. Small too, but the nipples are large and soft and their pubic hair is real soft – a bit like cotton wool.'

He paused as he savoured the memories. How sweet those moments were, how arousing to a penis untouched, unkissed, and unused.

'Go on.' Jamie had sat himself on the opposite end of the bench on which Thomas was stretched out. He was leaning forward, hands on knees, his pale eyes all attention. Thomas appeared to be listening, but his eyes were still closed and his head rested against the metal locker once more.

To Michael it was no longer of any importance who was listening. From deep within he dredged his thoughts and restarted his story. Once began, it was almost as though his two friends were no longer there. It was as though he were back at school again, and the games teacher from the girls' school had come to take the boys swimming because Mister Grant, the games master, had gone on honeymoon. He explained that to them and they mouthed noises of approval.

'She said she wanted us to do the breast stroke,' Michael began. 'Two lengths, green team only, then back to her.

'Even before she blew her whistle to start us off, I was struck by the way she said the word "breast". It was stressed as though she hoped that someone might notice. Well, I noticed. I smiled, saw her glance my way, then glance away again. She made me feel warm. I felt special.

'Like the other boys, I dived into the pool and, putting as much effort into my strokes as possible, I swam the required two lengths.

'I touched home first, and after shaking the water from my hair and face I thrust my fist triumphantly into the air and looked up. I couldn't believe what I saw.

'Miss Redpath was wearing a pair of navy blue items that were a cross between shorts and culottes. They had very baggy legs and came to about halfway down her thighs. She had white plimsolls and socks on as well and her legs were a very soft brown. I guessed she was that colour all over and just thinking about her naked body made me instantly hard.

'Her legs were spread to brace herself and she leant forward so that her whistle rested on her knees. Above, I could see her brown thighs going on and on until they met a cloud of dense black hair.'

Michael closed his eyes and took in a deep breath. 'For the first time I caught the mysterious sea-green scent of a grown woman and saw what she has between her legs. Crisp black hair curled over plump lips from which a small, pink button peeked through.

'Despite the title "Miss" I could not believe that she had not yet been invaded by a hard, hot penis. In fact, I was convinced that she had had many. But had she been bereft of such intrusion of late? Was that the reason for her lewd behaviour with a bunch of adolescent boys?

'She saw me looking, and I blushed.'

'Were you a wee bit embarrassed?' It was Jamie that asked.

Michael shook his head. 'I don't think so. I think it wasn't just my cheeks that were on fire, but my body too. Besides that, my swimming trunks suddenly seemed far too small for what was in them.'

There was a low murmur of ribald laughter.

Michael, encouraged by their obvious enjoyment of his tale, continued. 'She said, "Well done, Michael. You did that very well. No doubt you can do something else very well too.' Michael paused. 'My heart thumped as I considered what she might mean. "How about a crawl?" she said.

'Her suggestion was not exactly a disappointment. Like her intonation of the word "breast", I was sure there was something else meant by what she said. But I did the crawl just as she asked. I knew she was watching me every inch of the way. When I got back to where she was standing, I was doubly sure. Normally, a teacher would move and direct attention to other pupils. But not Miss Redpath.

'Again, I found myself looking up Miss Redpath's shorts, and, again, I caught the whiff and sight of her sex.

'At the end of the lesson, she sought me out, told me not to go into the changing room but to stay and do some more swimming.'

Michael broke off recounting his tale, threw back his head and intoned her name in a low, long moan. As he did so, his penis stiffened and moved slightly. 'Miss Redpath! Miss Redpath! Oh, I remember you so well. What a woman!'

He paused again and smiled dreamily as though he were recalling her more clearly to mind. Before they could get impatient with waiting, he resumed his story.

'She had chocolate-dark eyes. I remember them gleaming with admiration as they ran over me. I was a well-developed lad. I wasn't as fit as I am now, but I had a mature, taut body, good muscle tone, and strong thighs. I wore my hair a little too long. I remember it curling around my neck. Later on, when we came to know each other better, I remember her fingers squeezing the water out of it. But not then. That was later.'

'Never mind you.' It was Jamie again. He sounded impatient. 'What about her? What was she like? What happened next?'

Michael smiled smugly. Jamie was hanging on his every word. It was easy to imagine his penis erecting beneath the soft towel wrapped loosely around him.

Thomas, on the other hand was listening but seemed more abject, more thoughtful about what he was hearing.

Unperturbed, Michael went on.

'I remember her skin being as smooth and as silky brown as coffee laced with cream and brandy. I remember the huskiness of her voice.

'"You are a very strong swimmer," she said. "I think you could go far if you put your mind to it. Have you considered having extra tuition?"

'I couldn't believe what I was hearing. I was excited, but I managed to reply, "I would like to learn more if the chance arises. So far I've never found anyone willing to teach me."

'She smiled and suggested we start right away.

'What she taught me was not on the school curriculum.

'Being only a young boy, I was apprehensive as she locked the door to the baths.

'She told me to get out of the pool. Her look was appraising as she walked slowly round me in a complete circle. I remember that one finger tapped thoughtfully at her lips. Every so often, she raised her eyes and grinned impishly.

'When she spoke, I felt I would melt. "Now. Let me see all that you have. I need to know every imperfection in your structure, your bones, your muscles, every asset of your body."

'I knew what she might be implying, but did I have it right? I mean, I didn't want to do the wrong thing. After all, she was a teacher. Did she really mean she wanted to see me all over? *All over?* Was she really asking me to drop my swimming trunks? I plucked up the courage and asked her.

'She did not falter. "Of course. How else can I undertake a constructive critique? Take off your pants."

'With trembling hands, I carried out her instructions. I pulled my wet trunks to my ankles. She was behind me as I bent over so she had a full view of my hanging testicles. I could feel her eyes upon them and I wondered what she was thinking. Such thoughts made me hot and excited.

'I stood up straight as she came round in front of me. I was aware that my penis was thrusting forward. I could have hung a coat on it! She noticed too. Her tongue rolled along her lips and her eyes were very wide, very bright.

'Suddenly, her eyes narrowed. "I need to feel how hard you are. Do you mind?"

'Shivering with anticipation, I shook my head and avoided looking down. Something new, strange, and exceedingly wonderful was happening at the top of my legs. Balls that had been made of mere flesh, now felt as though they were made of lead. A penis that had mostly lain hidden among its crown of hair, except when coaxed into an erection under the sheets of my bed, now became hard.

'She looked and sounded pleased. "Your muscle tone is very good. Michael, my dear boy, you are so well developed for your age."

'I said yes. I remember it being hard to say, but I concentrated hard. As I concentrated, I smelt her again. The scent of her sex was in my mind. Blood rushed from my head to my cock as she ran her hand over my shoulder, down my arm, and across my chest.

'I trembled and closed my eyes. That only made things more intense. Without seeing what was happening to me, my other senses took over and my erection got stronger, more demanding.

'She slid her hands down my back. She moved behind me and placed both hands on my buttocks; fingered them, caressed them. As I clenched my muscles, my cock shot forward. I could almost have come at the feel of her fingers. She went on stroking my behind, then ran her hands around the front, slid them over my belly, then took my cock in both hands.

'I remember groaning. I remember closing my eyes then groaning again. I remember opening my eyes and seeing the top of her head sink away from me as she slid downwards and licked my foreskin so it crumpled away from the rest of my member.

'Her tongue licked me from the very tip of my cock to the very root. At any moment I could have spilled my load, but I didn't want to shame myself before her. I wanted her to be pleased with me, to heap praises on my head and tell me how good I was at it, and how much better I would become. I was like that when I was younger. I always wanted to be the best at whatever I did.'

Jamie and Thomas exchanged glances. Michael hadn't changed much.

So engrossed was he in his own story, that he did not notice their wry smiles.

'She licked between my thighs and sucked at my balls before she raised herself and took my cock into her mouth. I was shivering like a jelly and my knees would have knocked together if she hadn't been partly between them.

'Perhaps it was because it was the very first time a woman had done that to me, but I still look on that first fellatio as the best one I ever had. Or perhaps it was because it was the very first time.

'She held my balls in her hand as she sucked at me. Her other hand held my behind, gripping my buttock so that she could move me backwards and forwards to suit the dictates of her mouth and her inclination.

'When I came, I thought she would eat me. Again and again I felt her sucking on me with all the intensity of a high-powered vacuum cleaner.

'Not a drop of semen remained on my flesh once I retrieved it from her mouth.

'I sighed, and she kissed my lips as she patted my now soft member.

'I told her it was lovely and asked when she would do it again. I remember her raising her eyebrows.

' "Immediately," she said, and took off her clothes.

'Just as I had guessed, she was lightly brown all over. My eyes opened wide and my cock stiffened again as I looked at her. What a sight she was! Her breasts were like small plums tipped with purple nipples. Her belly had a gentle roundness about it, and her pubic hair was the most abundant I have ever seen.

'She told me to follow her.

'Up on the diving board, she turned, braced herself on the side bars, and spread her legs over them.

' "Look," she said. "This is what you are having now."

'That pungent smell was stronger. Her purple-red lips were now open to me. Her most secret place was mine for the taking.

'Already a decent erection was returning and, once it was hard enough, I approached and, with her help, pushed my way into her.

'The urge to fuck was upon me. It happened as if the skill to fuck had always been there, as though I'd been born with it. There I was, no longer a boy but not yet a man, jerking my hips backwards and forwards, burying my juvenile erection into her moist and wide-open vagina.

'All the while she hung there for me over those chromium rails whilst I pushed myself into her, rolled her breasts in my hands, and squeezed her nipples with my fingers.

'The heat of her sex, of her womanhood was all around me, drawing me in, devouring me for her pleasure. In return, the warm moistness of her sexual muscles coaxed my climax out of me as no hand or mouth could do.

'I came into her and my shouts of sheer joy echoed round and around the high-vaulted ceiling of the swimming bath. As I came she closed her eyes and groaned long and low.

'It was incredible. Incredible. Something I will always remember.'

Jamie shook his head. 'Incredible alright. Are you telling the truth?'

'Would I lie?'

'Why should you?' Thomas spoke quietly as he got up from the bench where he had been sitting.

Not once, Michael noticed, did Thomas look his way. It unnerved him, but he did not allow himself to be ruffled.

'I've no reason to lie. You asked, I answered.' He patted Jamie on the arm. 'Your turn next.'

Jamie laughed then smiled broadly. 'Sure. I'll tell you on Wednesday. That's when I'm here next.'

Michael slapped him on the back affectionately. 'Hold you to it.'

Chapter 2

Michael smiled to himself as he drove home. Those listening could not have known that he had put into words a fantasy he had enacted over and over again in his mind for very many years.

At school there had indeed been a teacher who stood spread-legged at the end of the pool. She had indeed been a lovely creature, her skin a tawny brown by virtue of her mixed parentage. Her eyes had been dark brown, her lips full and her hair a crinkly mass of blackness that fell to halfway down her back.

The boys, him included, had looked up her wide-legged shorts and imagined they could see far more than was actually visible in the musty darkness at the top of her legs. Miss Redpath had been the stuff teenage fantasies were made of, a useful adjunct to a throbbing penis and a hard-working hand. That fantasy had stayed with him. The story he had told his friends had been the imaginings of what they might have done together, not what had actually happened. The truth of his first time was far less exciting.

Deirdre Anderson, the sister of one of his friends, had been besotted with him. She had ginger hair and dusky green eyes. She also wore spectacles which left a red indent over the bridge of her nose. Curiosity had overcome taste when it came to shedding his virginity. Deirdre had been a lily waiting to be plucked, and he had plucked her. Because he didn't want to be seen out with someone who wasn't exactly top drawer when it came to looks, he had suggested that they meet in the garage at the back of his house which backed onto the same lane as hers did. It was the first time in his life that he knew himself to be on a sure thing.

His parents and her parents were out, and her brother had a passion for cricket. Michael had been given a ticket for the county match for his birthday. With saintly expression, he had handed the ticket over to his friend who was gullible enough not to doubt Michael's protestations that he wasn't really feeling up to it and, besides, he was looking forward to rugger and the winter.

Nothing could have been further from the truth.

In the garage, Deirdre allowed herself to be pressed tightly up against the cold grey of the concrete wall.

Fumbling beneath her school skirt, Michael had grown more and more excited, his kisses getting wetter and wetter as he rammed his tongue into Deirdre's open mouth.

In order to prevent her crying out, he had sucked determinedly on her lips as he slid his hand into her white cotton knickers and his fingers into the slippery flesh that nestled within her sexual divide.

Deirdre's one redeeming feature had been that she wore stockings rather than tights, and the feel of her adolescent thighs had fired his enthusiasm so his cock was good and ready to penetrate the unknown and untried.

Slipping his fingers beneath the crotch of her knickers, he had pushed her legs apart with his free hand and his knee. Elation had surged through his bloodstream as the head of his penis had parted the lips of her sex.

Freeing her breasts from the constraints of her bra was easy once his penis was in her. Big breasts tumbled into his hands and her nipples stiffened, reminding him of ripe acorns.

As the fierceness of his thrusts increased, her ample hips began to jerk towards him and her pubic hair mingled with his.

It had been the first time and Michael had been a novice in the field of human physiology and erogenous zones. But one thing he had been aware of, even at that age, was the fundamental facts of procreation. He was well aware that what went up could result in a nine-month foetus coming down, a fact he wished at all costs to avoid. He had no intention of becoming a teenage bridegroom. Neither did he wish to become a father.

Fast and furious, his semen began to rise up the length of his member. Excited as he was, breath quick, face hot, he kept his head. Just as his semen was about to spurt from his end, he pulled it out, leaving Deirdre sobbing with regret, and let his fluid fall into the pool of oil left on the floor by his father's car.

Deirdre continued to bemoan her dissatisfaction and he couldn't quite understand why. Clitoris was a name he only vaguely knew. He wasn't really sure where it was situated among those fleshy lips, or what its function was. Such information only became clearer as he got older. So poor Deirdre was left bereft of climax, her sex slippery with juice, and one leg of her knickers torn beyond repair.

Michael sighed and shook his head. Deirdre and the true story of his first time was not for repeating but, thankfully, Miss Redpath had still been in his head.

His eyes sparkled and he began to laugh as he remembered the envy on the faces of his friends.

Chapter 3

Soft white curtains were billowing over a honey-coloured pine floor in a white-painted studio at the house Michael shared with his wife, Josie. Michael was being the perfect host, refilling glasses as he explained his wife's paintings and sculptures to his business guests.

True to form Josie had provided a superb dinner. As well as being a skilled artist, Michael's wife was also an excellent chef. Her Seafood Thermidor had been exquisite, her Steak Italienne tender and tasty. After the refreshing contrst of melon and apricot sorbet, the brandy and coffee had gone down well – very well indeed.

'Lucky you,' said Alan Frinton, Executive Director of Far East Investments, the company Michael was presently wooing. 'What joy it must be to have a wife who is gifted, a good cook and beautiful.'

He said this as he admired an erotic terracotta figurine that stood on an ebony plinth. He did not see the lie in Michael's eyes, he only heard him agree.

'You are so right. Josie is a treasure in more ways than one. With each showing of her paintings, her own personal treasure trove increases. I can honestly say her bank account is bigger than mine. If I didn't do what I do, you could almost term me a kept man.'

Alan Frinton laughed as his eyes followed the slender woman with the striking red hair. He was not entirely fooled. In his head he was comparing the dynamic, extrovert Michael with the ephemeral Josie. She was too pale for Michael, he decided, too sensual, and far too clever. *If only*, he thought to himself, smiling benignly, but he did not comment. He was not alone in admiring Josie.

'Has she shown her work in many exhibitions?' asked Doug Hammond, the most important man in the company – Managing Director and Chairman all wrapped into one.

Hammond was admiring a pastel nude that echoed the cubism of Picasso but had a certain originality; triangles of colour and light accentuated the curves of the woman's body. It was titled Ashanti.

'Three so far. But there will be more. In fact, she's off to Cornwall shortly to make a personal appearance at the new place in St Ives. It should be very successful if her previous exhibitions are anything to go by.'

There was a certain pride in his voice when he spoke of his wife. Josie was part of his success story. When he'd first met her and asked her out, she had turned him down, told him he was much too much of a womaniser for her. And anyway, she told him she loved someone else. But he'd been persistent; had even given her the impression he'd become celibate on her account. Of course he hadn't, but he'd never let on that he seldom went to bed alone when he was away on business trips.

The day came when the man Josie loved seemed to have disappeared from the scene.

Always adept at turning a sad situation to advantage, Michael had swooped. With a keen resolve he didn't know he had, he pursued her, wore down her resistance until making her his own became as fixed an objective in his mind as being top salesman, most promising executive, and probable director. Josie had become his wife.

Michael's success within the company had soared. So-cialising and entertaining became a way of life. Josie had been a worthwhile investment, but Michael's tastes were diverse and wide-reaching. Eventually, he had succumbed to more colourful women and more vigorous sex. His life had divided into two. Josie was home, and home only melted into his professional life when he allowed it to.

Dutiful as she was, Josie played her part well. She came up behind them as they admired her paintings and asked if everything was alright. Asked them if she could get them anything else – anything at all. She smiled warmly as if she were there just to be beautiful for them, just to be willing.

After the guests had gone, the phone rang. Josie heard it from the kitchen; heard Michael pick it up; heard his voice drop in volume.

Eyes blinking rapidly and face flushed, she walked out into the garden, the white curtains swirling behind her. Shoulders rigid, she stood still on the patio and waited for his footsteps, for the hesitation in his voice.

'The roses look so beautiful,' she said softly. 'And their smell is quite impossible to describe.'

He came up behind her, rested his hands just below her shoulders. His palms were warm, yet she wanted to shiver.

'I have to go out. That was Alan. Our guests have got more stamina than we gave them credit for. They're having a drink at the Hyperion and fancy having a flutter. They've asked me to join them.'

'I see. And you have to go, of course.'

'Of course I do, darling. It's business.'

Not once did she turn to look at him. Not once did her voice betray what she might be feeling.

The fact that she hadn't seemed to notice what he said unnerved Michael. Just because there was no accusation in her eyes didn't mean he didn't feel guilty. On the contrary, receiving no response made him feel more guilty. But why should he? Hadn't he given her a plausible excuse? He'd been to the Hyperion before, and so had she. While he had played the tables with Jamie and Crystal, she sat on a bar stool with Thomas, Crystal's husband, and Mariana, Jamie's wife – until Mariana had gone off to dance with some young black stud. Calm down, he said to himself. The

Hyperion is a plausible enough excuse.

But that was it. That was all it was. An excuse, and although Josie never questioned the truth of it, she never voiced any objection. Such disinterest made Michael suspicious that she knew.

Before anything could be hinted at, he left.

Josie heard his car start and, as it drove away, the squareness of her shoulders lessened.

From beneath her folded arms, she pulled out a mobile phone, dialled a number, and heard a well-loved voice.

'He's gone. I'm in the garden.'

That was all she said.

Placing the phone on a garden table, she threw back her head and smiled up at the moon. Then she kicked off her shoes and let the green dress she was wearing slide to her ankles. She wore nothing beneath it. Michael had not known that. It was enough for her to know it, just as she had known that Michael would take advantage of having important business guests and go out after dinner.

Kicking the dress to one side along with her shoes, she threw out her arms, let out a yell and ran through the wet grass like a happy child.

In the dark shadows beneath a Japanese maple, she lay out on the damp grass, rested her head on her arms, and stared at the moon.

At first the only sound around her was the rustling of the trees.

Then there were footsteps; light and swift on the long grass that prevailed in this part of the garden.

He came into her vision and stood between her and the moon so it seemed to form a halo around his head.

She opened her eyes and smiled. 'My love. Here at last. Let me worship you.'

Silently, he took off his clothes and lay down beside her. Although the grass was chill to her back, his body was warm against hers.

18

Chapter 4

Michael ran his hands around the steering wheel as he drove. They were sweaty – mostly with excitement. A throbbing expectancy ebbed and flowed in his lower torso.

Swiftly, he switched his lights from main beam to dipped. Ahead of him was the lay-by – their usual meeting place. Her car was already there. Just thinking about her dark hair, her sparkling blue eyes, made him breathe more heavily. Thinking about her perfectly round and very full breasts, her voluptuous abandon when he made love to her, increased the aching throb between his legs.

Accompanied by a cloud of expensive perfume, Crystal, Thomas's wife, opened the car door and slid into the seat beside him. His hands left the steering wheel and grabbed her shoulders. He clasped her to him as their lips met in a hot and passionate kiss.

'It's so good to see you,' he said, his lips still pecking at her cheek, her ear, the soft waves of her hair. He smelt her freshness, her warmth permeating through his shirt to his skin.

The firmness of her body excited him. The smell of her invoked an odd feeling in him of wanting to ram himself into her as a knife slides into butter. He wanted to eat her, mould with her, savour her body in such a way that all his senses would be satisfied.

'I want you.' That was all she said.

As her hands ran down over his chest to his waist and his zip, Michael threw back his head. Murmurs of ecstasy emerged from his throat as she pulled his erection from the front of his trousers and began stroking it. Her head dropped to his lap.

Michael groaned. 'Crystal! Darling! Can't you wait?'

A murmured 'no' drifted upwards. Through narrowed eyes, he could see the top of her head bobbing up and down in a steady tempo as her lips sucked on him. Her mane of dark hair hid his sex and what she was doing to it. Never mind. He didn't need to see. He could feel what she was doing, and it was absolutely delicious.

'That is so good.' As he groaned with pleasure, he rested his hands on her head and adjusted his pelvis so she could get to him better.

Hot, moist kisses fell from her lips and all along his stem. Her tongue licked at his pubic hair and her hands pulled on him with a steady rhythm.

'Crystal. Oh Crystal!'

His voice had a drifting quality about it – like a breeze blowing rushes along a river-bank. Like the rushes, he was helpless to do anything about it.

'Oh, Crystal, I'm coming,' he moaned.

The moment of no return was nigh, but just as he was about to ejaculate, she brought her head up and kissed him.

'Crystal,' he moaned once her lips had left his. 'I was coming.'

'Have you told Josie yet?'

Instead of replying, he kissed her. It was a short kiss. She pushed him away.

'Have you told her, Michael?'

'Oh come on, Crystal. I had guests tonight. Big-shot guys who I had to impress. Josie did a great job and, anyway, before I could get her alone you rang and demanded I get out to see you.'

She turned her head as he tried to kiss her so his mouth landed on her ear.

'You're full of shit, Michael. I don't know why I love you. I should hate you, the way you treat me.'

Michael sighed and despondently rested his head on one hand. When Crystal had called earlier that evening, he had immediately wanted sex with her. He had come out with that specific intention in mind. Now, his penis was softening as the wetness her mouth had left turned chilly. Would she change her mind and stop pressurizing him to leave Josie and go off with her? He doubted it.

Crystal sat and glared through the windscreen. She folded her arms in front of her. It made her look quite formidable.

With red, glossy lips, Crystal pouted like a self-willed child. Michael suddenly felt very vulnerable.

'Well? When are you going to tell her?' Her voice took on a certain cutting edge.

Michael groaned. 'It's not that easy, darling.' He reached for her.

'Don't you darling me!' She hit him away.

Michael's penis was turning cold and his stiffness was going fast. He had an urge to put it away, but had a greater longing for her to go back down on him. The likelihood of it happening did not look too promising – not for the moment at least.

But Michael wanted his own way and meant to have it. He softened his voice. 'Look, Crys. Tonight was full of business. The moment wasn't right, but it soon will be. Soon Josie will be off to Cornwall. Instead of just screwing each other ragged during that time, why don't we go over things and get everything in proper order. What do you say?'

When she turned the full force of her eyes on him, he felt like melting – or coming in his trousers. Crystal was beautiful and knew it. Sometimes he felt as though he were falling into those eyes of hers. It was as though each sparkling glint was a chip of glass that burrowed into his flesh and pulled him nearer to her like some weird magnetic field.

Slowly, the wilful glitter left her eyes. Her jaw loosened and the sculpted perfection of her cheekbones seemed softer.

A smile returned. 'Alright, Mike. When Josie's away, you and I will play. But we'll also make plans, plans for us; for me and for you.'

'Oh, yes.' Michael placed his hands on either side of her head. He ruffled her long, silky hair as he gazed at her, then sucked in his breath as her hands ran down to his open zip. 'Oh, yes,' he said again, his eyes half closing as his mouth met hers.

He was hot, he was hard again, and he was pretty sure that Crystal was about to resume what she had been doing so well.

With no care for his pride or his comfort, he felt his penis being pushed back into his pants. To his great surprise, this was followed by the sound of his zip being closed.

His lips left hers. 'What are you doing?'

She grinned and patted the bulge that pushed against his jeans.

'Keeping it for a rainy day.'

'But, Crys . . .!'

She wagged her finger at him, tapped his nose, then kissed it.

'Save it, buddy. Save it until Josie's away and we can get down to things a little more seriously and in far less restricted a space.'

'But, Crys . . . '

Crystal was already outside the car. He got out and ran after her before she had a chance to get into her soft-topped, sporty Merc.

'I told you before,' she said to him loftily. 'I want you full-time. So get to it. Stop messing me around.'

Michael stood with his mouth open, hands hanging useless at his side.

Panic suddenly grabbed hold of him. 'I will see you when Josie's in Cornwall, won't I?'

Crystal tossed her hair so it fell over her shoulder and down her back like a black fountain. Her attitude was unyielding.

'Of course you will. I fully intend to have you Michael Warner – one way *and* the other.'

He watched her go, her headlights searing through the darkness and making the tarmac of the road look wet as she drove swiftly out of sight.

There was a hollow feeling inside him, as though she had drained him dry. Crystal played with him. She lifted him up, and she let him down. She aroused him, then left him stranded high and dry with a full-blown erection. It was still there now, hot and throbbing in his pants.

He walked back to his own car and drove home. When he got there, the house was in darkness. Josie had already gone to bed.

There was a blueness about their bedroom, a soft ghostliness as the same sort of curtains that hung in the studio wafted gently before the open window.

Her shoulders were bare and gleamed almost silver. The sheet barely covered her breasts. No matter that it was Josie and not Crystal, his penis responded to the sight of her. Crystal had left him high and dry. Now he wanted Josie.

Naked, he slid into the cool sheets beside her.

Her back was towards him. He kissed her between the shoulder blades and drank in the scent that was all woman, all warmth and understanding.

Josie was sweet. She was like a flower – a neat carnation wrapped into itself with a silky stalk and slim-limbed leaves. She was fragrant and sweet but not as wildly heady as Crystal; not as dark, not as compellingly beautiful but she didn't have the other woman's prickly thorns.

Oh Josie was sweet alright, and tonight he was glad to have her.

He ran his hands down her back, felt the angular form of her shoulder blades, the nodules of her spine only barely covered by flesh.

As his hips pulsed towards her and the tip of his penis nudged at her behind, his fingers followed the soft curve of her hip and the sweep of her thigh. Between kissing the nape of her neck and the indent between shoulder and ear, he murmured sweet nothings, told her how glad he was to have her.

What he was saying was only truth. He *was* glad he have her – at that moment. But it was Crystal who had aroused him, Crystal who had egged him on, played with him like a cheap toy and then left him wanting. It was Crystal who had set him ablaze.

Josie did not waken. But Michael didn't need to have her awake. He was enjoying what he was doing; feeling her, using her without her knowing. It was a very singular thing. With closed eyes, he jerked his pelvis against her, and when at last his moment came, he let his semen seep betwen the cheeks of her behind and run down to stain the sheets, just as Crystal was staining their lives.

And that was how Josie was thinking of Crystal: she was like a stain spreading, contaminating each person she touched. Thomas, her, Michael. And who else? Perhaps Jamie and Mariana too, though in what way was not clear.

I'd like to wash her out of our lives, just as I have to wash this sheet in the morning, she thought to herself.

Michael sighed and turned over, and Josie felt the semen run in a warm, sticky stream between the cheeks of her behind.

Chapter 5

JAMIE'S STORY

All three men had jogged themselves to a sweat on the treadmill, pushed up the poundage on the arm curling equipment, then rocked from the waist, counting beneath their breath as one abdomen crunch followed another. After that, they had left the health-giving torture of the gym behind, dived into the pool, then partaken of a sauna. Glowing and self-satisfied, they were now back in the changing room in various states of undress.

Jamie was stretching and rolling his shoulders in that casual way he had. He was the only one who was still completely naked. His towel, which was usually wound tightly around him, had fallen to his ankles. He made no attempt to pick it up.

'Show-off bastard!' Michael, who had completed his habitual stretching exercises and so was half dressed, flipped his towel at the tightness of Jamie's stomach as he went past. Briefly, but regretfully, he let his gaze fall to Jamie's rod which stood hard and erect. Like Jamie's muscles, it was well developed.

'Do you ever use it for pole vaulting, Jamie?' asked Thomas, his gaze barely lingering before opening his locker.

Jamie beamed proudly. 'You're just jealous, my dear Tommy boy. Jealous that your John Thomas – *Thomas* – is nothing near the size and length of mine.' He laughed at his own joke. Jamie always laughed at his own jokes. 'If you'd led as sporting a life as I have, your muscles – all your muscles – might be as big as mine!'

Michael, who had now donned his underwear and pulled a polo shirt over his head, rejoined the conversation. 'Was your prick that well developed by the time you lost your virginity?'

Jamie looked down at his proud member and puffed out his chest. He badly needed to go to the lavatory, but not yet. Not until he got dressed and they could no longer see that his erection was the result of a full bladder and would shortly disappear down the drain. Until then he would bathe in the warm balm of their admiration.

He rolled his shoulders again as he answered Michael. 'I've always been a sporting man, my lads. Rugby, cricket, rowing. Still did plenty of sport when I joined the navy. Went all over the world then. Plenty of sport, plenty of women!'

He chuckled as though he were gathering his memories together.

'So? Are you going to tell us about the first time, or were you that crap at it you're keeping it to yourself?' Michael was zipping up his chinos and looking sidelong at the big, sandy-haired man.

Jamie guffawed and stood straight and tall, fists clenched above his head, biceps bulging, member standing hard and proud from his body.

'I was late in the sex game,' he began. 'All that sport took up a lot of my time, so sex got sidelined. I finally lost my virginity in Cairo. Like many ports all around the world, there are certain places frequented by navy personnel. We'd been at sea a long time and, perhaps because I had not been indulging myself in sport, I was pretty randy.

'The chief petty officer pointed me in the right direction and towards the right establishment. They vary, he told me. Quality and sexual preferences are geared to all tastes, all classes, and all pockets. Because I was an officer, the particular one he sent me to was of a pretty good standard.'

Jamie's voice seemed to drift slightly. There was a faraway look in his eyes, and those listening replicated in their minds what they thought he was seeing in his.

'I remember there being a smell of spice and flowers in the air as I walked down a shady street. It was a very narrow street. Looking up I could see a strip of blue sky barely separating the white wall of one house from another. It had a lovely calm feel about it, that street. It gave me a sense of magic, as though I was walking into a dream. High, whitewashed walls ran down on either side of me. From the other side I could hear the sound of fountains in hidden courtyards like they have in hot countries.

'The address I'd been given brought me into one of those courtyards. I was let through a heavy wooden gate by a very tall black girl who smelt of musk and tobacco. I explained to her what I wanted. She looked at me as though I was stupid. She didn't understand, you see. The first mate, who had travelled with me but was going on to a bar further down town, explained in Arabic exactly what I wanted. I squirmed when he told me that he had informed her that I was still a virgin. I could have killed him. But he laughed and went on his way, and I went in.

'The coolness of the place fell upon me and the mix of smells made me dizzy. The sound of running water mixed with the swishing of silks and the tinkling of jewellery. It was a lovely sound. Lovely smells. All perfume and women and lemon trees.'

Jamie sighed and shook his head. A faraway look came to his eyes. 'I can still see it now – and smell it.'

'Are you kidding?' Michael was making an effort to be mocking. The truth showed in his eyes. He was fascinated with Jamie's flowery descriptions. But Michael hated to think that someone had led a more exciting life than he had. He sneered as he spoke. 'I don't believe a word of it. It was Hannah's Whorehouse on the docks in somewhere like Amsterdam or Istanbul. All red lights, big tits, and ten minutes for ten Deutschmarks!'

'Piss off, Michael! Do you want to hear this or not?' Jamie's face had turned red. He glared and seemed unbelievably flustered by such a trite comment.

Michael blinked and took a step back. After all, Jamie had big muscles and a broad chest. He didn't doubt he knew how to use them.

It was Thomas who interceded. Gently, he patted Jamie's arm. 'Take no notice, Jamie. He's jealous.'

'He'd better be. It wasn't Amsterdam! It bloody well wasn't no two-pfennig whore either.'

'Of course it wasn't. It was Cairo, and it was sheer Arabian Nights.' Thomas's voice was as calm as his eyes.

Jamie nodded. 'That's right.' His voice was less angry, his face less red.

'I'm sorry,' said Michael. 'I was only joking. Go on. Tell us the rest. I'm intrigued. Really I am.' He shrugged and spread his hands palms upwards.

Although it was meant as a mark of regret and apology, Jamie fixed him with a stare before continuing.

'I was led up some stairs and along a shady verandah. There were blue and red tiles beneath my feet but, once I entered the building, the tiles were covered with thick carpets in the same colours.

'The smell of flowers and the sound of jewellery was more obvious here. In the bluish haze of shadow and smoke, I saw many young women lying half naked on piles of cushions. Some smoked the hubble bubble or Turkish cigarettes.

'I remember their dark eyes looking me up and down. It felt as though they were looking through my clothes – as though they could see my body underneath. Their lips were dusky pink and their skin seemed to gleam despite there not being much light in the room.

'Dark fretwork shutters hid the glare of the sunshine outside the windows. I could smell the wood – cedar, I think. And sandalwood, I'm sure I could smell sandalwood.

'I was a man in a room full of women, and I could feel the blood surge through my body. I felt powerful – powerful beyond words.

'There was a light titter of laughter as my dark-skinned companion told the girls of my requirements.

'Being only young, I began to feel embarrassed. I was in two minds to go, but the dark girl who had come with me turned and held my hand. "*Premier*," she said, and shook her head as she smiled.

'I took a deep breath, told myself not to be stupid, to hurry up and get it over with. Soon, I was entranced by the room, by the women, and by my predicament.

'I remember the electric fan whirring overhead. I remember thinking that except for that one sound of the twentieth century, I could have been swept back in time to some fabulous place straight out of a fairy tale with genies and djinn, and princesses, sorcerers, and weird birds and vicious monsters. I could have been in a harem.

'Here they all were, dark eyes, half dressed and smiling, and all waiting to do my bidding. Each one was there to fulfil my every wish, my greatest desire. Which one would I have?'

Jamie stopped telling his story and began to do arm-flexing and back-stretching exercises. He was smiling as he did so. His eyes gazed up at the ceiling.

Michael blinked. It was easy to see he had been hanging on Jamie's every word, and Jamie knew it. Now he was punishing Michael for his earlier behaviour.

Thomas smiled secretively to himself as Michael began

to show signs of impatience. Jamie appeared not to notice and continued his exercises.

At last, Michael could wait no longer. 'Well go on then! What did you do? I mean, which girl did you choose? What was she like? We want to know, don't we, Thomas?'

Thomas said nothing. An amused smile played around his lips. Jamie stopped throwing his arms out from his muscled chest. He took a deep breath, grinned sidelong at Michael, winked at Thomas, then went on with his story.

'There was this soft little thing with big dark eyes looking straight at me. I thought she was beautiful and she looked fairly young. I thought, right, Jamie old boy, that's the one for you. She's young, and can't have had too much experience, and you're completely inexperienced. I thought she seemed the most sensible choice. After all, I didn't want to appear a complete fool now, did I?'

Michael gave a curt nod. 'No more than you can help anyway!' He burst out laughing.

Jamie got riled. 'Do you want to hear this or don't you?'

Michael held up his hands defensively. 'Okay, okay!'

Again it was Thomas who intervened. 'Go on, Jamie. I'm listening. I've always envied you navy boys and your experiences.' Thomas was sat with his legs up on the bench, a towel still around his waist and his brown back gleaming. His arms were crossed over his chest and he was looking thoughtfully down at them. But he was listening. Jamie could tell that by the tone of his voice.

He beamed and continued his story. This time Jamie purposely looked in Thomas's direction as he told it, rather than at Michael.

'As I said,' Jamie went on, 'this beautiful young girl was looking at me and I thought, that's the one for me!

'I pointed to her and the black girl beside me said something to her in Arabic. The girl got up, took hold of my hand and led me out of the room.'

Jamie gave a big sigh and shook his head. 'Her hand

seemed so small, so fragile in mine. You know, like a butterfly does when you've got it trapped in your palm and you're trying to throw in out into the garden. That's how it felt.'

He looked suddenly thoughtful. 'Strong, though. Incredibly strong.' His voice faded and even his penis seemed to wilt slightly because his attention was focused on some picture in his memory, a picture provoked by his words.

'Go on, Jamie. Tell us what she was like,' Thomas urged softly.

Jamie blinked rapidly as though someone had just woken him from a deep sleep. 'Yes!' he said. 'Yes! Of course. I'm sorry. I got a bit overcome. It all seems such a long time ago now.' He smiled. 'The product of a misspent youth. Happy memories, eh?'

The others smiled too, but said nothing. They were waiting for Jamie to continue.

'The passageway she took me along had no windows. The only light came from a dark blue glass door at the very far end and a brass filigree lamp hanging from some sort of scrolled bracket high on the wall.

'We stopped outside a carved wooden door and she turned and smiled at me. "Please," she said. "*Entrez*."

'Fretwork shutters hid the room from the outside world, though shafts of sunlight came through the screen and repeated its pattern on the floor.

'Beyond the reach of the sunlight was a low, round bed. It was piled with cushions. She drew me to it, lay down on it and motioned that I should join her.

'I tried to kiss her, but she put her hand across my lips. "*Non*" she said. I asked her why not. She pointed to glasses and wine. She poured me some, raised it to my lips. It wasn't Chateau bottled, but then it wasn't wine I really wanted. It was her. I was on fire for her, my cock was hard for her, and she was giving me wine.

'I drank most of it and she put the glass back. This time she let me kiss her, let me feel her breasts and run my hand up her skirt.

'Her breasts were big and round, the skin soft as satin, the nipples as hard as hazelnuts.

'As my hand went up between her legs, she got onto her knees and parted them as wide as she could. Then she lifted her skirts and treated me to the sight of her pussy. My, but pussy was the right word. A mass of black hair ran halfway up her belly and hung like streamers between her legs. Even so, I could still see the lips of her pussy and something else besides. I couldn't believe my eyes at first, but I swear before you now, if my name's not James Ewen Campbell, her clit hung a full inch below her lips. What a sight! What a girl!'

Jamie paused enough to take in the effect of his declaration. For once, Thomas was looking keenly his way.

Michael's eyes were wide open and his jaw was hanging slack. 'Good grief.' Michael groaned it rather than said it. He looked stunned, and Jamie was pleased. He licked his lips before going on.

'I reached out and touched it. It moved, jerked towards me as if it were erecting. I was astounded.

'At first I was wary of going too near. Not because I was afraid of it. In all honesty, the opposite was true. I wanted to take a closer look. But I had heard that Arab girls take pride in having a strong smell, so I held her clit between my finger and thumb, rubbed it gently, and laughed as it danced over my fingertips.

'She laughed too as I played with it and ran my free hand over her hairy belly and tangled my fingers in her hanging hair. It was a bit like stroking a collie dog. You didn't really know where the hair stopped and the flesh began. But I was enjoying what I was doing, and it seemed she was too.

'So far I was still clothed, though my pants felt as

though they were strangling me. I wanted to lay her down and get into her, but I was fascinated with the sight of her sex. Each time my fingers went to my buttons, her clit danced around as if excited by the prospect of me poking her, and each time my fingers went back to it.

'By now, she must have been thinking that time was going on and I was getting nowhere. "*Mange*?" she said suddenly.

'I looked up, and she pointed at her mouth. "*Mange*?" she said again.

'My eyes went to her pussy and then back to her face. I shook my head vigorously. "No," I said. "No." I shook my hand in front of her pussy and patted my cheek in an effort to make her understand that I had a rotten toothache.

'She laughed. "*Non. Non. Premier.*" She pointed at me, then tucked her skirts around her backside. Her sex still exposed, she reached behind her.

'My God! I thought to myself. My God! I don't believe this. She had a small cucumber in her hand. You know. A courgette.'

Michael and Thomas were all attention. Neither had been in the navy, so abroad meant beaches and bars in well-known tourist resorts. Jamie, they both realised, had seen the more gritty aspects of foreign lands.

'She took me for a complete beginner! She leaned back on her legs – a bit like a limbo dancer. With one hand she opened the lips of her sex. My eyes nearly popped out of my head. Her clit was so prominent, so amazing.

'As she opened the outer lips, she slid the courgette along the length of her inner lips. All the time she smiled and watched me watching her.

'"See, sailor boy? See?"

'For the first and last time in my life, I was being given a lesson in female anatomy on a living and very willing subject. I was amazed.

33

'In her hand, the courgette had become a penis. She was running it along her flesh, swaying on her haunches and moaning as she nudged this green vegetable into her vagina.

'I gasped. This girl thought I was so green, that I needed to be instructed as to exactly what was expected of me. She was showing me the exact postion of her vagina.

'But no matter what her true intention was. My cock was hard and hot in my pants. This time there was no denying it what it wanted.

'By now, the courgette was half hidden in her vagina. I caught at her hand, pulled the thing out, and immediately shoved myself into her.

'Her legs were still bent beneath her, but the angle I entered her at was quite delicious.

'As I thrust into her, she balanced at that angle beneath me. Luckily, at that age, my arm muscles were good enough to support me.

'Her breasts, which up until then I had only felt, were now exposed.

'I sucked on her nipples and, pressing my full weight against her, I used my hands to bunch her breasts into two manageable halves. Then I showered her face with kisses, wrapped my arms around her and, falling backwards, brought her to lie on top of me.

'She rode me then. Her breasts jiggled, I remember, and the hair of her sex lay like a ragged mat across my stomach. All the time she rode me, she held her skirt up so I could see it all more clearly. Then she lay flat on me, her breasts fleshy on my chest, her legs closing tightly around my prick. I could have died. I could willingly have died and gone to heaven. It was sheer bliss!'

Jamie let out a big sigh and stopped doing his Charles Atlas poses. 'Well, there you are,' he said, and reached for his trousers.

Michael shook his head and smiled. His expression

34

betrayed a hint of disbelief, but also more than a fair portion of jealousy.

Thomas looked surprisingly noncommittal, although warm; as if he had just listened to very good story.

Jamie, pleased at their response to his narrative, sauntered off to the lavatory.

Once he had obtained the necessary solitude, his semen flowed from his member and bubbled happily off down the drain. As it went, he stared at it and shivered. Like his teenage years and his virginity, it was all gone, though not in quite the way he had described.

He rememberd Cairo, he remembered the place, and he remembered the girl. All that had been true. Details of his erection and his performance were not entirely accurate.

No matter how often the girl had pushed the courgette into herself, and no matter how often she had taken his flaccid tool into her mouth, his erection did not last.

As he tucked himself away inside his trousers, the young girl stayed his hand and had helped him out of his clothes.

At first he had resisted, but then realised she was only trying to help. *Perhaps*, he thought, *I might be harder once my clothes are off.* Accordingly, he went along with it until he was sat naked among the cushions. The other women looked on, faces implacable, but eyes interested.

It did no good. No matter how much the girl stroked him, kissed him, and pulled on his penis, it refused to stand up.

In the end, she had got very annoyed and had muttered rude words to him in a broad mix of Arabic and French, before flouncing off. Titters had run through the watching women.

He recalled with shame the return of Biblay, as the young girl was called, and Ashara, the tall black girl who had escorted him from the wooden gate. Both held their heads high as their dark eyes gazed down on his nakedness which he was trying his best to hide by bundling his clothes before his stubbornly soft penis. With more shame, he remembered reddening from head to toe as his eyes met those of Ashara.

'*Anglais.*' One word and her teeth flashed in a wide smile and she'd arched her eyebrows. 'English?'

He had nodded. 'Yes. I'm English.'

Ashara had spoken quickly to Biblay, whose face quickly flooded with understanding.

Jamie did not have the guts to say he was Scottish. He knew well enough what they meant by the word 'English'.

Ashara pointed to an iron-bound chest that sat before a highly painted cotton tapestry. Biblay went to it and Jamie caught the aroma of old wood and sweet lavender as the chest lid had creaked open. What he saw next brought sweat to his brow and a sudden hardness to his member. All at once, those twilight events at boarding school came flooding back to him. As the memories returned, his penis hardened.

Ashara's long fingers and bright red talons snatched his clothes away from his groin as her other hand hit his face and sent him flying.

It knocked the breath out of him. He lay there among the scattered cushions breathing heavily, his eyes bright, his member upright. The watching women hit him, scratched him, and punched at his shoulders. Shivers of excitement ran over his body like warm seams of sticky toffee. This was the moment he had waited for. This was the kind of sex he wanted.

Biblay bound his wrists and ankles with leather and dragged him along the floor, over the cool tiles, the rumpled carpets. The tip of his penis just barely kept contact with the ground. The feel of the tiles was cool, the roughness of the carpets almost cruel against the head of his shaft. It felt quite delicious.

Then they had forced him to do all the things he could never in a million years tell his country-club friends about. All he could tell them was how it had felt to see Biblay and the courgette, to feel her vulva sucking on his penis.

He could not tell them of how Ashara had sat on his face at the same time Biblay had sat on his penis.

Even now it was sheer ecstasy to recall that very first time when two women had given him the same sort of treatment he had received and enjoyed at boarding school.

The smell of Ashara's sex had seeped onto his nose along with her juices. He had taken a deep breath and drawn the fluid up into his nostrils. Divine was the only word he could think of to describe it.

There he was, bound with leather, his mouth covered with the sex lips of a tall, young black girl whilst his penis was used by another young woman without any dictates from him.

As he drank of Ashara's sweet offering, Biblay's thick labia had sucked at his penis. The extraordinary clitoris that had danced over his hand now danced among his pubic hairs.

Again and again they had used his body. In between each bout, they sat on their haunches; talked and drank coffee. It had been almost as if he was not there. Almost as if he were just a tool to be used. No more nor less than a pestle to pound grain, a flail to thresh wheat. And, in between each bout, they had also whipped his flesh with wet twists of cloth. His buttocks, back and thighs had stung. Cries of protest had been stifled by one woman grasping his head between her thighs. His flesh had been red, but not bruised or cut, and at the end of his treatment they had massaged his body with sweet-smelling oils. One girl held his length between finger and thumb whilst the other applied oil to her palms and then to his member.

How sweet the memories of youth, he thought to himself. How sweet and how well they shape our lives.

Exercise over, he now looked forward to getting home. Telling such a tale had left him with a yearning to enjoy the same treatment again. Home was where he wanted to be.

Chapter 6

Still thinking of the story he had told the others, Jamie pulled into the drive of a pale cream house that had big glass windows. Their wide open aspect was contradicted by Venetian blinds. The house was of contemporary design and boasted a sweeping roof. 'I think your architect was inspired by the ski jump at Innsbruck,' Josie, Michael's wife, had observed.

He had not been too sure whether he should have taken exception to her comment, or should have welcomed it. Because he had been unsure, he had pretended he hadn't heard her. It seemed the best strategy at the time and, anyway, no matter about other people's remarks. The house suited him and Mariana very well indeed.

Brick and cobble steps led down from the front of the house to a lawn of two-tone stripes. Between the lawn and the road, a battalion of upright conifers gave shade and complete privacy.

To the postman or any other casual visitor, the house was opulent, very private, but perfectly normal.

A rosy picture was presented through the window that looked out over the lawn. Comfortable furniture and dark wood proclaimed that the residents were not hard done by but were still perfectly ordinary.

An oblong shadow ran between the house and the garage. The shadow was not ordinary. It fell from a window at the side of the house, a window designed of lead and bits of coloured glass that formed a swirling pattern to deceive the eye and present a picture of flowing form and natural colours. And the eye was easily deceived. But not Jamie's eye, because Jamie knew better.

Rather than actually seeing the picture formed by soft lead and multicoloured glass and cut into shapes of leaves, petals and pretty little birds, he saw the colour beyond that. He saw the blue from the lamp in the back room which told him his wife was waiting for him. It told him she was ready for him and knowing that made him shiver.

His trembling was accompanied by a feeling of heaviness in his balls, especially in the places where two red dots gave witness to past torment, past ecstasy.

Mariana was waiting for him, and he couldn't wait to be with her.

Once the car was put away, he went round to the back door, paused, took a deep breath, swept his hair back from his face, polished his shoes on the back of his trousers, then went in.

There she was, her honey-gold hair swept up and piled on top of her head. She was dressed in a way that their friends at the country club never saw. Memories of another time and another place were resurrected by the way she looked. Her hands were on her hips and her head was held high, chin tilted and firm. There was that look in her eyes that said she was in the mood for him. There also was that certain hardness about her lips that made him want to drop to his knees then and there, crawl along the floor and kiss her pink-varnished toenails.

'About time, my English sailor. About time you came to see me. I hope you have plenty of money. I hope you are going to be very good to me in return for me being very bad to you – very bad indeed! Now come along. You have kept me waiting long enough.'

In a flurry of flimsy veils and tinkling jewellery, she turned away from him and passed into their special room.

As she went, Jamie took a deep breath and drank in the smell of sandalwood and musk.

Drawn like a moth to the flame, he followed her, his limbs trembling, his flesh prickling with a thousand goose bumps as he imagined what she would do to him tonight and what she would want him to do to her.

Incense burned in a copper and brass receptacle which sat on a cast-iron stand in one corner. Copper planters which once used to glow in the Arab quarter of Marseille, or the back streets of Cairo, cast a silvery light through blue-tinted glass. Music was playing. Not soft, romantic love songs, or even raunchy, highly erotic numbers, but simple, lilting strains accompanied only by the tinkle of cymbals and the beat of bare fingers against stretched skin.

There was no bed in the room. Jamie and Mariana's sexual tastes did not require one.

There was a chair, a long settee with scrolled arms that was perfect to lounge on but totally unsuitable for sleep. But, then, neither of them intended sleeping.

Strands of pearls circled Mariana's head and they jiggled as she moved. One strand looped beneath her chin, and one beyond that rested on her bare breasts. Falling from her hips, a flurry of veils floated around her thighs but did nothing to hide their form or the triangle of hair between them.

Jamie, his mouth open, his breath now catching in his throat, stood still as he awaited what he knew must come.

'Take off your clothes!'

His cheek tingled as his wife's hand made contact with it. He fell to the ground, not because her blow was that hard, but solely because it was all part of the act.

He attempted to rise from the floor in order to undress that much more easily.

His wife interpreted his intention. 'Stay where you are!' Her toes dug into his side as she slapped him about the head.

Staying as low as he possibly could, Jamie removed his clothes. Once he was completely naked, he looked up at her, his eyes shining with love and with trepidation. His penis looked up too. It was hard and becoming moist at the tip.

He lay there as she circled him, not daring to move, not daring to speak. Each muscle bulged with the effort of not moving, of avoiding her displeasure.

Smiling, Mariana bent down and picked up his clothes, which he had placed in a neat pile. Holding each one at arm's length, she examined it, then shouted that they were dirty and she didn't like having dirty washing. With that, she threw each item to a different part of the room.

'Now pick them all up,' she ordered. 'But stay on your hands and knees.'

His face red and his penis swollen, Jamie did as she ordered. She insisted he pick them up with his teeth and place them in a pile.

'I should think so too!' Her tone was cruel, but Jamie was in ecstasy. Strong as a bear he was, big as an ox, and this was the kind of treatment he liked. He blessed the day he had found his wife. She was the one thing that had made his life complete.

'That's a lot of washing,' she snapped. 'I'm not happy about it. You deserve a good beating for getting your clothes so dirty. Don't you agree?'

He didn't answer. He wasn't supposed to.

'Dumb!' As she said it, she raised her leg and placed her foot on his head, forcing him downwards until his forehead was touching the floor.

Palms and fingers pressed flat to floor, Jamie snatched at his breath. Shivers of warped pleasure seeped like a spreading stain over his body. The sole of her foot pressed cruelly into the nape of his neck.

'You are nothing but a great dumb man. A stupid

mariner who can't even keep himself tidy.' She removed her foot. 'Now. Stay where you are.'

He did as she said. The position was quite delightful. His forehead was touching the floor and his naked behind was high in the air. Vulnerability was the spark that lit the flame of arousal.

Veils whispered and silver jingled as his wife walked around him, her bare feet soundless on the red, blue and green tiles of the floor. Imprints of her soles, her heels and her toes dotted the shiny tiles with dampness. He had an urge to lick them up, to take even this most humble part of her into his body.

At last she stopped pacing and stood directly behind him. His heart thumped in his chest as he imagined her eyes surveying his hanging balls and their covering of golden hair. As her fingernails dug into his scrotal sac, he cried out, then groaned, his thighs trembling. Mariana did not require him to groan with pleasure – only pain.

His buttocks clenched tightly together as her fingers slid all over his testicles and his backside. Not once did she pass her hand through his open legs and touch the weapon that rose so hard and erect in front of him.

Arousal soaring, Jamie continued to bite his bottom lip. Her nails were scraping across his backside now, dipping down to his sac, cupping it, squeezing it, digging into it with outstanding ferocity again and again. His voice, usually so deep, was now nothing more than a whimper, a series of mewing sounds.

All the while, his piston pulsated of its own accord. Not for his weapon the touch of soft fingers or softer lips. Jamie needed only his mind and this scenario to spill his seed. And this was what he did.

But before he did it, Mariana slid a towelling bag over it as a groom would slide a nosebag over the head of a horse. This bag was one-third full of ice.

Jamie cried out as the tip of his penis became embedded

in the nest of crushed ice. Every muscle of his body strained to keep still despite this new cruelty. Every vein stood proud of his flesh.

With one hand, his wife squeezed and released his scrotal sac in a constant rhythm as though he were a cow and she were milking him. The fingernails of her other hand scraped down the divide between his buttocks.

There was no time left to do anything else, for the sharpness of her fingernail to dig into his anal portal, for her fingers to scrape the inside of his thighs. An orgasm had come and had taken him. Jamie bucked as his semen rose along his stem then discharged into the ice.

Jamie glowed with satisfaction. It didn't matter that he now had to scrub the kitchen floor before he ate dinner. That he had to load his clothes into the washing machine without getting up off his knees.

After that, he became her footstool, naked and curled up beneath her feet as she watched television, a glass of wine in one hand, and the dog lead attached to his collar in the other.

Jamie was content to do this for his wife who was also his mistress and confidante. There were no secrets between them – which was how Mariana came to know about Michael encouraging the telling of tales in the changing room.

'How very interesting,' she said thoughtfully. 'Tell me more, my little slave.' To add encouragement, she tugged sharply on the dog lead. Jamie told her everything.

'There's a good boy,' she cooed once he had finished. 'I will reward you for this later, but for now I think you should feel some chastisement for being such a naughty little boy.'

Jamie knew exactly what her words meant. Later Mariana would want him to bring her to orgasm, and he would be pleased to do that too. But for now he was happy to do just as he was told.

Chapter 7

THOMAS'S STORY

It was Friday in the changing room, and Thomas was running his towel across his back in a diagonal movement designed to mop up the last damp patches of water.

As usual, another towel was tightly bound around his waist. It was white and its tightness around his behind and hips seemed to exaggerate the broadness of his back. His hair was still damp, clinging to his head and gathering in crinkled curls over the nape of his neck.

'Well, Tommy old boy. Your turn next.' Michael slapped the broad back, but retrieved his hand smartly as he felt Thomas's muscles bunch beneath his touch. Sudden tension worried him. Not for the world did he want his friend to imagine he might have 'left-hand' designs on him. Not him. Not Michael. Didn't he go out of his way to flout his masculinity, to boast of his sexual prowess?

Thomas turned to face him. 'Don't call me Tommy. I'm Thomas. Let's keep it at that. It's my preference, okay?'

Michael winced and coloured up slightly. 'Sorry, Thomas. I forgot.' He held up one hand, palm outwards. 'Pax?'

Thomas nodded. 'Pax – Mickey.'

'Alright, alright. Sorry again.' Michael waited a few minutes to let the tension in the atmosphere and in Thomas's muscles dissipate. 'Now what about your tale of woe. How did you first get your end away, Thomas?'

Thomas smiled that secret little smile of his – the one

that infuriated his wife because he usually did it when she was angry and trying to provoke some response from him.

He sat down on the bench, stretched his legs out in front of him, and lay his back against the locker. There was a certain translucence to the gleaming brown torso, the chiselled muscles of his chest and legs. His smile persisted. There was something secretive about it – almost as if he knew something they didn't, but which they should.

'I remember it well. We were sweethearts. Had been since we were children.

'I remember her being six and wearing pretty angel tops in lacy materials, and one of the colours in her top matching her trousers.

'I remember her being ten and wearing jeans that matched mine and shirts that she stole from her brother's bedroom. She liked being one of the boys and used to climb up with us and play in our tree house. We used to tell stories, sing songs, play dares and even ran to doctors and nurses. That was the best game of all – especially if her brother wasn't around.

'She was fourteen before I realised I loved her. She was sixteen before we kissed and fell in love'.

Jamie interrupted. 'Love? I thought we were talking about sex.'

Thomas crossed his arms and continued to talk without bothering to acknowledge Jamie's comment.

'It was a warm Sunday afternoon. Her brother was out doing good deeds with the church and the boy scouts.

'It was hot, but the top branches of the trees were swaying in a reasonable breeze. She suggested we climb up our favourite tree and sit in the shade of the leaves up in the tree house. So that's what we did.

'Signs of neglect were all over the place once we were inside it. After all, we hadn't been up there for ages. We'd got older.

'There was an old mattress up there and, once we'd given

it a good shake, it looked decent enough to sit on. As we shook it a whole load of leaves fell from the branches above and floated in. The mattress was covered in them, but we didn't care. We lay among them, our heads resting on our hands, our eyes gazing up through the leaves to the sky.

'It was then that I became aware of her as a girl; as a woman. Somehow her body seemed more warm than I remembered it and, even though she was lying still, shadows from the moving tree dappled her body. Her smell seemed more tantalising and the feel of her hair against my bare arm made my breath catch in my throat. Instinctively, I knew she felt it too, knew that the sky, the leaves, and the birds singing around us, were all part of what we were feeling. It was as though we were blending, mixing together like ingredients in some sort of natural recipe.

'She asked me if I loved her. I said I did.

'She asked me if I'd ever kissed a girl.

'I said I had.

'What about making love to them?

'I didn't know how to answer that. One half of me wanted to lie, to tell her I had gone to bed with loads of girls. It irked me to think I was still a virgin, you see. But I couldn't lie. Not to her. To her I had to tell the truth.

'"No," I said. "I haven't." I couldn't tell her that I'd tried on several occasions. I couldn't tell her that some girls had condescended to let me finger them, to suck me off, to jerk me off. Somehow, I couldn't tell her any of those things. So I said no.

'She turned to me and looked me straight in the eye. She told me she was glad. Told me that many boys had asked her, but she'd held out. There was only one boy she wanted. That's what she told me. So there, beneath a canopy of green leaves, we kissed, softly, gently. Then we took off our clothes.

'I couldn't seem to move once I saw her naked. I stared as if she was something strange, not something beautiful. As the breeze rustled the leaves overhead, the dappled shadows caressed her body, the sweet curve of her breasts, the pink teats of her nipples.

'She broke my silence when she asked me to kiss her again. So I did. Her lips tasted sweet. Once she was close to me I could smell her femininity, her freshness and her willingness. I poked my tongue into her mouth and tasted her. I reached for her, ran my hands down her shoulders and cupped her breasts moaning as I traced my thumbs across her nipples and felt my penis hardening against my thigh. I smelt the perfume of her hair, the slight, girlish sweatiness that rose from under her arms and between her legs.

'I ran my hands down her back and felt the roundness of her behind, her buttocks placed neatly together like two halves of a meringue.

'I was fired up with the urge to fuck her, to take her virginity and to give her mine. But I was scared. Like any other technology, it's all very well reading the theory, but there's nothing like doing the practical. Inexperienced as I was, I did my best.

'I lay her among the thickest part of the leaves, kissed her lips, her breasts, her belly and the thicket of soft fur between her legs.

'Very, very lightly, I trailed my fingers over her breasts, down over her belly, and down the inside of her thighs. I saw her shiver.

'"This is so good," she said in a sweet, trembling voice. "So good that I feel I could let you go on doing it forever and ever."

'Her words were like music to my ears. I was doing it right and I wanted her to want me always. There was no one else in the world for me except her, and no one else should be around for her except me. I told her this and she smiled sadly. "Perhaps," she said.

'It was all I gave her the time to say. Gently, I played

with her breasts and the soft wetness between her thighs. I knew she needed that wetness, needed as much of it as possible before I attempted to enter her body. In an effort to make things as easy as possible, I eased my finger into her. She cried out at first, then mewed like a kitten and rolled her hips from side to side. Soon, she was begging me to enter her. I did as she asked.

'Being careful not to hurt her, I pushed myself into her vagina. The tip of my penis nudged against a natural barrier. She gasped as I hit against it. It wasn't easy, but I held myself back. I felt my cock pulsating inside of her, surging with a need to push forward, to ram against the barrier that stretched before it. It was almost painful. I asked her if she was ready for that final thrust. She said she was, so I pushed myself into her.

'Like two people rehearsing the first steps of a very famous dance, we moved tentatively against each other until natural forces took over.

'No matter the coolness of the breeze, the sky, the leaves and everything else, we were lost to it all, dizzy with our desire for each other and this new thing we had just discovered.

'I remember coming into her, how I felt that we were no longer two people but one, and would be forever. I remember her breath rushing against my ear as she climaxed and said that she loved me.' He paused. There was a faraway look in his eyes. 'She meant it, and I meant it too. I never forgot her, and she never forgot me.'

Encompassed by a strange silence, the three men began to dress and get themselves ready to go home to their wives, their wide drives, and their up-market houses.

Somehow the story recently told was endemic of their lost youth and the open door through which they had passed to become men.

Michael was the first to recover. 'See you on Wednesday, Thomas, Jamie.' He grinned and patted both his companions on the back. 'I'll tell you something more when I see you next. I'll tell you about the first woman I fell in love with. That'll get your blood going!'

Crystal was not at home when Thomas got there. He hadn't expected her to be. Although they had arrived at the country club at the same time, she always arrived straight from work in her own car, and he in his. And she always stayed later than him, giving him the excuse that she had either talked too long, or that she had a business meeting to rush off to.

He knew none of it was true, but it no longer mattered to him whether she told him the truth or not.

Tonight it mattered even less. Tonight he lay out in the suspect comfort of the garden swing, his body half comfortable, and his mind full of the memory of a red-haired girl with dark green eyes, creamy flesh, and a beguiling smile. His only companion was his mobile phone.

He wished, as he had so many times before, that he had never got that place at Plymouth University, that she had never got hers at Reading. Never in all these years had she left his mind, and never in those early days had he ever expected her to leave his side. But she had.

She had married first, and in time he had married too.

Wasted years, he thought to himself. *Too many wasted years. But they did say it was never too late.*

With that thought in mind, he closed his eyes and smiled into the night. He hoped with all his heart that it was true – just as his story had been.

His phone rang before he could drift off into dreams and memories.

'Thomas?'

Her voice was as soft as the rustling of those leaves that first time.

'I was just thinking about you.'

'Were they loving thoughts?'

'They're never anything else.'

Chapter 8

MARIANA'S STORY

Crystal, Mariana thought, *might be very beautiful, but she also had a large behind. When she stood up straight it wasn't so noticeable and matched her generous breasts, but when she bent over it seemed to spread. Or smile,* thought Mariana smugly; *her crack is smiling above a bushy black beard. As if it were made to complement a very large behind, Crystal had a lot of pubic hair.*

They were in the women's changing room at the country club and Crystal was pushing her towel in and out of her toes.

Learning that the men had been talking about losing their virginity had rekindled old memories in Mariana, so naturally she was the one who set things going for the women. She did not, of course, tell them that the men had been discussing their sexual exploits in the changing room. Such information was sacrosanct. They would want to know how she had found out, and that was something she could not divulge. Her relationship with her husband was a private matter, so she steered the conversation in the right direction.

'Sex,' she stated firmly, 'is a very funny thing. You can give it away, and yet you still keep it. Except of course as regards virginity. Once that's gone, it's gone forever.'

Crystal straightened and laughed that loud, bell-like laugh that drew people to look and, once they had looked, admire. Crystal had tumbling black hair and bright blue eyes. Some Caribbean forebear had also blessed her with a skin colour that resembled dark honey but gleamed like satin.

She eyed Mariana over her shoulder. 'Where there's demand there's always supply. Market forces, you could say.'

'Not everyone gives it away. Aren't you forgetting that some women charge for it.' Josie was drying her hair, running her fingers through it with one hand and holding the hairdryer with the other.

'True.' Mariana looked at Josie and did her utmost not to appear entranced by her friend's body.

Josie was standing naked, arms slightly raised, red hair tumbling before the warm breeze of the dryer. She was slim – almost boyish. And white, very white. Like the marble she sometimes worked with. In fact she could almost have been a statue herself stood there like that.

Josie did not appear to notice her interest. Behind the veil of red hair, she went right on talking. 'But most people – even those "in the trade" give it away the very first time. Didn't you?'

'Didn't we all!' Crystal straightened, threw her towel to one side and began doing stretching exercises. Her breasts quivered and rose as she did them. Her buttocks clenched tightly together as though they were kissing each other.

It's still big, thought Mariana before resuming. 'Well I most certainly did. I remember it well.' Mariana wrapped herself in towels, sat down on a bench and drew her legs up under her. 'He was older than me but that isn't necessarily a bad thing, is it? At least he knew the ropes.'

'How much older?' asked Josie who had finished drying her hair and was getting her clothes out of her locker. She was still naked and Mariana noticed, as she had many times before, that Josie's pubic hair was as red as that on her head. *Josie*, she thought, *is as much like some of her paintings as she is her statues.* Dramatically romantic – other worldly.

'He was about thirty-five and I was sixteen. I remember his eyes being very dark – darker than yours Crystal. But then he would be. He was Turkish and he made me think of harems and the Arabian Nights. All those sort of things.'

'Was he a sheik?' It was Crystal who asked. She was lounging naked on a bench, one breast nestling in one hand, one nipple between forefinger and thumb. She was frowning at it. *As though*, thought Mariana, *she is checking it for flaws.*

It was Josie who answered. 'Turks don't have sheiks. They used to have caliphs, but now they only have tour guides who show you around for a minimal fee and tell you they're only doing it to improve their English. Then they tell you that they've fallen in love with you and what chance is there of sleeping with you tonight.'

'True,' laughed Crystal and her hair floated around her shoulders as she nodded her head.

Aware that she could lose control of this conversation, Mariana stepped quickly back into her story. 'He was a banker. My father was sent to Turkey on a three-year contract by the bank he worked for. Ahmed was his Turkish counterpart. The first time I saw him was at my parents' home. They were having a dinner party for about twenty or so people. I stayed in my room and tried to study, but it was difficult. I could hear them all talking downstairs – but only indistinctly of course. I remember hearing a door close and footsteps, very stealthy footsteps, outside.

'My room had a balcony that was absolutely stuffed with terracotta pots full of an amazing assortment of flowers. I remember the smell of it all. Down below was a garden. Full of roses, if I remember rightly.'

She took a deep sniff and half closed her eyes. 'Wow!'

she exclaimed. 'I can still smell it now.

'I heard voices, protests, then moans. I turned off the light and quietly made my way out onto the balcony.

'The moon was full. Its light sprinkled the garden with a shower of silver rain.

'Immediately below the overhang of my balcony was a small circle of dark red tiles. It was completely surrounded by bushes, flowers and small, sweetly scented trees. It was the area where my mother read in the afternoons. By day, thanks to my balcony, it was very shady. By night each detail seemed more stark, more precise in the light of the low-hanging moon.

'I remember covering my mouth with my hand when I saw what was happening below. I could see two people. One was lying out on the sun lounger where my mother usually read Graham Greene or Hemingway. Now it was being used for something entirely different.

'I remember him standing over the woman. I remember him lifting her dress. I could see the whiteness of her thighs, the strip of white suspender holding up each stocking. I could also see what was between her legs.

'I heard her speak. Her voice was muffled, yet I could still make out the words. "Look, my love," she said. "Look. I'm not wearing any underwear. I'm ready for you, for you and you alone."

'She held out her arms to him. He stood over her. Nothing moved except his fingers which tangled in her pubic hair. Her legs seemed to fall apart as if they were melting away from a great heat. I heard her groan as he pushed his finger between her furry lips. I heard her gasp, then a squelching sound. I presumed his finger had entered her.

'The woman began to beg him to put it into her. I heard her using words that I had understood to be vulgar. I sank down to my knees, my eyes wide with interest. This, I knew, as making love. But I was very confused. Where was the romance between this man and this woman? Where were the words of love that I had been taught to expect when people were as intimate as this?

'Accompanied by the downward swipe of his zip, the woman began to throw her head from side to side, bent her knees, and opened her legs so wide that her feet were on the floor to either side of her.

'Moonlight made the fairness of her pubic hair shine like a cluster of Christmas tinsel. I did not see this for long.

'After sliding his trousers down to his knees, the man lay between her thighs, the rounded strength of his muscular bottom brown and hard against her whiteness, her softness. And then it began.

'Again and again he rammed into her. His pace never altered. It was fierce, rapid, and made her wail long and low as if she had been pierced by a particularly sharp needle.

'At last I saw his buttocks clench more tightly, her legs wrap protectively around him. The sound each of them made suddenly ran along the same track, heightened, then decreased steadily until fading to a mutual softness.

'The light from the house caught his face. That's when I recognised Ahmed. I could not see the woman's features.

'As they returned to the dinner party, I slunk back into my room.'

'Was the woman his wife?' It was Josie who asked.

Mariana avoided her eyes, shook her head, and went straight back into her story.

'The next time I saw him it was the fault of my mother. He had offered to show us around Istanbul. It was an odd sort of outing. My father spent most of his time taking snapshots of my mother. He loved taking pictures of her. He had hundreds. Once or twice he took photographs that included me, but most of the time I was left in the safe hands of Ahmed, the man I had seen bending over a half naked woman.

'He talked to me about the city, its history, its places of interest.

'His eyes were very dark and I remember his mouth being very wide. He smiled at me a lot and laughed at my embarrassment when the light cotton shirt I was wearing got soaked as I walked past a fountain. The wind had caught the spray and sent it washing over me. I remember it clinging to my breasts. It was cold and made my nipples stand out. There was a different look in his eyes from then on. It intrigued me and I began to feel a strange excitement that I had not felt since I saw him in the garden. This time, of course, because he was near to me, my excitement was far more intense.

'He watched me closely. I could see the look in his eyes that posed a question. Why were my nipples so obvious, why were my breasts so enticing? Oh yes, I could see it there. I can still see that look in his eyes even now.'

Mariana bit her bottom lip and closed her eyes. She let out a long breath. Crystal and Josie were still and silent. Their eyes were fixed on her. She was safe. She could go on and tell her tale and they would hang onto every word she said as though it were certain truth.

'Ahmed had a yacht. He invited us onto it regularly and one day, when my parents were stretched out sunning themselves on the deck, he took me swimming.

'We got into a small motorboat and he drove us to a hidden cove where the water was very blue and clear. The cliffs enclosing it were a burning yellow and were dotted with clumps of green that reminded me of cabbages.

'The water made a hushing sound against the shingle. I imagined it was telling me to be quiet; not to disturb the tranquillity of the place where only the waves and the seabirds made music.

'I remember I wore a black bikini. You know how I love black. I loved it then as much as I do now. It's the best colour possible for blondes.'

56

She tossed her head as if to emphasise the point, but not with any sign of vanity. Mariana was not a conceited woman.

'What did he wear?' Crystal purred her question and her eyes were half closed. She was stroking her body and obviously enjoying it. 'Was he wearing anything at all, or was he showing you exactly what was on offer?'

Mariana blinked a few times before she answered. 'No. He wasn't naked. He wore green trunks with a black slash across the front. The black slash sparkled slightly from the water and the sun. It was hard not to look at it. Harder still not to gaze intently at the bulge behind it.

'We lay down on the beach. He asked me if I wanted to get my back brown without a strap mark. I said I did, so he undid my bikini top for me.

'He had brought lotion and warned me against burning my shoulders. His eyes never left me as he said it. I felt them wandering over me in the same way his hands would.

'I knew what he was going to do even before he did it. I gasped slightly as the coldness of the cream was spread in slow, ever-increasing circles over my skin.

'His hands were warm and his breath was quickening. It was very soothing – comforting. I felt his fingers leave my shoulders and run down my spine. Even though the sun was hot on my back, I shivered. But I was slightly afraid.

'I was a child who had been brought up on romance, not sensuality. I was confused by what he was doing, but I was also helpless beneath his touch.

'He asked me if I liked what he was doing to me. I told him I wasn't sure. He called me a silly goose and kissed my back. I remember the feel of his lips upon my skin, the roughness around his chin, the silky softness of his moustache. I remember his chest hairs tickling the middle of my back. I remember a tightness in my stomach and a curling ticklishness between my legs.

'Because his shadow fell over me and his body pressed

on mine, I felt trapped by him. I closed my eyes and pretended to feel tired.

'"Rest awhile, little girl," he said to me. "Rest awhile and dream, and I will soothe all your fears away."

'He lay next to me, one hand resting on my behind as if only carelessly placed there. Yet I knew it was not carelessness. It was a deliberate act. He was enjoying the feel of my buttocks. I was convinced he was hoping I would get used to his hand being upon me, the warmth of his fingers arousing my body just as the warmth of the sun was soothing it to sleep.

'Warmth and the dreams of what might happen made me fall into a light doze. My mind entered that hazy area between full consciousness and deep sleep where all things happen and anything is possible. I was Alice wandering through my own Wonderland. Not the fairy-tale one with white rabbits and novelty playing cards, but one that burned brightly on the frontier between puberty and adulthood.

'In my dreams the sun itself had sprouted hands and was trailing its warm fingers down my back. I murmured something wordless. So strong was the warmth of those fingers that they slid enticingly beneath the fabric of my bikini pants.

'I liked the sun doing that. It made me wriggle my hips and moan in my sleep. It was only as I felt those fingers dividing one buttock from the other that I knew they belonged to my companion, Ahmed the banker, and not to the sun.

'Inexperience made me feel confused. What should I do in such a circumstance?

'I decided to continue with my pretence of being asleep. Better that than show my ignorance. The vision of him in the garden pleasuring the woman was still in my mind. I recalled the whiteness of her limbs, the tension of the suspender that gripped both her flesh and her stocking. I also recalled the deep vee of golden fleece pointing between her thighs. It made my body burn with desire.

'The subterfuge seemed to suit him well. Each time I jittered – as though I really were sleeping and still dreaming – his hand paused. And yet, I did not want it to pause.

'I felt him ease my pants down over my bottom. The sun kissed my newly exposed flesh in the same friendly way as it would kiss twin melons growing from the same stalk. As I murmured some unintelligible utterings, my dark-eyed banker kissed one buttock then the other. He slid my pants down my legs. He did it very slowly, very gently. He left them loose around one ankle. My body was naked except for that forlorn piece of blackness around my ankle and the matching shred that divided my bare breasts from the gritty sand.

'I did not move. I did not want him to know I was compliant with what he wanted of me. So, even as he eased my bra top downwards, I did not protest. I merely whimpered slightly as the sand reformed around my bosoms.

'"You like that," he whispered. "I can see you like the roughness of the sand against your pretty pink nipples. I can see you like the feel of the sun on your bottom too."

'He was right, but something inside me would not admit it – not even to myself.

'His hand ran down my back in a soft, gentle sweep. It was the sort of touch you would use to soothe a young horse that is about to take a rider for the first time. It made me hot, but it also made me tremble.

'Because there was a large hump of sand beneath my hips, my buttocks were raised slightly.

'I heard him moan as he pushed my legs apart. Ignorant as I was, I did not know whether he was doing this because he liked what he was seeing or because he was experiencing pain. I only knew I liked the touch of his fingers skimming lightly across my flesh and dividing the lips of my sex.

'I felt his tongue, warm as the sun, wet as the sea, run down the crease of my behind. Where his fingers had been, it too went. Soon I was cooing as he probed the lips of my sex. His fingers became wet with my juices.

'"That's it, little girl," he said. "Enjoy what I am doing to you. Many other men will do this to you in the future. Some you will remember, most you will forget. But not me. You will never forget me because I was the first and took what no one else will ever take.

'I didn't know what he meant. As I said, my ideas of sexuality were based upon syrupy novels and films that were all chosen by my father. Right up until that moment, my father had treated me as a child and my mother, being pretty disinterested anyway, had gone along with him.

'The sun was hot upon my body. At first I was grateful that Ahmed lay over me, his arms rigid, his shadow cool upon me. The coolness did not last. I squeezed my eyes tightly shut and gritted my teeth so that I would not cry out. Something very hard and very hot was pushing its way into my body.

'I suprised myself and him. Had my hips acquired a mind of their own?

'Without any real effort I bent my knees, raised my buttocks, but still I did not open my eyes or make a sound.

'Ahmed sighed with happiness. "That's it, little girl. Push yourself onto me and I will open the gate to your perfumed garden."

'At first I felt the hot tip of his member prod at my moist, aching lips. They opened and let him in. Hard and alien as he was, the muscles of my vagina welcomed him, gripped him as if encouraging him onwards.

'What tension I felt left me. He did not ram himself into me as he had the woman in the garden. Bit by bit, little by little, he eased himself gently and smoothly into my body. And I welcomed him, willed him to go further.

'But I still had a hymen and he had not reached that yet.

When he did, I felt a hot, searing pain. I cried out and took a deep breath which quickly became no more than a whimper.

'His breath was hot and rapid against my fear. The consideration he had shown me gradually went. Now his thrusts were more urgent.

'"All of your life," he said, "I will be the one man you will always – always – remember. I am the man who took your virginity." And he was right.'

'Wow!' Crystal looked genuinely impressed. Confident as she was of her own sexuality, her own power to seduce, she now regarded Mariana with more respect than she had prior to the tale being told.

'Did you ever see him again?' asked Josie.

'Yes. Many times.' Mariana smiled. There was a look in her eyes that suggested there were other things she was remembering that she did not want to talk about. Before anyone could press her to disclose further details, she got up, dropped her towels, and began to dress. 'I'll tell you another time. Bowls this evening.'

'Lucky you!'

'Not that kind, Crystal baby. We're going to watch Jamie's father play bowls – not play with balls, though I wouldn't say no if someone offered.'

They laughed, gathered their belongings together, and left.

Josie joined Michael in the bar for a drink and a quick bar meal.

Mariana met up with Jamie and they made their way over to Redcatch Park where Alex, Jamie's father, was playing for his company team on the silky green of the bowling club.

Chapter 9

'Glad you could come.' Alex kissed Mariana's cheek. Jamie asked who wanted drinks then went off to get them.

Alex squeezed Mariana's hand. As he did so, he winked and his bright blue eyes twinkled an unspoken message to his fair-haired daughter-in-law. He said just two words, trying to encapsulate everything that his eyes were saying to her.

'Everything alright?'

'Everything in the garden is lovely.' Her mouth stretched in an insincere smile.

What was so lovely about her life? she asked herself. Her eyes narrowed as her smile disappeared and her jaw line became tense.

To all intents and purposes she was watching Alex as he stepped forward to the green. He hitched his white flannel trousers at the knee before bending and aiming for the jack.

I wonder if Jamie will end up like his father, she thought to herself. Jamie, who was not particularly lovely. Jamie, whom she was fond of and had married. But *why* had they married, a small voice in her head piped up. *Because we suit each other,* she answered. *We thought we had something to give each other*. That was all.

No, Jamie was not lovely. Lovely was a term she could apply to Alex, his father. Alex reminded her of her own father, a father she had adored. A father who had let her down as much as her mother had.

As shadows lengthened across the bowling green and a stray grey cloud temporarily cloaked a glowing sunset, Mariana wrapped one side of her thigh-length sweater tightly over the other. She hugged it to herself, as if that would make her warmer and chase away a chilling memory.

Once she had drunk the St Clements Jamie had bought for her, she made her excuses and wandered off around the park.

'I've got a bit of a headache,' she said to Alex.

Jamie looked at her askance.

'First time I've ever known you to have a headache,' he said in all seriousness.

Alex laughed. 'Good grief, son, you certainly are a lucky man if that's the first headache you've ever known your wife to have. Your mother had one of the bloody things every time I reached across and touched her thigh or let my gaze wander to her bosom rather than look her straight in the eye.'

He laughed again and put his drink down before rejoining his cronies down on the green.

Mariana did not meet the look in Jamie's eyes.

'You alright?' he asked.

Mariana took a deep breath of air and nodded quickly, jerkily, like some ancient tin toy whose clockwork is slowly running down. 'Yes,' she repeated again as though Jamie needed some serious convincing. 'It won't last long – not once I've had a swift walk around the park. I'll come back when the game is over.'

Briefly she patted Jamie's arm as she swept past him then pecked her father-in-law on one soft cheek.

'Enjoy your walk,' he said to her.

'I will.' She smiled warmly at him, this man who was as big as his son, but whose hair was white, his flesh pink and as dimpled as the rind of an orange.

Despite the advance of twilight, the evening was a pleasant one.

As she left the bowling green and the white-clad men and women behind, she allowed her cardigan to swing open. The evening air encouraged her to walk taller and straighter, to stick out her chest so that her shape was easily discernible. Like cherries on top of the roundest and most well-risen of sponge cakes, her nipples thrust defiantly against the clinging black top she wore.

The sun was beginning to streak the sky and gild the edges of fat-bellied clouds. Summer was in the air and all the scents that went with it; flowers, grass, heat and dust. It reminded her of Turkey. It also reminded her of Ahmed, that night beneath her bedroom window, and that other time, the time when she had found out what sex felt like as well as what it looked like.

Walking with her eyes half closed, she could again easily imagine the moon dappling the leaves of that time, the earthy red of the floor tiles that provided such a rich bakground for the white flesh of the woman exposed to Ahmed's gaze.

At first the woman's arm had shielded her face from view. Mariana had leaned further out of the open window, her mouth slightly open, her breath hot with the need to discover. Such a heat, that heat of youthful curiosity, of youthful arousal.

Still she had not been able to see the woman's face but, even so, each person has individual traits, familiar characteristics by which they are and forever will be known.

Perhaps it is the way a woman holds her body or holds one leg against the other in a clichéd pose she might once have seen in *Vogue*. Perhaps it's the angle of a toe in relation to its foot. The slimness of an ankle, the dimple of a knee – whatever. Mariana could not discern exactly what it was that was so familiar about this woman. But she had paused as she watched, her face impassive as a hive of confused thoughts had buzzed in her head. She had been convinced that the woman was known to her.

Impassive though her expression had been, Mariana's heart had thudded against her ribs. Even now as she walked through an English park all those years later, just thinking about that time brought back the echoes of that thumping heart.

It had been the dress the woman was wearing that had been the trigger to knowing. The slim shift of black crepe studded with jet had been new.

Even so, she had not been able to bring herself to tell her friends the woman's identity. That was for her to know. That was the pain for her to carry. Much water had flowed beneath many bridges since then, yet still her face flushed when she thought about it.

Groaning as the man's fingers probed her sex, the woman had thrown back her arm and a gold bracelet had flashed in the moonlight.

The bracelet had been enough to send Mariana's heart racing more quickly. She knew that bracelet too well and thought she had known the woman to whom it belonged.

Curiosity had made her throat dry. Her breathing had quickened and become almost painful as it rasped over the dryness of her tongue and her throat.

She managed to swallow as she focused her eyes on the woman who lay beneath the man. She immediately recognised the features.

Although her eyes were closed and her mouth had hung open in the manner of someone who has totally taken leave of their senses, her identity was confirmed.

Heart beating like a drum, Mariana had hung there, eyes wide with amazement. The coldness of realisation had mixed wtih the heat of untried adolescent sexuality. Down below, in the light of the moon, surrounded by the lush greenness of a Turkish balcony, her mother was having sex with another man.

Of course, she could have run screaming into the house, shouting at the top of her voice that her mother's knickers were around her ankles and Uncle Ahmed was lying in between her thighs.

She could have rushed crying to her father, eyes and nose running as she tried to blurt out the details of what she had seen.

But she did not do those things. Instead, she watched, her eyes wide, her knuckles whiter than the stone balustrade she was gripping so tightly.

And inside, something had stirred. Something she had not understood, and yet had enjoyed. Feathery light tingles of something resembling butterflies seemed to flutter between her legs and float upwards into her belly.

There was a stirring between her legs, a more persistent fluttering as though something had just hatched out and was about to spread its wings. The strange thing was that no matter how much that presence might try, it would never truly leave her body.

She never questioned how she had known that. She just had. One thing she was sure of was that from that day on everything in her life would never be the same again.

As she plodded the dented tarmac of the path through the park, Mariana contemplated how it had been after that.

She remembered it being hard to be civil to her mother. Incivility had led to outright rebellion, and not just that. That other something that had been aroused besides the contempt for her mother was also becoming more and more demanding.

After her mother had complained about her behaviour, her father had taken her into his study and given her a lecture about being civil to one's elders.

She had stared at him, her jaw firmly clenched, wanting to tell him exactly what she had seen and not knowing where to begin. Her father's blue eyes had twinkled once the dressing down was over. He'd hugged her. She'd hugged him back as tightly as she could. There had been so much she had wanted to say, and so much she couldn't. But the cold fingers of shock that had first gripped her heart had changed to fear. What would be gained by her father knowing? He might go away and leave her entirely with her mother and Ahmed. And how could she face them? How could she talk to them and laugh and joke like they used to. Living with them would be like living at half volume.

No, she had decided and, with the naive logic of the young, she had bitten her lip and hugged her father that much harder.

'Steady on,' he had said, as her hands had clutched at his trousers. She remembered the embarrassed look on his face as he pushed her away, the slight flush that had come to his cheeks and a certain furtiveness to his eyes. 'Steady on, girl. Save that for all the young men that are going to come after you. They'll all want your love and if you give it all to me, you'll have none left for them.'

'I don't want them!' She had tried to hug him closer, her hands gripping his buttocks, but he had pushed her away with more force than before so that she fell back onto the floor. Tears had stung her eyes. All the love she had for her father had been as bruised as her body – more so perhaps.

His jaw had become more solid, eyes more stern, lips set in one even line. 'Oh yes you will,' he had stated, and then he turned away.

She had lied to her changing-room friends about the trip into Istanbul. Her father had not been with them. Her mother and Ahmed had laughed a lot together and she had felt like some piece of unnecessary baggage they would rather have left behind.

All the same, the strange fluttering that had been ignited on the night she had seen them having sex beneath the balcony was still with her. Only it wasn't so much a fluttering now, but a bigger, more solid presence. It was like comparing what had been a mere butterfly to an eagle.

On the trip into Istanbul that presence began to assert itself as she watched her vivacious, blonde mother and the darkly romantic Turk.

Their hands kept touching, their hips bumping as if neither of them could contemplate being separate human beings.

Mariana had trailed on behind, her eyes following each furtive movement, each sexual signal.

Ahmed had long brown fingers that seemed as dextrous as spiders' legs. Mariana's gaze had followed them as they curled over the soft rise of her mother's behind, up over her waist and her ribs so that they rested beneath the curve of her bosom.

They had sat at a table outside a whitewashed cafe and, as Ahmed and her mother drank thick Turkish coffee, she had sipped at sherbet, her eyes studying them from under the flaxen fringe that fell over her eyebrows.

Again she had followed the progress of Ahmed's fingers. They had lain almost immobile in her mother's lap, the long fingers pointing down between the deep valley between her thighs.

As she looked, she heard Ahmed whispering to her mother.

'What are you looking at, Mariana darling?'

Her mother's high-pitched voice had made her start and look up, leaving the straw she had been sucking twirling in the midst of her drink.

She had flushed and mumbled a muted 'nothing'. She had blinked, glanced at them, and seen them exchange looks that told her they did not believe what she had said.

Ahmed made a comment about it being time she had a man of her own.

Her mother protested that she was too young. 'She's only sixteen.'

'Old enough – especially in Turkey,' Ahmed remarked.

Mariana did not hear what he whispered to her mother. She only watched, hands clasped tightly around her drink, eyes wide and apprehensive.

Her mother tried to argue, but Ahmed gave her no chance to utter more than one word at a time. At last, her mother – poor, weak soul – seemed genuinely swayed by the logic Ahmed presented to her.

It was a day or two later that she had accompanied her mother to Ahmed's house.

The house wasn't his matrimonial home where he lived with his family in the crowded heart of the city. This house was white and square, its base built on the yellow dust of the earth, its top half framed by the blue of the sky. Yellow dust trailed behind their car as they approached it; like a veil, Mariana had thought to herself, or a curtain that hides this side of Ahmed's life from the other.

They entered a hall with a high ceiling and floors of terracotta red.

From the outside the house appeared to be a simple square, but its heart was cut out. In the middle was a courtyard.

Sunlight filtered through damask blinds and broad-leafed plants. A fountain played in the middle of the courtyard beyond arched doorways in walls of blue tiles.

Smiling, Ahmed approached from a set of steps that curved from one side of the room.

'Welcome!'

His voice echoed around the blue, grey and green of the place. It was the only sound except for their breathing and that of the fan which disturbed the air and their hair.

'I hope you are well.' His teeth flashed white against the sleek brown of his face and Mariana thought how handsome he was. The feeling inside her that had started so small was now taking over her body, responding to his dark eyes, his captivating smile.

In that one moment she became a woman. In that one moment she also became jealous that this man lad lain with her mother before lying with her.

There was a sudden electric charge in the air. All three of them had stood immobile, holding their breath for the next thing to happen, the next word to be said. But something did happen and something was said. Mariana remembered it well – too well. Word for word, she remembered what her mother had said next.

'It's so hot out there. I'm quite faint. Do you mind if I lie down out on the terrace. I've brought a book with me'.

A book. She always brought a book, always had a world to escape into. In a book, she was forever young, forever sexy, and always the heroine.

'Perhaps you could take my daughter over the house. She likes old buildings.' There had been a distinct nervousness in her voice. Her eyes had flitted onto her daughter then quickly away.

Her footsteps had echoed off the cool walls, the blue tiles, the green blinds, the redness of the terracotta floor.

Mariana had not protested. She had looked boldly into Ahmed's eyes, so boldly that his seemed to light with excited fire.

Vague impressions from memory came back to her as the shadow of a plane tree fell across her path. Its shadow was solid, black as she made her way through the park. She shivered and wrapped her woollen jacket back round her again. The sun was less warm now and the clouds were getting darker.

She shivered again, but not so much because of the fading sunlight, but because of those things she remembered.

Ahmed had taken hold of her hand. She had gasped at the coolness of his fingers, the softness of his palms. A sweet ache came into being below her belly.

'Are you going to seduce me?' she asked him.

His eyes opened wide in surprise. 'Seduce you? My dear girl, do you know what that word means?'

She nodded. 'Yes. It's what you did to mummy out on the terrace. You seduced her.'

Ahmed looked at her in amazement, then frowned. 'You saw us? Did you tell your father?'

She shook her head. 'No. I didn't.'

'But I thought you were daddy's little girl. I though you told him everything.'

'My mother said so?'

'Yes.'

'Perhaps. But you haven't answered my question. Are you going to seduce me?'

He paused. 'Do you want me to?'

'I don't know.' She trembled.

Still holding her hand, he came close to her. He touched her face with his free hand, the coolness of his fingers running over her cheek and leaving a fire in their wake.

'It will be good for you. It is meant to happen.'

That in itself would have been acceptable. That in itself would have been a tale to tell – if Mariana hadn't found out the other thing. But the other thing would stay hidden. The other thing was something she did not like to repeat.

'You are hot,' he said to her when they at least reached the sleek coolness of the upstairs rooms. 'You must have something cool to drink.'

Mariana licked her lips and swallowed as she remembered the taste of raspberries and something else, something slightly bitter.

'Drink it all up,' he had said, and she had done so.

A feeling of wellbeing had come over her. The room around her seemed less crisp. Bright colours became more muted, hard lines were softened. After that, her arms and her legs seemed suddenly lighter than they had been. He bade her lie down. She couldn't recall the colour of the walls or the floor in the cool room. She only remembered that the bed was soft, the headboard behind her fashioned from dark wood. Grapes, vines, nuts and small birds with unseeing eyes rambled, tumbled and flew across the headboard. The carvings were slightly yellow in places where, perhaps, hands had rubbed or nonchalantly followed the form of the carving or the grain of the wood.

The main thing she remembered was the rich ochre of the ceiling and the waft of air from the overhead fan. She also remembered the look in Ahmed's eyes as he bent over her. His teeth looked like small pearls above the moistness of his tongue. He smiled.

'Let me make you comfortable.' His voice was as provocative and as irresistible as the sound of the waves kissing sand. 'You are too hot. Let me make you cool.'

She vaguely remembered trying to protest as her clothes were taken from her body. She tried to wriggle, but her hips merely undulated with a sensual slowness. Her voice did not obey her. Neither did her limbs. Only when she lay naked did she moan as her nipples hardened and her flesh dimpled beneath the coolness of the overhead fan. Suddenly, she had been grateful for his consideration.

Silent and unmoving, she had watched everything Ahmed had done. She had taken in the details as a bystander might watch an accident occur, or a crime happen. Such things seem to take place in the smallest of moments, so minute a time frame that the bystander can make no movement. Or at least, that's how it seems. The moment itself drags by in slow motion and each detail is remembered as if it took forever.

As she walked through the park all those years later, she found it all so easy to recall.

His lips had kissed her mouth and his tongue slid between her teeth. The smell and taste of him gave her pleasure. The silk of his shirt caressed her breasts before

73

his hands did, before his fingers tapped, then squeezed at her nipples.

They're getting harder, she had thought to herself. She could feel them responding to him.

Above her the fan had whirred and turned. Below her breasts, his head bobbed around her belly. A wet warmth had circled her navel. What was he doing there? she had asked herself.

Strong, yet delicate, his tongue had dipped gently into her navel as though this small, fleshy cul-de-sac was something far more feminine, far more virgin than anything else on her body.

Feelings never before experienced had swept over her. Even as she walked through the park now, she remembered how exciting those feelings had been. There never is a time like the first time. Never is a moment so indelible in the mind. But she also remembered indignation that something precious was being stolen from her without her permission – almost without her taking any starring role in it.

Suddenly, despite the cool air, her cheeks burned and her eyes turned a more chill blue than they usually were.

In the park, two teenagers were strolling along the path in front of her. They were giggling, cuddling, the boy's hand slipping onto the girl's bottom, his fingers squeezing. The girl did the same to him.

Later, thought Mariana, they would do more. Within the park they would find a grassy mound among a clutch of shrubbery and there they would make love. It might be for the first time, or it might not. But at least the girl was likely to be given a choice whether to respond or not – whether to push him away or not. Mariana had not had a choice.

Ahmed's dark eyes had smouldered with passion as he had looked at her over the flatness of her belly. His hands had pushed her legs apart. She had been too weak to protest. The drink he had given her had done its job.

'You liked that, didn't you, little girl. You truly liked that. I can tell because you are wet.'

She had tried to say something. Only a whimper came out.

He had laughed. 'You do not believe me? Then I will show you.'

Long, artistic fingers slid through her hidden flesh. She trembled at their touch and small cries fled her throat like a clutch of startled birds.

Tingling, tantalising electricity gathered in one particular spot as his finger dipped into her. The sensation around where he entered was not unpleasant. She had found herself wanting his finger to go in further. She had found herself wanting this man to do whatever he wanted.

'See?' He had held his finger up before her face. It glistened with her own juices.

The story she had told Crystal and Josie was partly true. He did say that he was taking her virginity and that she would rememer him all her life. She had remembered him. She had adored him.

'I will show you the weapon that will take your virginity,' he had said. He had knelt between her legs, unzipped his pristine trousers and released his member.

Wide-eyed, she had gazed at it. She saw it move as if it were trembling at what it was about to do. Thick veins stood proud of the dark tan flesh. She could almost feel its heat, wanted to reach out and touch it, but her arms felt like lead. She had then mewed with pleasure as its hot tip had divided her sexual lips.

He used one hand to hold her hip and steady her. He used the other to guide himself into her.

Bit by bit, she felt this alien intruder slide into where no one else had been before.

'I will be gentle,' he said, his voice trembling, his eyes bright with excitement. 'I will push in gently at first until the barrier is breached and I am inside your womb, invading your body.'

'I remember it well,' she whispered to herself on her walk through the park. There was an ache between her legs that reflected the thoughts in her mind.

Ahmed had pushed himself into her just like he said he would. At first, as he had promised, he was gentle, then there was searing pain, tension and a rigidity in her limbs as he ripped through her hymen.

She had cried out for her mother and had tried to move her legs, to force him from her. Tears had rolled from her eyes. The fluttering that had caused her to do this had suddenly stilled as though regretful of what it had instigated.

'There, there,' he had said softly. 'Take it easy. Breathe slowly. Let it wash over you like the waves of the sea. Soon the pain will be no more and only pleasure will remain.'

He had lain still on her then, kissed her tears and, as he kissed them, she felt him throbbing within her, his sac hot between her thighs. Then it began again.

Once he knew that her barrier was broken and her tension released. His pace quickened and became fiercer.

Her cries became groans as the first tremors of pleasure replaced the searing pain of his initial intrusion.

The heat of his belly and the coarseness of his pubic hair had slapped against her as he rammed himself into her. He gripped her hips, his hair against her mouth. The smell of it made her both sick and excited.

Something was released from deep within her. Something that fluttered and spread over her body like the touch of butterfly wings, rising ever higher, making her close her eyes because it felt so beautiful, so pleasurable.

She opened her eyes and stared into the sweating face of Ahmed. His expression was intense, his lips wet as he groaned more deeply with each thrust of his loins.

He looked fierce, frightening; like a brigand, a thief that comes in the night and takes something that is not his. He had taken from her, he had given her only pain but, at last, her own moment of triumph came as she took something from him.

His body had stiffened against hers. She had felt a pulsating deep inside her womb, a cascade of warmth as he moaned gratefully against her ear. He had taken from her, and yet, she had also given something. Both left her with a feeling of power – the power to provoke, to arouse, to give pleasure.

That had been the first time, and just thinking about it made her feel hot – and also regretful.

If only that had been it; pure sex and a simple taking of her virginity and the coupling that followed. How different she might have been. How different a man she might have married. But her life had not been as simple as that. Other things had followed.

Chapter 10

CRYSTAL'S STORY

The three of them were having lunch in the sharp black and white surroundings of Luigi's Trattoria.

Mariana was smiling at a pretty little waitress. The waitress blushed and looked away.

'Sweet little thing,' proclaimed Mariana. With neatly manicured fingernails, she pushed her blonde bob away from her face.

'Not my type.' Crystal raised her eyebrows and threw a shocked glance at Josie.

'Don't knock what you've never tried.' Mariana poked her tongue through a circle of red pepper and wiggled it provocatively.

'I'll carry on as I am,' returned Crystal. 'I started out with cocks and I'll finish with cocks.'

Mariana grinned as she let the piece of pepper fall back to her plate.

Josie merely shook her head and smiled.

'So how old were you the first time you opened those long legs of yours and let in the first vessel?'

Crystal snorted.

'Oh, come on, Crystal.' Josie nudged her elbow and smiled. 'Don't be shy. Tell us how he approached you and how good-looking he was. Come on.'

Thoughtfully, Crystal sucked on a piece of cucumber that she held between finger and thumb. She endowed the action with a certain sophistication, almost as though using cutlery was vulgar. Rolling her eyes as she considered the question was typical Crystal. Enigmatic was the word to describe her smile, though smug might be just as good. The message was clear. No one in the whole world had experienced such a delicious deflowering as she had.

Josie held a finger across her mouth, perhaps to hide her own smile. Green eyes shone intently above her white hand. She gazed into Crystal's face as if willing her to open her mouth and let the details come out.

Crystal avoided looking at Josie, lest Josie see the guilt in her eyes – as well as the pity.

Poor Josie, so dull compared to Michael. No sex life before him. So single-minded about her career, so good at being the dutiful wife, the courteous hostess. Poor Michael, having to live with her; him, the successful executive and Josie the suitable wife. Not the sexy wife, the exciting wife, the woman who made his breath come in short, sharp gasps along with his penis. It was Crystal who fulfilled that particular need.

Poor Josie. Crystal smiled. Why shouldn't she tell her just what a foxy woman she was? The red lips parted, the blue eyes sparkled, and Crystal began her tale.

'He was a rugby player. A big bruiser of a man with thick thighs and great big shoulders.' She emphasised their width with her hands. 'And he was black as night. Hard as nails. Wow, what a moment! What a dick!'

Josie smiled softly and glanced at Mariana. It was Mariana who urged Crystal to go on.

Crystal adopted uncharacteristic coyness. 'Oh I don't think you would find it that interesting. I was just a young girl and he was just a muscle-bound man. You know the sort of thing. Everything was so completely irresistible!'

Crystal laughed her strident, confident laugh, a laugh that seemed to tell everyone else that there was no point them even trying to be sexy when she was around because she was the best and they'd better believe it!

'Cut the dramatics, Crystal darling, let's have the facts – pure and simple.'

Josie joined her in the not-so-subtle art of persuasion.

'Come on, Crys. You've whetted our appetites. We're all ears.'

Madame Giaconda could not have outdone the beguiling smile that swept over Crystal's smug features. The audience was waiting. 'Oh, well . . . ' she purred seductively.

Mariana touched her hand. 'Come along, Crystal darling. Don't keep us in limbo. What happened? Who propositioned who, and was his weapon really the stuff that legends are made of?'

At last an expression of contrived resignation spread over Crystal's lovely face. From the very first she had wanted to tell them about how she lost her virginity. She had listened, enthralled, to how Mariana had lost hers – not entirely without jealousy. But she could easily outdo that maudlin tale. Mariana was handsome, but not beautiful. She was cynical rather than sexual. Those were Crystal's considered opinions, but then, Crystal had to be better than anyone else, so she was keen to tell them. But she also thrived on attention. There had to be a build-up, a perceived longing to know on their part. Coddled in the shallow depths of her ego, their encouragement added greater value to the adventure she was about to impart.

Her breasts heaved against the blue silk of her blouse as she sighed and directed her gaze to the blackened beam that hung low above their table. Her voice dropped to a level that might possibly be overheard and even remarked on.

'As I said, he was a rugby player, black and built of grit and muscle. He had a chiselled face, coal-black eyebrows, and eyes like chocolate – melting chocolate.'

'Runny?'

Crystal ignored Mariana's trite remark and sceptical expression. She carried on, her eyes fixed on the bowl of blue anemones that sat in front of a lead-paned window.

'It wouldn't have been that difficult to sit in one of his hands – that's how big he was. Six five – perhaps more.'

As though she had said something really wicked – really wild – she paused for effect and another heave of her generous breasts. The blue silk rustled. Her nipples left small dents in the delicate fabric.

'I wasn't really interested in the game as such, but one afternoon my brothers persuaded me to come along and watch. Some friend had given them tickets and the third one would have been wasted if I hadn't agreed to go.

'Like brothers do, they did their best to lose me once we were inside. I didn't mind at all. I was too busy watching these great big men rushing into each other over the frosty ground. Just looking at them made me feel as randy as hell – me, that had been educated in one of the strictest convent schools in the country. But, oh boy! It was a sight worth seeing!

'I remember the cracking of heads and the crashing of bodies as they threw themselves at each other. I remember the way their thigh muscles quivered as they strained at the scrum. It was lovely.

'When the game was over and the teams were about to leave the pitch, my brothers suddenly found me. They were grinning and I wondered if they'd been plotting some mean trick. They were always doing things like that. Being the only girl was pretty tough with those two, much as I loved them.

'They asked me if I was alright and did I want to go to the loo or anything, or did I want something to drink. I said I could do with going to the lavatory if they could direct me in the right direction.

'"We'll take you," they said. Like a fool, I believed them.

82

'Pushing our way through the crowd, one brother in front and one behind, we came to a blank door that had no notice on it, but it did have a handle. My brothers informed me that this was exactly what I wanted.

'"It's not marked ladies," I said to them.

'"Ain't no ladies or gents," my brothers informed me. "Everyone shares the same lav at a rugby ground." Like a fool, I believed that too.

'I went in and closed the door behind me. The place was not at all like any lavatory I'd ever seen before. I stopped and stared.

'There was a bank of showers along one side, and white china basins along the other. There was no one about, and everything was white tiled, steamy and smelled of sweaty boots and soap.

'Beyond the showers and basins, I found some toilet cubicles. The varnished wooden door opened to reveal a matching toilet seat. Connected by lead pipework to a stained white bowl was an overhead cistern. Cast in iron, it came complete with dangling chain and willow-patterned handle. It looked too good to be doing service at a local rugby ground. I couldn't help thinking of it being the official lavatory style for the Victoria and Albert – you know, all pristine whiteness and Victorian mahogany.

'I lingered too long. I'd done what I had to do and had pulled up my knickers. But the pattern on the handle and the ornamentation of the overhead tank were quite intriguing. Perhaps that was the first time I became interested in antiques – I don't know.

'Anyway, I heard voices. My heart sank. They were deep voices that said things to turn the air blue. I stopped in my tracks, my hand on the door knob. Voices became muffled as jerseys were pulled over heads. Boots knocked against tiles as they were kicked to one side.

'It was then that I realised that I'd been had. At that moment in time, I could have killed my brothers. The little swines had done it again!

'Luckily the brass bolt was firmly across the cubicle door. I stared at it, I remember, as if I were daring it to move. Stupid, I know, but it was all I could do.

'Water gushed from showers in the room I would have to go through to get out. I imagined them there, all those hunky men I had seen slamming into each other out on the rugby pitch. I began to feel excited.

'The thought of their mighty bodies naked and water running down and dripping off the end of their willies was too much for a young girl such as myself. I could hear them, hear their banter, their remarks about who had the biggest and the best, and who was going to go for it that night with their wife, their girlfriend, or a casual acquaintance.

' "I'm real ready for it!"

' "Come on, brother dick, get refreshed. Get ready for supper!"

'There was the sound of a slap, a whoop of pretend pain. I could tell from their conversation that some horseplay was going on. I could also tell that they were admiring each other's equipment.

' "What the fuck's that, Jason? You going pole vaulting or something?"

' "You're a jealous prick, Roger, cos that's all you got. Six inches fully extended and no good to nobody."

' "Come and see this, guys. Look at what he's got?"

'Despite the laughter, the voices of the other guys seemed to subside as they inspected the penis of the guy called Jason.

' "Wow!" I heard one say. "Can I borrow it?"

' "What woman could take that?"

'The comments just went on and on.

'Well, I can tell you, girls, I was more than curious. I'd been propositioned by some real good-looking men but had always kept them at a distance. Now, I was maturing fast and in desperate need of having my first fuck. If I was going to have a good one first time round, it sounded as if Jason's mighty member fitted the bill.

'Young as I was, I took my courage in both hands, took off my coat and undid the top three buttons of my blouse so that my cleavage showed. Bold as brass and with my breasts bouncing, I slid back the bolt and left my hiding place.'

Crystal threw back her head and laughed. 'Boy, were they surprised! Some just stared but others, probably those who had been so full of themselves, were stunned and silent.

'Head high, I walked past them all. They stood completely still and stared at me as I passed. Their mouths were hanging open. None had attempted to hide their cocks. Now and again I glanced down to where a stiff member stood proud of a naked body, then I stopped.

'"Which one of you is the super-stud?"

'They broke out into laughter and all tried to lay claim to the name. One or two swayed their hips and sent their lengths waggling before them. I can remember their lewd comments even now.

'"Anytime, darling."

'"All yours if you want it!"

'I stood with my hands on my hips so that my blouse gaped and my cleavage bubbled out of my bra.

'"Okay dickhead," I said. "Let me put it another way. Which one of you is Jason?"

'Groans and sniggers echoed through the steam.

'"I'm Jason," he said, and I knew he was. I recognised his voice. He smiled as he stepped out of the shower cubicle. He was gloriously naked, gloriously black and gloriously erect. I couldn't take my eyes off him.

'"I'm Jason," he said again.

His voice was as dark as brandy. I took a deep breath. It was hard to tear my gaze away from his rod. It was such a beautiful sight to behold; too thick for a hand to encompass, and long enough to tickle the deepest of throats.

'His skin glistened with water as the steam hit his flesh and ran in slow rivulets down his black-satin chest and the hardness of his inner thighs.

'Eventually, I did manage to let my gaze wander up over his flat stomach and the muscles of his chest. Eventually, I also looked into his face.

'His jaw was very square, his face was sculptured like some Greek statue. Like his body, his head was hairless and shone with health and with water. He looked me up and down. My legs went to jelly.'

The women she called friends watched as Crystal shivered in a flowing, floaty sort of way. As though inclined to kiss, her lips formed a perfect pout as she recalled the sight of the naked man and his huge erection.

Mariana had to make comment. 'Did he still have this hard-on, or had it turned to jelly like your legs?'

'It was magnificent. Still hard. Still huge. I could have fallen on my knees and worshipped it then and there, but I had other things on my mind.

'To this day I am sure that Jason read my thoughts. His smile dazzled and gave me strength. In return I gave him the bravest, most brazen smile I could; the sort that conveyed everything I was feeling.

'Leering faces were all around us, yet I knew he only had eyes for me and I for him.

'"Come here, hon," he said, and took hold of my hand. "Let me show you out."

'I didn't really want to go, but I didn't like to say so. Anyway, I couldn't take my eyes off him. He was making my knickers wet and I wanted the problem cured.

'The other men did not jeer and shout out like I would have expected them to. They stood aside as he led me beyond the changing rooms. Behind a green plastic curtain was a door. He opened it for me.

'"Stay in here till they're gone," he whispered. "I'll come for you."

'The room he left me in was lined with strips of pine and there was a cauldron near the door. It was very hot in there. I know now that it was a sauna. I hadn't a clue at the time.

'"If you get too hot, take off your clothes," he said, then the door closed and the curtain beyond swished against it. The room did get a lot hotter.

'Well you know what sauna heat is like. It tastes as though there's a layer of powdered graphite lining your mouth. Sweat began to creep from every pore of my body.

'Of course, there was no reason why I *had* to stay. I *wanted* to stay. I ached to have that hard, black body against mine. Just thinking of his gleaming skin and his massive muscles sent my head spinning.

'Like the heat of the sauna, the heat of my desire had a most definite effect. I laid my coat down on a bench, ran my hand inside my blouse and felt the heat of my body. My nipples that had lain so long inside my maidenly bra were hard as hazelnuts. To touch them made me tremble.

'His words were still with me. "If you get too hot, take your clothes off." I did just that.'

Crystal was a very physical as well as a very vocal person. As she continued her tale, she ran her hands down over her breasts and followed the sweep of her ribs, the narrowing of her waist, and the flaring arrogance of her hips.

Between words and accompanying her actions, Crystal's tongue flicked out and over her lips like a woman on a diet drooling for the taste of double cream.

A foursome at a nearby table had noticeably fallen silent. Platefuls of olive oil and pimentos sat untouched and stagnating in front of them.

Crystal glanced their way before continuing.

'Naked and glistening with sweat, I lay out on the lower

bench and waited for Jason to come back.

'Because it was so warm, I dozed, and as I dozed I imagined how his penis would feel in my hand. Lovely, delicious thoughts came to my head. I imagined he was stroking me. In my half sleepy state it suddenly came to me that he *was* stroking me, but not with his finger.

'Something much thicker and much hotter was running up over my thighs, its weight and heat rubbing softly against my skin. Its head tangled in my pubic hair and left a glob of wetness behind it. I clenched my stomach muscles more tightly as it rolled onwards. Over my rib-cage it went before lingering just beneath my breasts.

'I did not open my eyes, but enjoyed the heat of this thing against me. I knew instinctively that he was going to take his time with my breasts.

'I murmured, arched my back and opened my eyes. He glanced briefly at me before his eyes went back to what he was doing. He never touched me with his hands, just his beautiful black prick.

' "What are you going to do to me?" I asked him, but he didn't answer. He seemed to be concentrating very hard on what he was doing.

'Like a rolling pin having trouble with a heap of rebellious dough, his member rolled backward and forwards over my breasts.

'My eyes were transfixed by his length. I was certain it had grown from courgette to cucumber length. I gulped on my fear and told myself to be brave. I could cope. I was sure I could cope.'

At this point Mariana and Josie exchanged another glance. Knowing Crystal, they were sure she'd coped perfectly well.

Crystal's eyes blazed. They also flitted from one crotch to another each time as first a short waiter, a tall waiter, an old waiter, and a young waiter passed their table.

Josie wondered if they had caught snatches of what

Crystal was saying. The foursome at the next table had sent their plates back untouched. They were now drinking coffee – or rather they were slowly stirring it and not even taking the cup from the saucer.

'The very tip of it touched my lips. I smelt his maleness and wanted to taste it. I poked out my tongue and for the first time ever, I licked the tip of a man's sex. I ran it around his crown, then tasted the full length of his stem as he leaned forward so that it slid between my lips.

'I grabbed each end with my hands and about halfway down its length, I clamped my mouth over it, sucked on it, nibbled it as if it were a fresh corncob.'

Mariana suppressed a giggle. Josie looked down into her lap.

It didn't matter. Crystal wasn't telling them this tale, she was telling it to the foursome at the next table. She had a new audience. The waiters seemed more attentive too.

'He let me go on exploring and playing with it while he reached down and ran his fingers between my legs.

' "Pretty," he said, and looked adoringly at me.

'His fingers made me wet. Instinctively, I opened my legs and let him in.

'Lovely feelings built up in little waves, then tumbled down as he explored my little bits and pieces. The more he fingered, the wetter I became.'

Mariana stifled her giggles with her napkin.

Josie went pink as she stared down into her lap.

One of the foursome at the next table choked on a mouthful of coffee, and two waiters collided, the noise of their metal trays bringing a temporary pause to Crystal's story.

But she soldiered on regardless.

'It was as though I was turning into a water melon – all water, no substance. I was melting beneath his touch.

'I was glad when his fingers at last went inside me. I

could hear my flesh slurping as he dipped and dived, retreated and progressed again and again.

'By now I was moaning against his sex and my eyes were half closed.

'Perhaps he thought I was suffocating – what with the heat of the sauna – or perhaps he could wait no longer. Anyway, he lay full length on me, his hands either side of my shoulders, his arms braced. His veins stood like thick tendrils from his arms. His muscles bulged.

'Yet even though he was holding himself above me, there was barely room to accommodate the length of his penis. It was hard to concentrate. I looked up into his face; down at his penis. My heart was throbbing. I was about to lose my virginity and couldn't wait for it to happen.

'"I won't hurt you, sweet thing," he said. "I promise I won't hurt you."

'I willed myself to relax and enjoy the warmth of his rod as it caressed the inside of my thighs. I willed myself to lie there, open to him and to what he was pushing inside me.

'So well was I prepared that he barely had need to pause when he came to my barrier. So firm was his onslaught, and so pliant my muscles, that he was almost totally in me in no time at all.

'"You're so beautiful," he said. "Your eyes are so bright and you have the most luscious lips I have ever seen."

'For the first time since we had met, he kissed me. So intense was our passion that we barely noticed the heat and the way our sweat was combining and making noises as we jerked against each other.

'My breasts were lost in his enormous palms. I felt he was devouring me, and I wanted to be devoured. I wanted to be part of him.

'The waves of sensation that had gathered between my legs now became mountainous. They soared in time with the rhythm of our bodies. Faster and faster, higher and higher until, at last, they peaked, curled into themselves and flooded over us.'

Crystal sighed. 'There! That was my first time.'

She then scraped a crumb away from the corner of her mouth with her smallest fingernail. Perfection, to Crystal, was like a religion. Being the best was paramount. In her opinion, and judging by the silence of her friends, she had achieved all she wanted.

'Yours next,' she suddenly said to Josie.

Josie's mouth dropped open and her pinkness deepened. 'I don't know that I . . . '

'Of course you can,' corrected Crystal. 'Mariana told us her story about her first time, and I've told you mine. Now it's your turn.'

'Did you believe her story?' Mariana was giving Josie a lift home. Josie was about to get out, but paused to answer the other woman's question.

Josie was noncommittal. 'Did you?'

Mariana shook her head abruptly. 'No. I think our Crystal can be a liar as well as a right cow!'

She didn't meet Josie's eyes when she said goodbye. She didn't know whether Josie knew about Crystal and Michael. It wouldn't be her to let the cat out of the bag. Ignorance was bliss and might make a marriage last longer – if it was worth the lasting.

Chapter 11

Heels beating an even tempo on the shiny wet pavements, Crystal held her head high as she made her way down the High Street. Her hair was damp and clinging in thin tendrils around her face. Her mouth was set in a tight line and her eyes looked straight ahead.

Usually, a particularly attractive window display might have made her pause. If it was that enticing, she might have made a swift detour into the store itself. But today her mind was occupied with other things. Her flesh was burning with anticipation. She was going to meet Michael.

The last time they had seen each other, she had refused him sex. With all the allure of some old-time femme fatale, she had trailed her hands over his body, garnished his lips with the hottest kisses possible, and whispered wickedly and huskily into his ear.

She had aroused him with her words of seduction and teased him to erectness with her lips and fingers. Then she had left him high and dry.

He had sat open-mouthed as he watched her go and she had enjoyed his disappointment, enjoyed the feeling of power it gave her.

I am in control, she told herself. *Michael will do anything I want him to do, and that includes divorcing his unexciting wife.*

It hadn't occurred to her that she had been spiting herself until she got home.

Suddenly, the soft silk of her panties had been too

tantalising against her tingling crotch. Aroused and without Michael, she had crept up behind Thomas who was in
his study, working on his computer.

'Thomas, darling,' she purred, and ran her hands over
his shoulders. 'Have you missed me, sweetie?'

Her husband's muscles had tensed beneath her touch.
For one single moment, she had suddenly been regretful
that she no longer loved him. In that moment of feeling his
body, she had once again desired him.

'No.' It was as abrupt as that. 'No.' He hit her hands from
his shoulders. 'I've got too much work to do, Crys. You'll
have to find something – or someone else to amuse you.'

'Well you certainly don't! There's not an ounce of
excitement in you! Besides that, sex with you is like using
Yellow Pages as a bedtime read!'

'That's probably because I have no more desire for you
than I have for taking my summer holiday in the middle of a
traffic island in Milton Keynes.'

She had stormed out of his study, her fingernails digging
into the palms of her clenched fists as she tried to contain
her fury.

Imagine! Needing to have sex with Thomas! Her own
husband!

Her face coloured at the thought of him. How dare he
treat her like that. How dare he tell her that he no longer
desired her! Well she'd show him! She'd show him!

But of course, she would not. Her body was on fire and,
as much as she might imagine that Michael fucking her
would infuriate her husband, of course, it would not.
Thomas would not be there; not physically. He was purely
in her mind and it was there that she castigated him.

When she got to the town-centre hotel where Michael
had asked her to wait for him, she made her way to the bar
rather than sit around awkwardly in reception.

After hanging her wet mac up on a handy coat hook, she
made her way to the bar and a high stool with a raffia top.

She was vaguely aware of one other man sat on another bar stool.

'Crystal! I didn't know you were a lunchtime drinker.'

She recognised the voice even before she saw him. Her blood ran cold, but she managed to force a smile.

'Jamie!' she laughed nervously. 'What a surprise. I didn't know you were a lunchtime drinker either.'

Red in the face already, he nodded. 'Touché,' he drawled, his head continuing to nod. *Like one of those stupid dogs that sit in the rear windows of Ford Cortinas*, thought Crystal. 'Touché,' he repeated again, and pushed his glass towards the barman. 'Same again, and one for my friend here.'

Crystal tried to balance her facial expression between nervous smiles and downright dismay. She made a quick decision to toss the ball back in his court.

'A liquid lunch I take it.' She glanced expressively at the tot of whisky.

Jamie laughed and shook his head. 'No. No. Well . . . not really. An appointment I had was cancelled and I knew Mariana wouldn't be home yet.' His voice was thick.

Four whiskies at least, thought Crystal.

'Don't you like to go home when you know she isn't there?'

'Oh, no,' he said with ill-disguised bluster. 'It's not that. It's just that she likes me to arrive at certain times. On the dot, too. No excuses for being late or early with my darling wife, I'm afraid.' The barman pushed his refilled glass towards him. 'Will you have a drink with me, Crystal?'

She had to say yes, though it grieved her. She had been hoping that Michael would already be here with her vodka awaiting her. Her visions of having sex all afternoon in a hotel bedroom flew away. Michael would see Jamie without Jamie seeing him. And he would retreat.

Crystal was as sure of that as any woman indulging in a long-running affair could be.

As yet, Michael had not done the decent thing. The decent thing by Crystal's estimation was telling Josie about her. So he would play safe, turn round, and walk straight back to his office.

'Another?' Jamie asked after she had knocked back the first and the second.

Crystal glanced at her watch. Too late. It was too late. Was it her imagination or had she felt a draft from an open door, and had she just as quickly felt it a second time as the arrival had turned into a departure?

'Another,' she said.

There were others after that. Because disappointment made her feel empty inside, Crystal drank each drink Jamie bought for her. She noticed an extra sparkle in his eyes as time went on. She knew that look, knew what it meant, knew what he wanted. Jamie, her husband's friend, Michael's friend, was looking at her with lust. Suddenly all the anger she felt towards Michael began to boil up inside her.

Thomas had refused her advances, and Michael had left her stranded with Jamie.

But Jamie was looking at her as if he could eat her whole. Well let him eat her whole. What did she care if it was his cock inside her rather than the man she loved or the one she was married to?

Smiling provocatively, she leaned forward so that her cleavage was visible beyond the dark maroon of her blouse. She reached out and, with red-painted fingernails, she stroked Jamie's cheek.

'Thanks for all the drinks, Jamie darling.' She sighed and slid from her stool. He did the same. They stood side by side, too close for comfort some would say. Close enough to smell him, to feel the heat of his flesh permeate the fabric of his suit.

Crystal adjusted her body, thrust her hip out slightly and turned her body so that it brushed against his crotch.

'I feel like going to bed now, darling.'

'To sleep?' he asked slowly.

She shook her head as she ran her hand down over his chest. 'Would you let me sleep if you were in bed with me?'

Jamie swallowed nervously. His lower lip hung open. His mouth looked pink and wet like too little paint mixed with too much water.

'Oh no! No. Of course I wouldn't.'

She took the pre-booked room key from her handbag and swung it in front of his face. 'Then let's go to my room. I sometimes rent one to rest in when I'm shopping in town. Besides, the manager is a friend of mine.'

Explanations meant nothing to Jamie. She could see it in his face and his eyes as they skimmed down over her breasts and lingered there before continuing downwards.

There was indecision in his eyes for a moment, so she grabbed hold of his arm and pulled him gently towards the lift.

She held his hand.

'Looks like we could both do with a lie down, Jamie darling.'

Like a big, soft, limp teddy bear, he let her lead him along the carpeted corridor to the room she had been hoping to share with Michael.

Michael, she thought to herself, and wanted to hit him, scratch his face, bite his penis, even to kill him. He had let her down. He should have been here having sex in their pre-booked room, but he had seen Jamie and ran.

I'll kill him, she seethed, but instead she smiled at the dissolute face of the man walking beside her.

'I can take my drink,' he was saying. 'Don't think that I can't. Don't take advantage of me if you're thinking that.'

'I won't,' she replied.

What the hell's he on about, she thought to herself. *Take advantage of him! It sounds as though he wants me to take advantage of him.*

She let go of his wrist as she slid the pass card into the door lock of the room. The signal went green, so she turned the handle and opened the door.

Blue and beige was the predominent colour scheme of the room and the furniture was the sort of contemporary stuff that merely hints at being a bed, a dressing table, or a chest of drawers, rather than having any specific style.

Jamie's eyes seemed to glaze over as Crystal pressed her breasts against him and groped for his balls. He saw surprise in her face as she discovered no erection. By now, Michael or Thomas would have been stiff as broom handles.

'I think you could do with the laying on of hands, Jamie darling,' she cooed once she had thought about it. 'On your bare flesh, I mean.'

What she meant was that touching his bare flesh might result in a stiffer reaction. But she couldn't come right out and say it. Men only want to hear praise for their equipment and the way they use it, not criticism.

But Crystal knew how to treat men alright. As her tongue swept wetly along her bottom lip, she undid his zip and got his penis out from his trousers. It remained limp in her hand.

'What the hell . . .? Are you ill, Jamie?'

She had assumed that this man's erection would be much the same as her husband's or her lover's. Surprised and a tad disappointed, she stepped back from him. There was disappointment in her eyes and anger coloured her cheeks. Michael, Thomas and the drink she had consumed, combined to make her lash out. First she slapped one cheek, then the other.

'Damn you!' she cried. 'Damn all you bloody men! Damn you all!'

Her hair flew wildly about her head as she beat his chest with her fists until she was almost sobbing, tears of anger stinging her eyes.

Jamie stood impassively. He did not flinch. His eyes had closed and he was groaning slightly.

Crystal stopped hitting him. She caught her breath, and stepped back.

Jamie was still moaning, his eyes still closed, his head tilted back. He appeared to be in a state of near ecstasy.

'So who or what shook your rattle?' she asked softly.

Her eyes fell to his penis.

'Well I'll be . . . Jamie!'

It was hard to close her mouth, so she stood there, her eyes glued to his penis which was now hot, red and firm as need be.

'Jamie,' she said again and licked her lips.

'Yes, mistress,' he said weakly. Behind his closed eyelids this was not Crystal but Mariana, his wife, the woman who understood his needs.

Because of drink he did not care that his secret was now shared with someone else besides his wife.

Eyes wide and jaw slack, Crystal stared until her jaw ached and her eyes had to blink.

'So that's it,' she breathed, surprise giving way to wonder. 'That's it. You like being treated rough. You like being dominated! Is that it, Jamie? Is that it?'

He mewed slightly and his penis quivered. Crystal, being wary of losing this erection, and also intrigued to think Jamie was turned on by her beating his chest, caught hold of the pulsating appendage and gripped it tightly. With Michael, she would have caressed his penis, taken it into her mouth, kissed and sucked its essence into her.

Not Jamie, she told herself. Not Jamie.

What next? she wondered.

Her grasp of the situation was better than she realised. The words seemed to come easily to her tongue.

'Have you been a naughty boy, Jamie?' she asked in a strong, surly voice she thought suitable for a dominant woman.

She saw Jamie's throat move before he answered. 'Yes, mistress,' he replied.

Now what? Crystal asked herself, and rubbed at her head. God, if only she hadn't had so much to drink.

'Right,' she said resolutely. 'Right.' She transferred her rubbing to the nape of her neck as she carefully considered where this conversation should go next.

As a cruel smile crept over her lips, she reached between Jamie's legs and into his trousers. He half opened his eyes as his mouth fell open. Using her fingers like sharp talons, she dug them into his balls.

The response was dramatic.

He yelped like a kicked dog and, as he did so, she thought of how Thomas had rebuffed her advances and how Michael took her for granted. This was not Thomas, and it wasn't Michael. But it was a man and it was a man she needed to torture.

Her nails dug more cruelly. Vicious intent showed in her eyes as a sneer came to her lips.

'Like all men, Jamie, you are nothing,' she growled. 'You are a cur, a piece of something on my shoe. Do you understand that?'

'Yes, mistress,' Jamie whimpered as his penis grew and reddened.

'Good,' she growled again, and squeezed his balls that much more fiercely. Tears appeared from beneath his eyelids. 'I'm going to treat you so cruelly you'll ache all over,' Crystal went on. 'And you are going to do everything I ask of you. Do you understand that?'

'Yes, mistress.'

Was that a whimper of pain she was hearing, or was it a groan of rapture?

It didn't matter. Crystal was enjoying this.

She sat herself down in a chair and licked her red lips. She did everything very slowly, very deliberately. Her stockings lisped lightly against each other as she crossed her legs so that her skirt rode high up her thighs.

Jamie kept his gaze firmly fixed on the floor. He was trembling slightly – waiting, she guessed, for the next order, the next chance to be submissive and endure whatever torment she chose to inflict on him.

Crystal, who was beginning to enjoy this excursion into the role of dominatrix, adopted a cold, precise voice that she could hardly recognise as her own.

'Right,' she said. 'Now we will begin. First, I want you to take all your clothes off. You will remove each article one by one, fold it carefully and lay it on the chest there. The one next to the television. I want no untidiness. No scruffy pile. Everything must be done very neatly. Is that understood?'

'Yes, mistress.' Jamie trembled. He was pink with excitement and snorting slightly with the effort of controlling the extraordinary sensations that arose in him at moments like these.

Because she had said those key words, 'neat' and 'scruffy', he suddenly felt as if he were nothing but a worthless blob of untidiness.

His fingers felt as if they had turned to sausages; big fat ones that flopped in the wrong direction no matter what his brain told him to do. But he managed. First, he took off his shoes.

'Socks first,' exclaimed Crystal and began to laugh. But a laugh had no place in this scenario.

She turned it into an angry snarl instead. 'For goodness sake make sure you take your socks off first! There's nothing worse than a naked man left with only his socks on!'

It wasn't easy to disguise the laugh, but it had to be done, Crystal was sensitive enough to know that Jamie required her to be deeply serious and highly domineering at all times.

Mariana's husband was caught in a spell of his own

making, and that spell must not be broken.

Blood thundered against his temples as his imagination soared. Such was the power of what he perceived she might do to him, that he could imagine his climax even before it had actually occurred.

He followed her instructions to the letter until everything was piled on top of the chest of drawers with the exception of his shoes and socks. The shoes sat beneath the dressing table. Each sock was carefully folded and placed in the confines of its relevant shoe.

So there he was, this mountain of a man, all powerful muscles and soft, sandy hair.

As Jamie stood waiting for her next instruction, arms hanging limply at his side, his penis pulsated to a strict beat.

He glanced briefly at Crystal. She was smiling but, although her smile was cruel, it wasn't that which caused him to blink nervously.

'Beg your pardon, mistress, but the curtains are still open.'

Crystal glared.

Jamie bowed his head.

'And you want them closed? Is that what you are telling me? That you want no one to see me punish your naked body? Is that what you are saying?'

He mumbled a subdued assent.

Crystal's reaction was instant. Like a bolt of lightening, she stretched out and smacked at his cock.

'It's for me to make that decision, not you. Speak when you are spoken to in future. Don't you know the correct way for a slave to behave? All decisions are mine, and my decision is that the curtains remain open. Is that clear?'

'Yes mistress.'

Crystal felt suddenly warm. Her breasts were heaving and her need for sex was fast returning. *Could it be*, she asked herself, *that I am really enjoying this*?

She decided she was. *Now*, she thought to herself, *it's up to you to devise some outrageous treatment for this man, so be imaginative.*

'First,' she began, 'I will remove what clothes I care to. Of course, I will not disrobe completely. That would not be right. After all, I am the mistress. What I leave on is like a uniform, an insignia that proclaims my status. As I take off each item, I want you to fold it and pile it on the chest of drawers. But first, you will remove your pile of rags and place it with your shoes beneath the dressing table. Is that clear?'

'Yes, mistress.'

'Good.'

Slowly, Crystal peeled off her sharply tailored navy business suit.

Jamie watched her. He did not blink, did not speak, did not move.

All the same, she knew she was having an effect on him. His penis throbbed and grew larger with each item of clothing she discarded.

Once she had finished, she eyed Jamie in a way that told him she wanted everything done very carefully, and very precisely.

He bent to his task, and she watched him as he carefully folded her jacket, her skirt, and her blouse. His hands were trembling and, although he did not appear to be glancing in her direction, she knew he was perfectly aware of how delicious she looked.

Her underwear was red satin with panels of red lace set into the sides of her panties and over her stomach. Scallops of red lace hid little of her breasts and allowed her nipples to show.

Because she was wearing black silk stockings, she was also wearing a satin and lace suspender belt. Its colour accentuated the neatness of her tiny waist and the flaring voluptuousness of her hips. Satin suspenders ran from the belt to the tops of her stockings. Her shoes were black and had three-inch heels.

Crystal stood straight and tall, hands on hips as she tilted her head and tossed her long, dark hair.

Now, how brutal can I be? she asked herself, then made an immediate decision. In a flash, she had created a scenario that would please Jamie's predisposition to his own brand of sexual satisfaction and also purge the frustration she herself was feeling.

'Lie face down on the floor,' she ordered.

Jamie obeyed without a murmur.

Amazing, Crystal thought to herself. *I would never have dreamed of treating a man so despicably as this before.*

Thinking of men made her think of Michael. She pouted suddenly. *Perhaps I should have done this before,* she thought to herself.

She walked around the supine form, whose hands were either side of his head. She took pleasure from seeing him blink nervously as he wondered what she would do to him.

Crystal surprised herself with the pleasure she felt in just running the toe of her shoe up his leg, his calf and his thigh.

Silently, she walked round him twice before standing at his feet, from where she could study the muscles of his legs, the rise of his buttocks, and the broad sweep of his back.

Her eyes kept returning to those buttocks. She saw them clench apprehensively. She instantly knew what she could say that would arouse him.

'Open your legs,' she ordered, and kicked at his feet with the toe of her shoe.

Jamie obeyed.

'Wider!'

Jamie opened his legs that much more. Crystal could now see the softness of his scrotum lying in a soft mound against the carpet.

Despite having never fancied Jamie before, something inside ignited a new passion in her loins. Suddenly she wanted to pleasure this man. Suddenly, she wanted him to pleasure her. She shuddered with desire. If she wasn't careful she could become quite unhinged by what she was feeling. But then, if she suddenly grabbed the man and straddled him, she knew he would flee.

Softly, softly, she told herself. She took a deep breath and prepared to continue their game.

In this instance she thought, *I have to be cruel to be kind. How amusing.*

'A little wider,' she ordered again but in a more subdued voice than before.

As he parted his legs, she walked up between them until she could reach out with her toe and deftly poke it into the softness of his flesh.

His whole body seemed to tremble as her foot made contact with his scrotum. He did not protest. He made no noise at all. But he did tremble and his buttocks clenched and became as hard as iron.

Even through the suede leather of her shoes, she could feel the heat of his flesh, and she could not help but be aroused by it.

'Do you like what I am doing to you?' she asked.

'Yes, mistress,' replied Jamie.

'Then why are you clenching your behind like that. Relax as I want you to relax. Let whatever I do to you be pleasurable. Even if you are not feeling pleasure, remember that I am feeling it and be glad that I am.'

'Yes, mistress.

Crystal's eyes were shining brightly. Her tongue flicked over her glossy red lips as though she were licking at this man's body rather than torturing him with the toe of her shoe. It might have been strange before this had happened to think of torturing a man rather than pleasing him. But, of course, to Jamie torture *was* pleasure.

Once she finally removed her toe, the silky flesh of his scrotum fell once more to the carpet.

There was something in that happening which made her suddenly think of Mariana. *Just think of the many ways she degrades him in the privacy of their own home*, she said to herself.

It wasn't as difficult to imagine as might be supposed. Mariana was a cool blonde who was always in control of herself. She oozed confidence.

Crystal smiled as she imagined her friend's trim, six-foot figure striding through the weekend bar at the country club, her tight, tan flesh glowing with health as she smiled her brilliant smile and surveyed everyone around her as if she were queen Boadicea herself, about to have them all pulling her chariot.

Now she could understand why she came across like that. In her own home Mariana was not only queen, she was also Commander in Chief and mistress of all she surveyed. Jamie was merely a chattel, in much the same way as the BMW she drove.

To Crystal the situation was no longer just intriguing, it had become a challenge. No matter who the man and what the situation she had to be the best; the best suck, the best fuck, the best lay. In this field, the field of corporal punishment and domination of a man, Mariana had stolen a march on her. Crystal did not like that.

Slowly, with purposeful strides, she walked up past Jamie's head and, turning her back on him, she pulled the sash and looked out of the window.

'Lick my bottom,' she said over her shoulder.

She heard him getting up from the carpet.

'Yes, mistress. May I touch you?'

It was a question she had not been prepared for. She arched her eyebrows, and then she smiled.

'Yes,' she said, her voice ripe with desire. 'Caress my legs from the ankles up. Travel slowly until your lips meet what I have told you to lick.'

His hands were warm around her ankles, though his grip was strangely weak. But her ploy was working. She sensed a trembling in his touch as he began to raise himself. As his hands ran up over her calves, her knees and then her thighs, they trembled.

By the time they reached her hips, they were gripping her more tightly.

She heard him sigh.

Through narrowed eyes she viewed the rooftops and the busy roads that were spread out before her. Her own breathing was becoming affected by the frenzy of sensations left in the trail of his touch and his mouth.

This situation was becoming very pleasurable indeed.

'Do you like touching me, Jamie?' she breathed, her breasts rising and falling more quickly as delicious responses ran over her flesh.

'Yes,' he murmured between kisses. Even his lips had started to tremble.

'Then you will like licking me,' she said, and bit her bottom lip to stop herself from crying out. This was such an alien experience, yet such a tantalising one.

As the heat and moistness of his tongue seeped through the thin fabric of her knickers, she threw back her head, half closed her eyes and smiled triumphantly. She had judged Mariana correctly. Jamie's wife never allowed him to touch her. He was completely subservient to his wife's demands. She did everything to him, he was not allowed to do anything to her.

Discerning and devious as she was, Crystal had spiced up Jamie's perverted pleasure by allowing him to caress her tanned skin.

Being in control was the most powerful aphrodisiac Crystal knew. But so was tasting the more perverse practices of sexual arousal.

And next? she said to herself. *What shall I ask him to do*

107

next? What will give me the greatest pleasure?

She smiled and purred like a kitten as the answer came to her.

'Take down my knickers,' she said to him, altering her stance.

His sharp intake of breath told her all she needed to know about how she was affecting him. Even without looking round and studying his face, she knew a light film of sweat would be breaking out all over his body. He would be trembling, his muscles tensing as he raised his hands and bent his fingers, pausing, licking his lips before he dared feel the cool satin of her underwear. The knowledge excited her. Her flesh was on fire, her knees were shaking. She could no longer stop small moans of delight escaping from her throat.

But no matter how much she was enjoying this, she still had to appear to be in control.

'Get on with it!' she snapped.

A tingle ran through her body as the heat of his hands seeped through the lace panels at the side of her knickers. She sucked in her breath.

'That's it,' she growled in a low, menacing purr. 'That's it! Go on.'

His trembling increased. His fingers crept beneath the elastic of her waistband. The heat of his breath caressed her exposed buttocks. His palms rasped gently against her thighs as he slid them higher.

'Only pull them as far as my knees,' she ordered.

Trembling, Jamie did exactly that. The garment of red satin and lace stopped around her knees. It stretched as she opened her legs slightly and gripped her hips more firmly.

'Now,' she ordered, a new strength in her voice and excitement coursing through her veins, 'lick my behind.'

The command alone caused Crystal to tighten her stomach muscles. Between her legs she could feel a ticklish moving sensation as fluid seeped from her vagina and through the soft flesh of her sex.

Jamie groaned before his tongue deftly flicked over one buttock. Pain was in that groan, a sweet, gnawing pain that Crystal thought must reflect the severe engorgement of his penis.

Crystal closed her eyes and held back the murmur of pleasure that was sitting so impatiently on her tongue. Intuition told her that showing any sign of enjoyment would put an end to Jamie's erection. And she wanted that erection. She was determined to have that erection!

In order to keep exclamations to a minimum, she closed her eyes and pursed her lips. It was as though she were locking it all inside.

The warmth of Jamie's tongue aroused her flesh and left tingles in its wake. Her muscles tensed slightly as he licked over one firm orb and then the other. It was sweet indeed to be in control of a man. She liked it. She liked it very much indeed.

Especially delightful were the reactions radiating from just beneath her buttocks at those points where they joined her thighs. Her own hand went to her breasts. Slowly, she pulled each breast from its cup so it sat constrained and perched upright on the supports of her bra.

She smiled as she surveyed the windows of apartment blocks, offices and hotels in the city around her. Could they see her? Were they able to enjoy the sight of her bare bosoms and the look of ecstasy on her face?

She sucked in her breath through puckered lips as she fingered her nipples and traced the outline of her breasts. What a shame if no one could see all this beauty, all this sexual arousal.

But what other people might see or might want was of no real consequence. Her desire was rising and rising fast. Crystal wanted more of this sex, more of this perversion. Much more.

Another delightful thought came to her mind. It made her smile to herself. It also stimulated the excitement she was feeling. Passion grew from a quivering flame into a raging fire.

'Lick between the cheeks of my bottom,' she said, and then could not believe she had said it. Would Jamie really do it? Had Mariana trained him so well that he would obey without question?

Her mouth fell open and she threw back her head as Jamie's fingers eased between her buttocks and prised them apart. This was really going to happen! One half of her could not believe it. The other half was dizzy with desire and with power.

Jamie's tongue ran down the cleft between her cheeks and over the puckered opening of her behind. It was hard not to react to his licking, but again, she knew she must not do that. She knew she must appear apart from him; as though she were enjoying it on a different level to him.

Enough, she said to herself, only she did not tell herself this in a quiet way. The words screamed in her head. Even though Jamie had not touched her sex, the very fact that he was obeying her made that secret part of her tingle with a need for an orgasm.

She was wet and her body was ready to join with his but would he?

No, she decided. He would not.

'Enough!' she shouted, and turned round.

Jamie fell back upon his hands, his knees bent beneath him.

Crystal looked at him and eyed his penis. She did her best not to stare, not to linger. It was huge. Inwardly she groaned. What a beauty to have in her. She imagined how it would feel to have her muscles close tightly around Jamie's penis as its moist tip nudged against the neck of her womb.

It was a disappointment to her that this would be

unacceptable to this man. Yet she had to have him do something.

She gathered up every ounce of self-control she could muster.

'Well, don't lie there doing nothing! Lick me. Bring me off!'

Jamie's penis lunged forward and appeared to grow before her eyes.

Amazing, Crystal thought to herself. *Act nasty, sound like a right cow, and Jamie's penis looks fit to burst. What an odd one this is.*

Thinking contradictory thoughts helped keep her pleasure from her face. She adopted the hardest expression she could. Looking down her nose through half closed eyes, she saw Jamie's head moving towards her.

Gently, as though she were made of porcelain or fragile glass, he placed his palms on her hips and folded his fingers around her thighs.

Crystal tilted her hips towards his mouth. A strangled murmur of joy lay trapped in her throat as Jamie's tongue licked over her pubic hair so that it lay flat upon her flesh.

She was undulating against his face, her body fit to burst with all the most beautiful, most sexual sensations in the world.

Soon, the very tip of his tongue was probing the opening that ran between her legs. Like the flame of a flickering candle, it flitted on and around her clitoris and tasted the salty wetness of her labia.

The first tremulous threads of orgasm began to seep through Crystal's flesh and, as they did so, she thought of those who had denied her their bodies.

Damn you, Thomas! Damn you Michael! Her damnation of her erstwhile lovers was not vocalised. Her own power over herself and over Jamie was strong enough to keep it inside her.

But her passion was aroused. She could not help showing

some sign that she was enjoying what Jamie was doing.

Slowly, she began to rock her hips backwards and forwards.

'That's it!' she exclaimed. 'That's it! Keep licking me, damn you! Keep licking me! Give me pleasure. Give me all you've got!'

She heard him whimper and knew what he wanted.

As her climax began to rise, she slid her foot forwards and rested her toe against his stem so it stood upright.

Toe tapping against his penis matched the tempo of her hips as she elicited the ultimate of delights from her own flesh.

'Don't stop!' she cried out. 'Keep going till I tell you to stop.'

He did as he was told. Even after the last hushed breath of her orgasm had subsided to almost nothing, his tongue did not leave her. Muffled moans came more rapidly as his whole body trembled and his cock spasmed against her foot. She felt it jerk, felt it stiffen, then gasped in outrage as a warm stream of semen cascaded over her shoe and her instep.

Her outrage did not last for long. Thomas, Michael – and the way they had rebuffed her – came racing back to her mind. It was Jamie she ordered to lick every drop of his own semen from her shoe and her foot. But in her mind the face of her husband and that of her lover were interchanged with frequent rapidity.

Unbeknown to him, Jamie was the symbol of all men, and him licking his own secretions off her shoe was a symbol of her revenge.

Chapter 12

JOSIE'S STORY

Mariana, Crystal and Josie were getting out of Josie's car at the country club when the tall blonde went by, her breasts bouncing and her pert behind rolling like a snowball through snow.

Josie glanced at the blonde as she locked the door of the car, but she did not comment.

Mariana, on the other hand, could not help but make a comment. 'Now whose baby are you?' her eyes narrowed as they followed the lean tanned form as she strutted past.

'Bust, bum and no brain,' muttered Crystal as she caught her hair at the nape of her neck and wound a band around it. Eyes narrowed, she held in her stomach and thrust out her breasts as her gaze went with the young woman.

'You don't know that for sure.' Josie's voice was not accusing. Neither was her gaze. But Crystal dropped her arms and patted her hips and thighs in a casual way as if to say, 'Jealous? Me jealous?'

'She looks that type,' she snapped. 'She's not really that attractive. I've met her sort before. They know how to sell themselves, that's all.'

'Looks like she got a good price judging from the gold she's wearing all over her body.' Mariana grinned as she said it.

Josie threw her an accusing look, but a smile flickered around her mouth. 'And you can see what a bargain he's getting,' she added, a comment which seemed strangely out of character for her.

The others grinned as all three of them watched the blonde stoop and kiss a short, fat guy with grey hair and quick eyes. As she bent over, the cheeks of her behind peeped from beneath her bright pink dress.

Smiling as though he'd just hit the jackpot, the man opened the back door of his Rolls-Royce. The blonde's silk dress seemed to whisper as she slid over the buff-coloured leather of the back seat.

'Hope his purchase doesn't kill him,' muttered Mariana to the others. They watched the little man go red in the face as he sought to bend himself into a sitting position. Once he'd overcome his gross impediment, he slid in beside his leggy girlfriend, his bulky shoulders close against her lean ones.

He said something to her and the blonde seemed to glitter as brightly as the gold she was wearing. Red fingernails ran through his hair and down his cheeks. She kissed him as though she were wildly in love with him.

'Come on, girls. Let's leave them to get physical with each other while we get physical with the gym and the swimming pool.' Resolutely, as though she would entertain no hint of protest, Josie picked up her sports bag.

'Just a minute,' said Crystal. She bent down to unzip her bag. 'I'm not sure I've got my towel'.

As Crystal rummaged in her bag, and Josie looked on despairingly, and Mariana impatiently, a chauffeur came running, his face flushed. The short fat man threw him an order, but no rebuke. He turned his full attention back to the willowy blonde beside him.

'No guesses as to why she loves him so much,' sneered Mariana.

'Money, money, money?' cried Crystal as she closed her bag and straightened up.

'You don't know that for sure,' said Josie again as she

114

clicked the remote security device on the car. 'Anyway, he might be her father.'

'He's old enough!' exclaimed Crystal.

'Josie, you are as green as grass, my darling.' Mariana wrapped her arm around Josie as she said it and gave her a hug. 'My, but you are such a sweetie.' She added a quick peck on the cheek. Josie did not protest but, because she was embarrassed, she set her eyes on the double doors ahead, above which a sign stated COUNTRY CLUB AND LEISURE CENTRE – MEMBERS ONLY.

They pushed open the doors, exchanged greetings with the staff behind the desk, then made their way up the sisal-carpeted steps to the female changing rooms.

The warmth and smell of chlorine, busy bodies and the nearby sauna clung close around them.

'Phew! Warm in here!' Off came Mariana's clothes. She was always the first to strip.

Exhibitionist, thought Josie.

Lesbian, thought Crystal, but didn't let it worry her. She reckoned on it being some way near the truth, especially after what had happened with Jamie in that hotel room. In some odd way, knowing what Jamie and Mariana did together had made her feel less threatened by whatever the woman was. Josie – sweet innocent as she was – was still in the dark. Perhaps she would leave her there. Or perhaps she would enlighten her.

'I still think he could have been her father,' Josie repeated as her pale cream flesh became exposed, her nipples very pink and very large and constituting half of the total area.

'He might very well have been her daddy – her sugar daddy!' Crystal threw back her head as she laughed, then held it there so she could experience the sweet delight of feeling the ends of her hair tickling the small of her back.

'You're incorrigible, Crystal.'

'And you, Josie my love, are naive!'

Crystal's voluptuous body moved with an easy confidence as she slipped into her workout clothes – blue lycra cycling shorts, silver-blue leotard with the narrowest of thongs running between the cheeks of her behind.

'Not really,' returned Josie as she slid into her unitard, which was a mixture of pale, medium and dark green.

Briefly she surveyed Crystal from beneath her thick brown lashes. Crystal, she realised, had not heard her.

'Now, now, girls. No squabbling, darlings.' Mariana, shoulders angular, ribs countable, and pelvis as narrow as that of a young man, stood with her hands on her hips. Her eyes took in more than they appeared to. She desired each of them, but would never, not without encouragement, ever put her desire into words let alone actions.

'You have a problem,' she said, her accent after all these years of living in England still tinged with a hint of Austria. 'You are only jealous. Would either of you refuse the advances of an older man if he made it worth your while? Besides, an older man can initiate a young girl into the pleasures of sex far better than a younger one. Compare the sophistication of a mature lover with the fumblings of greener fruit. The pleasure would most definitely be greater.'

'Was that how you felt with your Turk?' Josie asked, her face veiled from Mariana's view as she pulled on one trainer then the other.

Mariana sighed. 'By itself, I would have to say yes. But other things happened around that time, things I am loath to talk about.'

Josie exchanged glances with Crystal. They had never heard Mariana sound as regretful as this before. But now was not the time to pry.

'Then don't talk about it, Mariana,' said Josie. 'Let's talk about something else. Let me tell you about an older man I became involved with.'

Mariana stopped fumbling with her shoelaces. 'You

116

were involved with an older man?'

'Yes,' Josie nodded. 'I was.'

'Are you telling the truth?' added Crystal. She was stood with one brown leg up on a wooden bench. She had been doing stretching exercises. Now she was immobile and all attention as Josie with the green eyes and red hair began her tale.

'I remember a tutor at university. He had kind eyes.'

She cuddled her towel to herself. A dreamy look came over her face.

'What else did he have, Josie darling.' There was a hint of disbelief, even mockery to Crystal's voice.

Josie did not meet her eyes. She went on with her tale.

'I wasn't a virgin when I went to university, but I suppose I was still pretty green. After all, my first lover had been my childhood sweetheart. We'd made love one summer afternoon in the shade of the tree house. It was idyllic, but I didn't know for sure – at least at the time – how it compared to other men. I found out at university.'

Mariana sat slowly down on the bench and, clasping her hands in front of her, leaned forward. 'This tutor taught you a few more things?'

Josie nodded. She blushed and lowered her eyes. For a moment it seemed as if she was unable to continue. The moment was short-lived. She took a deep breath and collected herself before she restarted.

'He lectured in Greek history. I'd always loved the subject so was conceited enough to think I would have no trouble finishing the course and passing my exams. I found out to the contrary.

'It was one thing to read Greek classics and history as they related to the legends and the Trojan wars and such like. It was different to be asked to dissect and diagnose occurrences and modern counterparts on paper.

'Besides that, I was being invited to a lot of parties and was enjoying going to them.'

'Were you getting laid?' Crystal asked. There was sarcasm in her voice but a hint of envy in her eyes. Was it possible that Josie was not quite so dull as Michael had led her to believe?

'Of course I did – once or twice. But they were one night stands and not terribly satisfactory. As you just said, Mariana, the fumblings of green fruit.'

Mariana smiled and rested her chin in her hands. 'And the tutor was definitely not green fruit.'

Josie smiled and a faraway look came to her eyes. 'Definitely not. His skin was as scored as an autumn apple. I used to think I would like to peel it away and find the smoother skin underneath it – the skin of his youth. I suppose thinking like that is all part of wanting to know someone better; knowing what's underneath and knowing about their past.

'His eyes were very blue and seemed to miss nothing. Like the students he taught, he wore his hair long and had a beard to match. It was bright blond – almost gold – but it had grey streaks running through it. Not that it mattered. It flowed around him like a golden halo, and it was soft; very soft, very silky.

'Some of the other students – especially the fellas – made comments about him trying to hold onto his youth, and why didn't he act and look his age. But of course they had their reasons for saying that. Whenever Cado was in the room he was the only man there as far as we girls were concerned.

'There was a husky harmony in his voice and an alluring brightness in his eyes. We were drawn to him and sat enthralled as he deliberated about the reasons why modern civilisation venerated the one that had flowered in Greece.

'He pointed out to us how many people and civilisations had done their utmost to prove descendence from those people and that time. Everyone wanted to have classic antecedents. Perfection, he stated, was seen in its teachings, its scions, even in its buildings. Mathematically

118

and aesthetically, the concept of perfection had flowered just once and no more. It had merely transcended the ages and shaped one nation after another, each one based on classic Greece.'

'But what about *him*?' Crystal asked impatiently. 'Never mind what he or you lot believed in, what did you get up to with him?'

Josie licked away the dryness of her lips. 'I will tell you. Cado, you see, wanted perfection in humans as well as discerning it in an ancient civilisation. We didn't always give him that perfection.

'I found myself wondering about him rather than listening to what he was saying, and that was how I found myself in his study, being ticked off for not completing an assignment he had set us.

'I remember gazing into his eyes when he came to his study door. For a moment I couldn't say a thing.

'Then he grinned at me and his eyes sparkled. "Will your tongue work better inside this room than outside of it?" There was a hint of wickedness in his eyes and his voice as he asked me this. He opened the door wider and, with a flock of butterflies playing havoc in my stomach, I entered.

'I became very aware of his presence behind me as I walked forward over the threadbare carpet. With a need to calm my fluttering stomach, I pretended to be genuinely impressed by the decor of his study. I gazed at the piles of papers, books and coffee cups. There was an ancient leather chesterfield in one corner. Most of the walls seemed to consist of nothing but book shelves.

'Feeling his presence was like being warmed by a coal fire. All I felt was the heat of his body on my back. I knew he was studying me. I knew his eyes were running over me and assessing my shape and how my skin might feel; how I might respond if he touched me. Just being alone with him made me tremble with trepidation.

'Once the door was closed, he moved closer to me.

119

'"Josie isn't it?"

'I replied that it was.

'He didn't say anything for a moment. He hung his head slightly as though he were examining the hole in the carpet. His hands were clasped tightly behind his back and I remember thinking, "I wonder what he's holding in them."'

'What was he holding?' asked Crystal.

'Idiot!' snapped Mariana.

'Courage,' Josie replied. 'He was holding onto his courage. Dare he seduce me or not?

'When he looked back up at me, he was frowning. He looked nervous and when he spoke he sounded gruffer than usual – almost as though he'd borrowed the voice from someone else.

'He told me he was most concerned that I had not finished my assignment. He said he had expected better of me, that he had considered me one of the brightest butterflies in his class.

'I thought it funny that he should use the word "butterflies" when imaginary ones were fluttering around in my stomach. I didn't mention that.

'I said I was sorry and that I would do better.

'"Will you?" He had sounded sad.

'"I will", I cried, "I will!"

He shook his head mournfully. "I'm not so sure about that," he said. "After all, you are only a butterfly."

'I didn't know what he meant and it irritated me. I had to ask the obvious question.

'"Why am I a butterfly? Why do you call us bright butterflies?"

'He straightened up and his eyes met mine. For the first time ever, I could not stop looking at him. No matter what I saw there, or thought I saw there, I had to hold his gaze. It was as if I were not just waiting for him to answer the question, but also challenging him.

120

'He briefly chewed at the hair on his upper lip before he answered.

' "Bright butterflies flit from flower to flower. Their life is brief and their heads are empty. The only outstanding feature about them is that they are beautiful, but, as I have just said, their beauty is as brief as their lives. Once they are gone, there is nothing to remember them by."

'His statement made me angry. I protested that I was not empty-headed. I loved the subjects I was studying. I had every intention of being successful in whatever field I entered.

'My breasts were heaving by the time I had finished. My face must have been flushed. It certainly seemed hot.

'Cado was staring at me in a different way now. His eyes ranged me from top to toe as if he were appraising me anew.

'At last he spoke, but very slowly. "If you truly mean what you say, then allow me to take you in hand. I will ignite your brain. I will force you to learn and make you into more than just a butterfly. I will make you into a perfect human being. Will you agree to that?"

'I had no idea what he had in mind, so I said yes.

' "First," he said, "there is the matter of this dissertation."

'With a solemn expression on his face, he lifted up my dog-eared papers by one corner. Then slowly, and with the greatest deliberation, he tore up each and every page.

' "Now we will start again. I will instil in you the discipline you need. You will accept that discipline and, in doing so, you will grow in stature. In time you will begin to appreciate the atoms of artistic and mathematical merit that are in each and every person, each and every stone, plant, star and drop of water. Do you agree to this?"

'I told him I did and it was then that my education truly began.

'First I was to take off my clothes. He would remain clothed.

' "And then," he went on, turning his back to me, "we will assess what you are in this mirror."

'I was trembling with excitement. This was a real man asking me to take my clothes off. The strange thing was that I did not feel used by him, or seduced. I felt I was getting the benefit of some truly monumental experience.

'He turned his back on me as he positioned a long cheval mirror.

'I caught sight of myself and blushed. I was surprised to see my reflection. There was something different about me to the person that had entered this man's study. I could not define what it was, but I knew he had already started having a phenomenal effect on me.

'I did as he asked, took off my clothes, and looked at myself again.

'I didn't question why I was doing this for him. I just stared at my reflection and told myself I was doing it for me and me alone. My flesh was tingling with a thirst for knowledge – not knowledge of ancient Greece, but a knowledge of my tutor's body.

'I never questioned the wrongs and rights of it. There were none. It was as done. It happened. I was naked, just as I really am beneath every item I have ever worn.

'The cool smoothness of his corduroy jacket briefly touched my back when he came to stand behind me. I sucked in my breath and saw my nipples get bigger. I transferred my weight from one hip to the other and felt sweet wetness erupt between my legs.

'This scenario was incredibly erotic. But of course it was erotic! How could it be anything else?

' "See?" he said as he placed his hands on my shoulders. "This is the real you, Josie. This is the flesh, this is all part of the butterfly. It is through this flesh that I will ignite your mind. When I have finished with you, you will see greater form, greater beauty and, ultimately, you will see perfection in everything you do."

'I hadn't a clue what he meant. All I knew was that I wanted to please him in everything. I wanted to be his best, his brightest pupil. I wanted to see the world through his eyes – its artistry and its exactitude.

'He took me by the hand and told me to bend over his desk. I did as he asked.

' "How does it feel?" he asked.

'Somehow I knew what he wanted to hear. He didn't want to know that I was frightened, aroused, or sickened by what was happening to me. He merely wanted to know what my reactions were to my surroundings and those things I was still in contact with.

'I told him that the leather of the desk top was cold to my nipples. I told him my breasts were flattened against the desktop and its edge was nudging against my sex.

'Besides telling him that the carpet felt gritty beneath the soles of my naked feet, I also told him that my belly was sticking to the desk.

' "And which part of your body is most in touch with the world around you, Josie?"

' "My mind?" I suggested.

' "Ultimately," he replied. "But your mind is gaining perception through your naked bottom. Your buttocks are merely in touch with the air around them. Because of that it is sending more explicit messages to your brain than any other part of your body. It is telling your brain that it is vulnerable. After all, it is only logical that the roundness of a woman's behind can attract a caress, a slap, or an act of buggery. So your mind is in tune with it . . . perfectly in tune."

'I closed my eyes as I lay there across that desk. He said sweet words. I can't remember them exactly. All I can remember is the impression they left behind.

'He spoke for some time before his hand ran down my back. I remember trembling as he fondled my bottom.

'By the time he raised me up from there, my flesh was tingling. Full of admiration for this man, I gazed lovingly up into his eyes. I remember him smiling before folding his arms round me and holding me close. And, most of all, I remember the lumpy springs of the old settee beneath my bare behind, and him, once he had removed his clothes, pressing me down against those spiralling contours as he entered me.

'The most amazing thing was that he did not touch my breasts or any other part of my body as he fucked me. Only his penis, his pubic hair and the outside of his thighs touched my body.

'I understood what he wanted me to do. With my arms thrown over my head and my eyes closed, I was to concentrate only on the areas of my body that touched his. And I did concentrate.

'Sex can never be the same with one man as another, and yet the differences are relatively slight.

'With Cado it was completely different.

'It's hard to describe exactly what an orgasm feels like. It's even harder to describe those initial shivers of apprehension as arousal becomes more intense, more urgent.

'Behind the darkness of my eyelids, I truly experienced my climax taking over my body. Waves of pleasure crept over my skin. I'm sure I could also feel it creeping along just beneath the surface. On one level it seemed to be touching me lightly, no heavier than the caress of a bunch of peacock feathers. On another level it was causing my blood to boil and turn to steam in my veins.

'When my orgasm came I shuddered but did not cry out. I held the experience within me. It had no sound because it had no form. It was part of me and would remain part of me forever.

'Cado gave me that.'

Josie smiled softly to herself. 'I don't care if I was only twenty and he was twice my age, he was one of the most enduring experiences of my life – perhaps the only one.'

Chapter 13

By the time Josie had finished her tale, the confident jut of Crystal's chin seemed a little noticeable.

'What a dark horse you are, Josie Clarkson!' exclaimed Mariana, admiration hanging in her eyes like smudged ink. 'Very interesting.'

'Interesting?' Mariana frowned as she looked sidelong at Crystal. 'That's a bit of an understatement, isn't it?'

Crystal sat up very straight like she did when she was thinking of leaving.

'I just meant that it was very interesting to hear something like that coming from Josie. I'm surprised.'

Josie was eyeing Crystal speculatively, though Crystal did not notice.

'That sounds a bit condescending. Why shouldn't Josie have had a relationship with an older man? Are you saying she's ugly or something?' Mariana looked puzzled.

Crystal flushed. 'Of course not! Don't be such an idiot! I only meant that I thought Josie was above that sort of thing.'

Josie smiled that soft, secretive smile of hers. Her green eyes met the blue ones of Michael's lover. 'I have never been a nun, Mariana, and my period of virginal puberty was short-lived.'

'Mariana is just making trouble!' Crystal looked daggers in the direction of the smiling Mariana. 'Ignore her. She's being cowish!'

And what are you being? Crystal asked herself. *A fool?*

Up until this moment, everything had seemed so straight-forward. Josie was – dare she say it – a mere shadow behind her dazzling husband. Wasn't that why Michael was so besotted with his mistress? Crystal had pitied Josie and sympathised with Michael's statement that his wife bored him. And of course she had done everything to exaggerate that contrast, to make herself more stunningly attractive and vibrant than Josie could ever be. In her mind's eye, not only could she see the slender Josie with her clothes off and hot as hell beneath the hands of her mature lover, she could also imagine her body against Michael's.

She's lying, she decided. *Josie is sexless; involved in her art and therefore in a fantasy world of her own making.* She took a deep breath, followed by a sip of coffee. *Change the subject,* she decided.

'Girls, have you seen that new designer shop down in Harrison Mews?'

'Do you mean where the antique shop used to be?'

'Yes,' nodded Crystal brightly, and went on with un-bridled enthusiasm to steer the conversation in the direct-ion she wanted it to go for the duration of her visit.

Later, as she lounged in the bath with her breasts bare and a wet towel over her face, she had time to think about things in greater detail.

She was feeling less guilty about screwing Josie's hus-band, but she was more concerned with analysing why she herself had found Michael attractive in the first place.

It wasn't enough to imagine that wicked glint in his eyes, his lopsided smile, and the way his hair curled over and around the nape of his neck.

Neither was it enough to recall how hot his body felt when he lay on her, his belly hard against hers, his chest squashing her breasts, and his hot, hard penis pushing between her legs.

To analyse the reasons why, she had to go back and

recreate each detail in her brain. To do that she must revert to the very beginning.

Michael had been playing tennis when she'd first seen him. Sweat was running down his face, clinging in damp crescents beneath his arms. He glistened with it and, because of the way he looked, because the sun was strong, she ran her tongue over her top lip and tasted her own saltiness.

Because he gripped the racquet so hard, the veins on his arms had stood proud of his muscles. Because he sprang so quickly and so resolutely to return the serve, his thigh and calf muscles had bulged beneath his tanned skin.

When he took a breather, he had wiped the back of his hand across his brow and their eyes had met. He didn't smile, but neither did she. She only knew, they both knew, that something had happened between them.

From that very first glance, Crystal had decided that they would talk later, and that when they talked, each would confirm that they were thinking the same thing.

She had crossed her legs as she sat watching him. Then she had uncrossed them, took deep breaths and leaned back in her seat so that her breasts thrust determinedly against her white shirt.

He pretended he wasn't listening or looking, but he didn't fool her. He would have seen a flash of inner thigh and the whiteness of her cotton knickers.

When he went back to his game, there was a new vibrancy to his serve, a certain flamboyant energy to the way he moved.

He knows I am watching, she had thought to herself, *and he wants to impress me.* She remembered smiling smugly to herself.

As a damp heat had gathered between her legs, Crystal had made no attempt to disguise her interest. She took in everything about him; the swatch of hair wetly plastered to his chest, the rippling prominence of his muscles as he leapt around the tennis court. She also imagined the heat of his body against hers.

The sound of racquet whacking ball reverberated continually around the tennis court and the tall conifers beyond that.

From the very start, it had been obvious that Michael was going to win the game.

But the man at the other end, who she vaguely recognised as being her last but one bank manager, was playing for all he was worth. As he tried to ape Michael's more agile movements, his thick, hairy legs landed heavily on large feet.

He cried out in agony as he reached and swung his racquet in the hopes of hitting the ball. He missed and the game was over.

Crystal had leapt to her feet.

'Well done!' she shouted. 'Very well played.'

He thanked her, then wiped the sweat from his face with a white towel. His gaze had fluttered back to her.

'You move well,' she said once he had come nearer, 'Are you a good mover in everything you do?'

Temptation was in her smile. He saw it, caught it, and the message he threw back at her was every bit as provocative as hers.

'Always. If ever you want to try me out . . .'

'I might take you up on that.'

After throwing him a winning smile, she had slowly turned and walked away, her hips swaying suggestively.

I have him, she told herself as she tingled with sensuous excitement.

Back in the clubhouse, still dressed in white shorts and clinging white halter-necked top, she sat on a bar stool, feet hooked beneath a rung, tanned legs gleaming. Slowly she sipped a long, cool drink. One should have been enough, but when it was finished and he had not reappeared, she ordered another one. She also ordered one for him and left it in a prominent place on the bar. How could he resist the misty look of the glass, the ice so tantalising among a sea of green lime and cool lemon.

Almost as though she were willing him to appear, she had eyed the pale wood and gleaming brass of the double doors that led to the gym and the male changing room.

The doors opened. Her heart skipped a beat.

Not him. It wasn't him.

Next time it must be, she demanded. *Next time.*

The brass of the door gleamed, blinked as it opened again and he entered.

Their eyes met. Neither smiled.

He looked sardonic, quizzical even.

She looked alluring, as though she had every intention of seducing him.

Even without her saying, he knew she was waiting for him. He walked straight to the bar stool next to hers.

'For you,' she had said.

Eyes she could have died for looked into hers before he smiled.

'Are you after something?' he asked her.

'Yes. You.'

He raised his eyebrows. 'What makes you think I'm available?'

'I don't care if you're not available. I'm going to make you wish you were available.'

He laughed and she had liked the sound.

'Enlighten me. How are you going to do that?'

She had tilted her head so a shower of black hair had fallen provocatively over her shoulder and framed her face.

'I'm going to seduce you,' she'd replied.

His mouth had dropped open. The hand that was taking his drink to his mouth jolted. Liquid was spilled.

'What a thought,' he'd exclaimed.

'A truth,' she'd retorted. She'd taken a deep breath and

smelt his freshness, the crispness of a body after the invigoration of a cleansing shower.

The sweat was gone and, in a way, she regretted that. There was arousal in masculine sweat, its identity heavy with the hormones that gave drive to his muscles and semen to her womb. It had a voice, she decided, it said, 'I am male. Taste me.'

From the very first sight of him, she had wanted to taste him. Oh, yes, she had wanted to taste him alright.

He had asked her how she intended seducing him and where.

'I'm not going to tell you,' she'd replied. 'I'm going to creep up on you and surprise you when you least expect it.'

She would have gone on, and so would he. He had been like a jackdaw blinded by her glitter. The sin of covetousness was on his face. It had touched his flesh.

Then Thomas, her husband, had come looking for her. But it wasn't all bad. Mariana and Jamie, who she and Thomas already knew, had also joined them.

A kind of sticky companionship had evolved at that moment. Before long they were talking business, dinner parties and meeting in the changing room at the country club.

The first dinner for the six of them was a candle-lit, atmospheric affair at the home of Jamie and Mariana.

In the glow of candlelight, Crystal had read the desire in Michael's eyes.

Perhaps it was the wine, or perhaps it had been her limited vision in the candlelight, but she was sure Michael had looked on his wife with a certain disdain. And did he talk *of* his wife rather than *to* her?

She had decided at that moment that Michael was a man with a wife who was both a business and social asset, but not necessarily a sexual one. Candlelight and heady wine had made her premise appear to be truth. Now she wasn't so sure.

She tried not to dwell on it.

In her mind she looked for the right signs to set her thinking straight.

Like a video on fast forward, her thoughts travelled onwards to other occasions when everything seemed to be going her way.

She remembered one night in particular. They were out on the patio at Michael and Josie's home. Warm sensations had spread from the palm and fingers that Michael had laid over one of her buttocks.

The sound of clattering cutlery was coming from the kitchen because Josie was filling the dishwasher. Thomas had gone to the bathroom. Jamie and Mariana were giving each other meaningful looks in the drawing room. Mariana was sat on the settee and was tapping fiercely at her knees in a constant spanking movement.

Jamie's eyes had been wide as saucers and his lips had been continually wetted by his flicking tongue.

Michael had followed Crystal out onto the patio.

'Let me fuck you,' Michael had asked quietly.

Crystal had sighed. She had been wondering how long it would take him to get round to propositioning her. She had also wondered what words he would use. She had now found out. Not love, not let's meet and have a few drinks, a meal by candlelight – a prelude to the main act. He had said exactly what they both wanted. Passion had blazed in his eyes. He wanted her. *Her.* Not just for physical relief, not like Thomas who might as well have been making love to a vacuum cleaner. He wanted to make love to her.

'Then fuck me,' she had replied in a low, husky voice, then she groaned as his hand had squeezed her behind.

Behind her towelling mask, Crystal remembered and murmured sweet sounds through closed lips.

Memory was not always reliable, but in her case she remembered every little detail.

'When?' he had asked.

'When you least expect it,' she had answered. 'Just as I promised you.'

'Wow!' He had said it very softly, but threw back his head and closed his eyes as if already savouring a moment that had not come. 'I remember you saying that. I dreamt about it that night.'

'Did you fuck your wife on the strength of it?'

He paused. She had sensed a certain reluctance to betray what was, after all, a close confidence. But eventually he did reply.

'Yes. I did.'

'But it wasn't her was it? It was her body beneath you, but in your mind it was me.'

'Yes,' he said softly. She shivered as his lips kissed her neck. 'Yes. It was you.'

Just as she had promised, Crystal surprised him.

There was an extra thrill in doing it in the men's changing room – not the modern one everyone now used which was integral with the main building, but the separate one behind the ancillary squash courts. Nowadays they were used only for overflow.

It had been very busy that day, so Michael and his partner for squash had been obliged to use the old changing room.

Crystal had watched Michael from the moment his car had pulled up outside, yet she had kept out of sight. She had followed the mud path that led behind the main building then ran down a steep slope to the back of the old changing rooms.

Taking great care not to be seen, she waited until Michael's squash partner had left.

As her pulse rate began to increase, she started counting. One, two, three, four. She had counted off the seconds in her mind. She had carefully judged the moment when he would be naked in the privacy of the old changing rooms. Then she went in.

He had turned quickly at the sound of her. Even now she could still see in her mind the look of surprise on his face, the wide eyes and open jaw, the sudden flexing of his penis.

He did not move. He did not say anything. He had kept his eyes fixed on her.

He had waited for her to approach, for her to make the first move.

She remembered how her eyes had dropped to his penis which swelled and reared beneath her gaze. Judging by its movements, Michael had been anticipating where his weapon would shortly be.

Naked, glistening with sweat, his scent compelling rather than offensive, he had moved towards her and kissed her.

Her flesh had been ignited with the scent and the feel of his nakedness.

Her fingernails had dug into his bare shoulders and he had yelled out, then clasped her more fiercely, more closely.

Her mouth had clung to his and sucked in the salty dew that lay on his upper lip. She felt the tip of his erect penis knock against her belly and she ran her hands down to clutch at it, to pull on it.

'I want it,' she had whispered, her voice echoing around the tinny emptiness of the whitewashed room.

His lips had suddenly left her.

'Wait. I need a shower. Will you join me?'

Crystal remembered she had murmured a throaty response. She was running her mouth and her teeth along from his neck to his shoulder as he said this, so his words were lost against her hair.

Before she answered, she had gripped him more tightly.

'No.' Her voice had been hushed, heavy with desire. 'No. At least not yet. Let me have you as you are. Let me have you smelling naturally.'

He had held her chin between his fingers and lifted it. She had liked the feel of his thumb pressing against her skin as her eyes had met his and her lips had parted. How striking his eyes had seemed, how straight his nose, how dark his hair and his eyebrows. Classic features. Michael always had a blue-black shadow over his chin, his cheeks, and his upper lip. It was never entirely absent from his face except in that short period immediately after shaving.

'I love the smell of you,' she had whispered as his hand roved over her thin cotton top.

She had groaned with pleasure, desire making her body sway against him as he lifted her tee shirt. Her skin burned as his palms ran up over her bare flesh.

'You feel good,' he had said to her, and she had tingled. 'Just as I thought you would. Just as I've imagined since the very first time I met you.'

There was a long wooden bench in the centre of the changing room. Behind and above it was a row of coat hooks.

Crystal gently eased herself out of his embrace, stood on the bench, and made a show of removing her top. As she did so, she tossed her long cloud of hair. Her breasts bounced and her nipples grew.

Except for his pulsating penis, Michael stood still and silent. Dark-lashed, his eyes noted each curve of her body, each breast, the definition of her collarbone, the dark mole on her left shoulder.

He had glanced briefly at the door as footsteps went past outside.

'I took the precaution of locking us in,' she told him.

'Who cares!' he murmured. His eyes did not leave her body.

Smiling and wriggling her slim hips and round bottom, Crystal slid her white linen shorts down to her ankles. Her white trainers followed.

Hips undulating, body trembling, she had spread her

arms along the row of coat hooks hanging there like some crucified offering. Her body had been ablaze with desire.

'Kiss me.' She had said it softly, invitingly, expectantly.

Michael had reached for her. With trembling fingers, his hands had grasped her hips before running in smooth, sweeping strokes down her thighs and on down her legs.

He had kissed her knees first then, with his tongue, he had traced hot lines over first one thigh, then the other. As she bent her knees, his tongue had prodded her belly, penetrated her navel.

Above him, she had groaned, tossing her head and letting it drop forward. Her hair fell over him like a perfumed veil. It tickled his shoulders as his hands had grasped her swaying hips and his tongue licked flat her crisp, pubic hair.

Contained within the confines of her hair, his scent wafted up to her. Urged by the probing of his tongue as it prodded into the place where her sexual lips began, she opened her legs.

She heard him moan as he drank in her scent and his tongue travelled further. The roughness of his chin scratched pleasurably against the smoothness of her inner thighs. His tongue was hard and wet as it wove its way through the petals of satin-soft flesh that enclosed her clitoris and ran through to her vagina.

So delicate were his probings, so accurate in their hunt for her most responsive flesh, she had to stand on tiptoe to accommodate it better.

When his lips had at last kissed her belly, she had known that the first chapter of their copulation was over.

He had lifted her down so that she was still clasping the coat hooks. She was stretched out between them and him, her legs wound around his waist. He had her fully extended so that her separated thighs fitted nicely over his pelvis and his erection.

Dizzy with pleasure, she felt his penis, hard and hot,

pressing against her sex, its tip nudging aside the cheeks of her behind.

Gripping her legs with his arms, he had reached for her breasts. He squeezed and she cried out. She recalled feeling as if two iron vices had been fixed over her breasts or, more accurately, as if they had been forced into a bra two sizes too small.

Friction was awakening all the nerve ends along her channel. Spirals of delight were sparking outwards and upwards, coating her body with an invisible cloak of sexual lust.

'Please!' she had cried, her voice full of the pain of wanting, of desiring.

He had seemed to know instantly what she was feeling.

He grasped her waist, jerked her body so that she let go of the hooks she was holding and her feet regained the ground.

Running her hands down his back, she drank in the perfume of his maleness, and lay her cheek against the sculptured hardness of his pectoral muscles.

At the time she had wanted to explore him further with her mouth and drink in the stronger smell that congregated around his genitals, but his voice had been urgent against her ear.

'I can't wait. I have to have you now!'

With his assistance, she had lain down on the bench so that her legs were dropped to each side and her sex was exposed to his view.

She looped her arms behind her so that her breasts were thrust forward and became more approachable for his mouth and his hands.

Gripping the bench on either side of her head, he had positioned himself very accurately and very carefully.

Arching her back, Crystal had levelled herself with the tip of his rod. She breathed heavily and murmured long and low. Her juices had trickled like honey from her vagina, seeping stickily down her inner thighs.

She had seen the intensity in his eyes, the slight looseness of his jaw as he began to ease himself into her.

'At last!' He said the two words in one rushed breath. 'At last I am fucking you! At last!'

Her breasts had trembled with each thrust of his loins. Their bellies met and made sucking noises as she brought her hips up to meet him. Desire ran through her like molten silver.

He had lain heavy on her when he came. He had mouthed expletives against her ear, words Thomas never used. Those words had made her want him to fuck her more, to bury her beneath him, for him to press her hard against the bench and to will her to come, to buck against him until the last eddy of pleasure was over and done with.

She had done just that. Her body had writhed with desire. Each organ within her, each nerve ending seemed to cry out with the unspeakable pleasure of it all.

No matter that she cried out for him not to stop, to keep doing it to her, to not do it to her, to do it harder, to do it softer, her cry was like pain, but also like pleasure.

And thus passed our first orgasm, she thought to herself as she lay soaking in her bath and, as is the way of such things, her thoughts went on to the second time.

In the shower afterwards, they had done it again. This time she had soaped him first until his body was covered with a white film of spuming lather.

She then knelt down in front of him so she could lather his penis and his behind more liberally before the running water and her tongue licked it all away.

Spray had soaked her hair and left it in gleaming rats tails. She had tilted her head back as far as it could go, looked up at him, moved her head forward and taken his balls into her mouth.

His erection had grown again. His flesh had pulsated with life as new fluid had been pumped along its length.

Almost, she thought to herself, *he almost came into my mouth, but he stopped himself.*

'Not yet,' he had murmured, his jaw more firm, his desire more controlled. 'I want to fuck you again. This time I want to take you from behind.'

Gently, he had taken hold of her shoulders and raised her to her feet.

After kissing her lips, he had turned her away from him. For a moment he had moulded the front of his body to the back of hers. Then he had pushed her head forward until she was bending away from him. Only his thighs had touched her then, and his penis and his pubic hair.

As the water ran over her head and through her hair, he steadied himself. The head of his penis divided her sex lips as with a groan Michael pushed himself into her for the second time.

She squeezed her eyes shut as the water from the shower head ran over her hair and down her face.

Michael had held her hips tightly as he eased her gently backwards and forwards to meet his hard member. His balls had slapped softly against her, and pubic hair slid like wet clay over and between her buttocks.

Being fully aware of the finer features of orgasm, Crystal had slid her hand between her legs and played in fairylike softness with her throbbing clitoris.

Thrilling sensations ran as quickly over her body as the water from the shower.

The sheer intensity of her climax had made her legs shake and she had cried out those unintelligible yet telling sounds that had left Michael in no doubt that she had come.

Eventually, he too cried out as his weapon pumped its essence into her. After that, his semen and the washed-off soap had mingled and run together down the plughole.

In the privacy of her mind, as she lay flat and sweating in the bath, Crystal came to no hard and fast conclusion about her relationship with Michael.

All she did know was that having it the first time with him had made a deep impression on her. There had been something almost virginal about it. It had been as though she had given herself for the very first time. It had been nothing like that when she really had experienced sex for the very first time.

His name was not important. Just as well, she couldn't remember it. But she did recall his rushed breathing, his sweating brow and his tunnelling fingers beneath the crotch of her knickers.

Only because it was the first time and her libido had been aching to be satisfied had she taken off her pants and let his youthful tool into her virgin chamber.

Amazed at its heat and its hardness, she had gripped his penis and steered it more skilfully into her. The youth had groaned and come into her hand. She had been angry but, being young, his penis had not remained flaccid for long. Again, this time without the aid of her willing fingers, he had thrust himself into her.

There had been a slight tightening inside her as the head of his weapon had butted her hymen. The barrier had been breached. The tightness had been fleeting. He was in her and she had raised herself to meet him.

Later that night in bed, she thought again about that first time with Michael.

As she lay in the darkness, she tried transposing the man beside her with the one in her brain. It didn't work.

Sighing, she pulled herself as close to the edge of the bed as possible, snuggled into her pillow and fell asleep, still thinking of Michael.

Lying beside her, Thomas was also awake. Crystal had been with another man again. He knew all the signs and also knew there was something different about this one.

He sighed and felt happier than he had for a very long time.

Chapter 14

There was a spot in the forest where Josie like to walk and make quick sketches that she could convert into water colours when she got back to her studio.

Along a narrow path between lines of whispering trees, she would walk until she came to her favourite place. Fallen trees left an open view and a grassy glade some way along it. At that point she could look down at the river meandering lazily through the valley below. She could see everything from there and yet be hidden from the path behind her.

The road far below followed the valley floor, but more directly than the river. A cluster of houses and other buildings mushroomed along its straightest length and wide fields fell like scraps of patchwork cloth towards a bend where the river formed a deep horseshoe into the opposite bank. It was a worthwhile scene to draw and paint – a composition contrived by nature itself.

Today she followed her usual habit. It was a warm day but there was enough of a breeze to rustle the trees and undergrowth. It was also enough to muffle the sound of approaching footsteps but not to hide them completely.

As a lick of red hair blew across her cheek, Josie smiled.

'I love the sound of rustling leaves. It reminds me of a certain Sunday afternoon when I was young and fell in love for the first time. The place was a tree house if I remember rightly.'

'You heard me. I had every intention of ravishing you before you even had time to notice.'

Thomas stepped up behind her. She closed her eyes as the warm strength of his arms enveloped her. His lips gently grazed her neck and made her shiver.

'That's a man's remark. A typical man. Here I am talking about falling in love for the first time and there you are talking about ravishing me.'

'The first time? How many more times after that did you fall in love?' There was a touch of amusement in Thomas's voice.

Josie laughed. 'Oh, a few. Or at least, I thought it was love. I know now that it was sheer lust. How was a young girl like me supposed to know about the surging of hormones and basic instincts, Thomas?'

Thomas laughed and she felt joy at the vibration of his voice and the roughness of his cheek against hers.

For a moment there was only the sound of rustling leaves.

Thomas spoke. 'But what about the first time? Was it really love?'

Josie detected a hint of apprehension in his voice.

'Yes and no. Yes, I think it was at the time, but I did not really recognise it, and no, perhaps even that first time when I lay naked in the shade of a clapped-out tree house, it was not the first time I truly loved. Perhaps that time is now.'

She heard him sigh with relief and knew he was remembering and regretting.

She narrowed her eyes and the scene in the valley below become less prominent, less important.

Thomas was still behind her and the feel of him against her back was too pleasant to disturb. But she did twist her head round so she could look up into his eyes. She smiled as she did so.

'And what about you, my darling Thomas? When was

the first time you fell in love? Was it really with a gawky, redheaded schoolgirl on that Sunday afternoon on a carpet of fallen leaves?'

A sudden silence came upon them both. Neither could tear their gaze away from the other. It seemed as though nothing else in the world truly mattered. No words were needed. In that one look Thomas said everything, and Josie easily understood.

'Why Crystal?' There was hurt in her voice.

Thomas's look of love turned to one of regret – almost of shame.

'You were lost to me.'

'I would have come back. You would have seen me again. I would have come home during the holidays and we would have carried on where we left off.'

There was pain on Josie's face. Thomas turned her round to face him and hugged her tightly. He spoke softly but urgently against her ear.

'It was sex, Josie. Pure sex. That's what Crystal is. Pure sex.'

'OK. OK. I can accept that. But why marry her? Tell me . . . Please.'

Her eyes looked sad.

Thomas tensed his arms so that she was held more tightly. It was as if he were afraid of letting her go. Then he sighed and released his grip as he began to explain.

'Crystal, as you well know, likes to have her own way. Once she sets her heart on something, she is determined that one way or another whatever it is will be hers. It doesn't matter that she might soon tire of her latest craze. She had to hold onto it even when her interest has waned. It's a bit like her clothes. Rather than take them to a charity shop or even one of those that resells them, she cuts them into bits and throws them in the bin or buries them in the back of a cupboard. She can't bear anyone else to make use of something she no longer wants. I'm like her old clothes. She doesn't want me, but she doesn't want anyone else to want me.'

'I want you.'

Thomas smiled and hugged her.

'I know. And I want you. But Crystal? No. Crystal doesn't want me, but she'll do everything in her power to hold onto me, unless we can work something out. You know Michael wants her?'

Josie nodded. 'Yes. He's besotted with her.'

'Then we play on his lust for her. Use it to fire him up and force him to make the first move. That way you can keep your house and your studio. The blame and the lust will be with them.'

'Did you lust after Crystal as much as Michael does?'

Thomas nodded. 'Yes, but I never loved her like he does. Crystal was built for lust, and I was young.'

'Tell me about it.'

Thomas hesitated, then nodded. 'Right. I will.'

He threw back his head and took a deep breath before he started. Then he looked straight into Josie's eyes.

'Crystal has always been good-looking. Long, thick black hair falling over her shoulders and a certain rhythm in the way she walked. In those days, she always dressed to tempt. Her clothes were explosively erotic; flimsy black or red underwear beneath a black lace trouser suit. High-heeled shoes or boots, low neckline, bright red lips and those flashing eyes. She oozed sexuality and made no secret of what she had to offer.

'I remember going to a disco. I vaguely recall glancing in her direction. Next thing I knew she was stood there asking me to dance. Her body was touching mine and, when I took her out onto the dance floor, she pressed herself against me so I could feel every contour of her body. Her hands were everywhere and I couldn't help responding. She was squirming against me, her hips moving, her pelvis tapping mine. I was in no doubt of what she wanted, and I couldn't help but give it to her. After all, I was only a young, red-blooded man.

'She took me back to her flat. I'd hardly got inside the door when she pulled me to her. I'd had a few to drink, but I remember how hot I felt. I was hard as iron and wanting her like hell.

'We seemed to tumble into her bedroom. I can barely remember our clothes coming off, only how warm and soft her body felt. My hormones were jumping and popping. I wanted sex with her. I *had* to have sex with her.

'Her hands were pulling on my cock even before I had time to touch her breasts. I remember her pushing me back onto the bed and holding my cock upright as she eased herself onto me. Her face was alight with sexuality. It was almost . . .'

Thomas's voice seemed to trail away as he swallowed and looked at the far scene in the valley below. 'It was almost as if she only wanted *that* part of my body. Not the rest of me . . . the real me. Just what I had between my legs.

'That was the first time.'

'And after that?'

'I continued to see her.'

'Why?'

'Sexual satisfaction. I felt no emotion when we did what we did. I thought she felt the same. And, anyway, I heard nothing from you. I heard you had hordes of boyfriends after you. I wanted to die. I wanted to use myself up or even bury myself in Crystal's body. I let her and my lust use me. I wanted to lose myself in lust.'

'I did have a lot of boyfriends and I had a few very exciting affairs.' Josie paused. 'But never mind me. Tell me more. You're not saying that Crystal loved you?'

Thomas shook his head. 'Not in that sense. Not in the way you mean it. Crystal collects men. To her they are things.'

'But why did she marry you? She didn't need to. And she certainly isn't faithful to you. Michael isn't the first.'

Josie saw his hurt look and bit her lip.

'I'm sorry . . .' She touched his cheek.

'No need to be.' He shrugged. 'Fidelity has no place in Crystal's life. I suppose you could say I'm like a tin of corned beef that's left on the shelf in case she should run out of fresh food. Yes . . . that's the best way to describe it.' He smiled weakly.

Josie's voice became quieter. Her eyes became wider, more confused. 'So why did you marry her?'

Thomas hung his head as he shook it. 'Because she told me she was pregnant and did not believe in abortion. I suppose you could say she appealed to my sense of decency. And I always did want a family.

'But she wasn't pregnant?'

He shook his head vigorously. 'Of course not. Crystal hates kids. She'd move heaven and earth so as not to get pregnant. I should have known better at the time, but I thought I could change her. Of course I know both her and myself better now.'

Josie stood on tiptoe so she could kiss his forehead.

'But you felt responsible. No matter about not loving her and not wanting to marry her. You felt a responsibility towards the baby?'

Thomas nodded then smiled sadly. His eyes met hers.

'Shame,' he said, 'when you think of what might have been . . .knowing you . . .knowing me.'

Josie let her fingers trail down over her lover's cheek as she smiled. Just such a story and such a commitment was the reason she loved him, and soon they would have to do something about it.

'Will she ever ask you to divorce her?' Josie asked.

He shrugged. 'I don't know. Has Michael mentioned anything?'

Josie shook her head. 'No. I know he wants to. It's just

a matter of time. We might have to push things along a bit.'

'Tell them outright?'

Josie cocked her head to one side. Thomas thought she looked like an inquisitive starling like that. 'Not exactly. After all, why should we go cap in hand to them. I think we will have to catch them in the act.' She smiled and her eyes sparkled.

Thomas let his hand slide to her breast. He squeezed it gently. 'That should be fun but, in the meantime, we are here alone and I love the feel of the breeze and damp grass against my skin. It brings back old memories.'

Josie laughed as she pressed herself against him. She ran her hands beneath his dark green sweater and felt the hardness of his back and the soft dots of raised moles. 'So do I,' she replied and, as his fingers traced the shape of her breasts, she brought her hands round to his belt buckle, released the catch, then pulled down the zip of his trousers.

She murmured with pleasure as his penis leapt out into her hand. She stroked and squeezed it as her lips met those of her lover and the world around them suddenly became less real, less dull.

He pulled off his sweater and she feasted her eyes on the hard contours of his warm brown skin. He threw back his head as she kissed each of his nipples.

There was an urgency in the way their clothes came off and their flesh combined.

She lay herself out on the grass, arms and legs spread as wide as possible. She closed her eyes and felt the dappled shadows of the leaves, alternate patches of light and shade over her body.

Thomas had broken off a length of goldenrod and was using it to caress her flesh.

She mewed with the subtle gentleness of its touch, the feather-light sensations that spread from her nipples, her belly and from between her legs when he touched her there.

'Is it nice?' he asked her.

She murmured her assent.

'How about your back?'

She rolled over so that the coolness of the damp grass was pressed against her belly.

Her body undulated against that coolness as the ears of goldenrod traced delicate patters over her back, down her spine, over each buttock.

Gently it caressed the lips of her sex sending thrills of delight coursing hotly through her body.

Then it was Thomas who was on her, the heat of his body pressing her tightly against the earth, the iron hardness of his penis pushing into her vagina as her love juice spilled out onto the grass.

Like their bodies, their cries of ecstasy and love mingled with the leaves of the trees that rustled above them.

Chapter 15

Jamie had received a good hiding from Mariana before leaving the house and driving off to meet the others at the country club.

Even now, as he sat in the comfortable driving seat of his BMW, he clenched his buttocks and felt the smarting of his flesh. He clenched his teeth as he sucked in his breath.

Of course, no one else would notice that his behind was pinker than it usually was. Jamie was always very careful not to expose his muscular frame to his friends until after they had exercised and used the pool and sauna. That way the whole of his body was somewhat pink. What was unmarked by whip or cane fused quite naturally with the pinkness of his much-abused bottom.

He shivered when he thought of what Mariana had done to him. They were lovely, delicious shivers that always remained after one of their sessions, sessions which were by necessity very personal and very secret. His friends and their wives might not understand his liking for such treatment, but it didn't matter. Jamie kept his habits to himself and was grateful that his wife did the same.

As he drove to the country club he thought about everything they had done before he had left the house.

Dressed in just a nylon overall he had carried out the cleaning of the bathroom. Everything was almost spotless but Mariana had, of course, found fault.

'Look at the old soap you've left around these taps! It's

hard and dry and should have been scraped off.'

With trembling gaze, Jamie had looked at the soap he had deliberately left around the bathroom taps.

'I'm sorry, mistress,' he muttered, his voice verging on a whimper as he had cowered low on the bathroom floor.

'You will be!' Mariana shouted. 'Bend over the bath!'

He had done exactly that. From previous sorties into the realms of white enamel, he knew precisely what position to take. He also remembered to pull his overall up at the front so that the coldness of the bath rim dug into his naked flesh just above his penis. Mariana wanted his head resting on his hands at the bottom of the bath, his behind high in the air. Accordingly, that was exactly what he did.

With cringing excitement, he felt her fold the thin nylon of his overall until it was resting along the nape of his neck. His head was almost covered by it. His bottom, which was higher than his head, was exposed to her view and her wrath.

'Open your legs!' she had barked, and he had immediately obeyed. With mounting excitement he felt the bristles of the lavatory brush hitting against the inside of his thighs. He whimpered long and low as the bristles crushed his scrotum to his body.

'Now I will show you how I want things scrubbed. Once you have been scrubbed as I want this bathroom scrubbed, you will remember it!' A delicious note of cruelty had rung through his wife's voice. Just thinking of it as he drove made the blood rush into his penis.

Of course he would remember how she wanted the bathroom scrubbed. But again and again in the future, he would avoid cleaning the dried soap from around the tap because feeling the bristles of the toilet brush on his scrotum was one of the most delightful sensations he could ever wish for.

'What would you do without me to keep you in order?'

Mariana had cried as the bristles of the toilet brush had smacked his behind. 'Imagine what you would do if you didn't have me but someone who let you do what you liked, like Josie or Crystal.'

Whether connecting the names of the other two women had something to do with it, Jamie didn't know. All he did know was that as Mariana spoke the names, visions of the two women came into his mind; Josie, slim, very white and with burning red hair and cool green eyes. And Crystal. Vibrant, sexual. Everything about her said take me in any way possible and, for the first time ever, Jamie wondered what it would be like to have another woman. As he thought that last outrageous thought, he cried out and, prompted by his wife, caught hold of his penis and adjusted his stance so that his semen had poured into the bath.

Later, whilst washing his deposit away, he had felt Mariana looking at him in a way she had never looked at him before. He sensed she was thinking, but said nothing. Mariana expected him to wait for her to speak her mind.

'Would you like to screw her?' she asked.

Jamie had paused in the scrubbing of the bath. 'Who?' he asked innocently.

'You know damn well who! Crystal. That little trollop with the big breasts and the open legs. Would you like to screw her?'

Jamie's mouth had gone dry. Did she know about him meeting Crystal in the hotel bedroom. 'I don't know.' His voice had trembled.

'Liar!' The flat of Mariana's hand had landed on his backside before she knelt beside him, her face close to his. Her fingers caressed his hair. 'Would you?' Her voice was suddenly sexual – almost kittenish. It surprised him. Mariana had many fine qualities and characteristics, but being kittenish was not usually one of them.

Jamie had swallowed hard before he answered.

'It might be interesting.'

Mariana snuggled closer and rested her cheek against his. She laughed. 'I think it might be fun, and I think she would be game. I would be there of course, my darling. Just imagine it, the two of us and you.' She kissed his cheek. 'Now that is something you would like isn't it, my darling.'

Jamie trembled. 'Oh, yes, mistress. Whatever you want, mistress.'

His mind did somersaults and his penis grew larger. Having one woman dominate him was wonderful. Having two would be out of this world!

As he pulled into the car park at the country club, he saw Crystal getting out of her low-slung red sports. She tossed her hair when she saw him and smiled.

'Hi, Jamie. Carry my bags for me?'

His penis, which was already hard on account of his lewd thoughts, got harder. It might sound like a question to anyone listening, but he knew an order when it was given.

Crystal's sports bag was down at her feet and, as Jamie bent down to pick it up, Crystal brought her foot to bear on his hand.

'Kiss my foot,' she said softly. 'Go on. There's no one around.'

Jamie tensed, then did exactly as ordered.

Two mistresses, said a voice in his head, and a mix of blood and hot sensations ran throughout his body.

Crystal flashed her chill blue eyes at him. 'Now, tell me what you are doing here without your wife.'

Jamie licked the dryness of his lips. 'I'm meeting Michael and Thomas. We're using the gym today.'

'And Mariana? Where is she?'

'Gone to see Alex.'

'A lover?' Crystal raised her eyebrows.

Was that contempt Jamie read there, or did she know something he didn't.

'Of course not. Alex is my father. She gets on well with him.'

'Of course she does. Of course. Mariana would be more likely to have a lover called Alexandra than Alexander, wouldn't she?'

Jamie swallowed. Wrinkles of confusion spread around his eyes as his brow creased thoughtfully. 'I don't know what you mean.'

It surprised her when he turned his back on her and marched off, but he just couldn't help it. His pale face was turning pink with confusion. Mariana liked what they did together. His kind of sex suited her. Girls had always interested her. He was aware of that. But girls were no substitute for the real thing.

'Don't worry about it,' he heard Crystal call after him. 'We all have our favourite girlfriends.'

'I'm not worried about bloody girlfriends,' Jamie muttered to himself as he pushed open the door of the men's changing room. And he wasn't.

Unknowingly, Crystal had sown a suspicion in his mind. For the first time he wondered just how well his wife got on with his father.

Chapter 16

Michael was his usual cocky self in the changing room. He was boasting about how he'd lifted three hundred and fifty pounds on the arm-curling machine.

'Really,' Thomas said. He didn't look in Michael's direction and certainly didn't sound convinced. All of them had heard Michael talking this sort of stuff before, and today Thomas had found him out.

Without appearing to, Thomas had watched Michael closely. Michael, of course, had not known he was being scrutinised so did not realise that Thomas had him sussed.

Thomas had always been suspicious that once Michael came to the end of a workout on any machine, he made a habit of pressing the plus button to add on a few pounds. The weight then read far more than he had actually lifted so that the next guy to use the equipment was suitably impressed. It looked good and suited his image. As yet Thomas had not accused Michael of being a liar.

Although Jamie was joining in with the conversation, his comments seemed a bit stilted, as though he had something else on his mind.

The fact that Jamie always had a rather red bottom had not been lost on Thomas. *I wonder if Mariana's been a bit heavy-handed of late,* he thought to himself as he caught a glimpse of Jamie's backside before his shorts hid it from view.

He did not dwell on the fact. He averted his eyes and left his mind open to what was going on around him.

'Ever had an older woman?' Michael was saying.

'Ever had a younger one?' Jamie added.

'Taboo,' said Thomas and wagged his finger disapprovingly.

'Not in some of the spots I've been to,' confided Jamie.

'Never mind the youngsters, an older woman can teach you a helluva lot,' argued Michael who was obviously unwilling to let the conversation shift away from his own personal experiences.

Thomas glanced sidelong as Michael ran his fingers through his thickly curling hair at the same time as he admired his reflection in the mirror.

'A lot of what, Michael?' he asked.

Michael jerked his head and patted the underside of his chin with the flat of his hand in a vain effort to keep a double chin at bay. He was smirking with satisfaction that the conversation would now go his way. He smiled knowingly.

'The right moves, the right sensations. An older woman knows which spot to pick, which move to make. They're great. I well recommend them. Now take Vanessa. She was the widow of a guy who used to own a company I dealt with; sixty if a day, but gorgeous with it. She had a look in her eye that told me I was in with the chance of giving her more than the company's standard attention.'

Michael whistled long and low. 'What a tasty woman she was! High-powered business suits and a shrewd mind didn't hide the fact that she still had a hot body and a lusty libido. I knew from the first that she was aching to have me. Wow!'

'Get on with it, Michael. We haven't got all day.'

Michael looked at Thomas with a hint of surprise. In his experience, Thomas didn't have an impatient or tactless bone in his body. It peeved him to think that he might have been wrong, so he directed the next part of his story towards Jamie who was sat quietly, eyes shut.

'So anyway, Jamie, I was saying. This gal had white hair that a bottle blond would be real jealous of. Her eyes were a deep, dark brown. So were her eyebrows. She had a good figure and a husky voice, and when she asked me to come to her house for dinner, I knew for sure that I was to be the main course.'

Michael waited until someone nodded before he continued. It was Jamie who obliged.

'Anyway, there we were, the food and wine inside us and the evening getting mellow. I remember her name was Vanessa. Van..ess..a!' He pulled the name apart slowly as if he would be more easily believed that way. He went on talking.

'I also remember that she was wearing a plain black dress with a low neckline. She had three strings of pearls around her neck, pearl earrings, a gold and pearl bracelet on one wrist and a gold Rolex on the other.

'I heard her stockings whisper like they do when a woman rubs one leg against the other. It made me want to have my hands between them.

'Anyway, she's flashing me messages over the top of her wineglass, and I'm sweating buckets and dying for her to make a move.'

He would have gone on, but Thomas interrupted him.

'Why didn't you make the first move? As old-fashioned as it might sound, women still prefer a man to take the initiative.'

Michael jerked his head abruptly and glared at him. 'I couldn't do that! This was an important business client. What if I'd read the signals all wrong? Bang goes the business and bang goes my bonus. Oh no. I couldn't afford to do that.'

Thomas raised his eyebrows in a mocking 'so what' sort of way. 'So what did you do?'

'I told you. I waited.' Michael laughed conceitedly. 'And then she did it. She couldn't wait any longer, so she did it.' He shook his head as he laughed again – longer and louder this time.

'Boy, did she do it. She got up from that table, took me by the hand, and led me out into a conservatory that was full of gym equipment and buckets of plants.

'"I've always wanted to *really* exercise," she said, and I knew exactly what she meant. Exactly! She pressed herself against me and put her hand against my trousers. As she kissed me I could hear my zip being undone and felt her fingers rolling my cock out from my pants. She began to pull on it as though it was some kind of elastic. Wow, but it was mind-blowing!

'Anyway, that was the signal I'd been waiting for. I unzipped her dress and slid it off her shoulders. She was wearing black lace beneath it and she smelt of expensive perfume and a musky female kind of smell.

'"I'll do anything for you at all, my dear boy," she said to me. "Anything!"

'Well, being a hot-blooded stud, I wasn't going to let this chance pass me by.

'I held her face in my hand and felt the softness of her hair. I kissed her lips. I remember that her lipstick was not only the colour of peaches, it tasted of them too.

'As I pulled my lips from hers, I gripped her head more tightly and pushed her gently but firmly towards the floor. She didn't protest. Wow!' Michael threw back his head and laughed. 'Quite the contrary. She sounded as if she hadn't seen anything like it for years and, when it was at last between her lips, she sucked on it as though she were starving.

'It didn't take long I can tell you. Her mouth was like a vacuum cleaner, sucking for all it was worth. I came and she swallowed.

'I can tell you, I certainly went there a few more times.'

'So the old bird could suck you off?' muttered Thomas.

Michael glared. His glare turned to a nervous laugh. It was a moment before he spoke.

'Why not? She was good at it. Besides, we didn't always do that. Sometimes I gave it to her over one of the gym machines or she would hang on one of them completely naked whilst I kissed her all over then put it into her. Of course, I didn't go on using the gym. Only for six months or so. She remarried later on.'

'You mean she dumped you?' This time there was no doubting the mockery in Thomas's voice.

Michael reddened. 'No she did not! Not really.' He coloured up a bit more. 'I was already courting Josie. I couldn't go on seeing her.'

'So who was the guy she married?' asked Jamie. He didn't sound particularly interested, but he was glancing nervously from Michael to Thomas. He sensed tension between them. Had Michael noticed it?

Jamie's urge for him to continue was enough for Michael. He turned his blazing eyes away from Thomas and shrugged nonchalantly. 'Just some zombie she met on holiday.'

'You mean that not only was he younger than you, he was also black.'

Michael's towel flew to the floor. 'No that wasn't what I meant! What the bloody hell is eating you, Thomas?'

'Nothing that a few home truths won't cure!' Thomas got to his feet. His voice was low but strident.

Jamie got between them. 'Now, now, lads. Calm down!'

He slapped a palm on each chest to hold them apart. They were both glaring at each other. It was unspoken, but all three of them knew why.

Chapter 17

When he was at last alone, Michael flushed as he remembered what had really happened between him and Vanessa. Even now the truth about the scenario in the conservatory was painful to bring to mind.

How could he tell his friends, his very macho friends, that Vanessa was nothing like he had expected. Even now he shuddered to think of the raw truth of that night.

The dark huskiness of her voice had been ever more enticing than her looks.

When they first met they had talked mostly about him, which suited Michael fine.

It was almost as an afterthought that he had asked about her husband and why she had married a man some twenty or so years older than she was.

He remembered how she had fidgeted in her chair. There had been a knowing look in her eyes that had unnerved him. Her red-lipped mouth had smiled and the red silk suit she was wearing had lisped in a very satisfactory way as she crossed and recrossed her black-stockinged legs.

'You could say I regarded him as a father figure,' she drawled. 'He was a man I looked up to.'

Before he started going to dinner at her home, he used to visit her at the office. He was usually waved straight in.

Only on one particular occasion was he kept waiting in the outside office.

As he sat there patiently, wondering just how far things

might go with her today and when exactly she would proposition him, he was aware of sniggers and knowing glances coming from behind computer terminals and filing cabinets.

Because he had been sitting long enough, and also because he hated being laughed at, Michael got up and started walking up and down in a rather purposeful manner.

He smiled at the receptionist and, hands in pockets, he shuffled up to her desk.

'Been working here long?' he asked.

She glanced up at him. Her smile had been almost nonexistent. 'Long enough.'

A compact answer.

Michael would not be put off. Persistence was what got results, he told himself and, if he was to get on in this job, it was persistence that would do it for him.

'She's a great woman, isn't she? Mrs Van der Boor, I mean. Incredible for her age.'

The woman's mouth dropped open. At that moment the door to Vanessa's office had opened and she came out with a dark-skinned young man who had beautifully aquiline features and an earring in one plump lobe.

Michael had the distinct impression that if they had not been interrupted, the receptionist would have burst out laughing, though he was not sure why.

It was only later, in the conservatory, that he found out the truth.

Everything had happened just as he had told his friends. Vanessa had fallen to her knees, her eyes wide as she had taken in the superb erection she pulled out of his pants.

She had indeed kissed his penis, licked it long and lovingly as though its taste was nothing less than heavenly. Everything, exactly as he had outlined, had truly happened. He had received a most magnificent service from those bright red lips which had left a thick ring around this climaxing flesh. In no time at all he had recovered and was ready to explore Vanessa's body.

Despite her age and the fact that she was a favoured client of his company, he would have done so.

Vanessa did indeed lie back over some piece of gym equipment and Michael had fondled her breasts. They didn't feel like any other breasts he had ever touched. He put that down to her being older than any of the women he had previously had sex with.

It was only when she had rolled her skirt up that the dreadful truth became clear. 'Vanessa' was in fact Vince who had not only never been married but who was also a transvestite.

Michael immediately broke out in a cold sweat. Horrified by his discovery, he had stood and stared. At the same time as he stared, his penis retreated into his pants.

His response was immediate. Loyalty to the company and personal ambition were suddenly of no consequence. No matter the valued client status, Michael had fled from the place. So speedy had been his exit, that it wasn't until he was two miles away and about to fill the car up with fuel that he realised his flies were still undone.

Not that it mattered. There was no sign of that firm length he was so justly proud of. In fact, it took a fair while to recover its previous virility. For days after, he had been in a state of celibate shock.

How could he have been so stupid? How could he have been so enthused with lust that he had failed to notice any sign that Vanessa was not what she purported to be.

During those days of shock, he made excuses at work for no longer handling her account. A replacement was easily found. 'Hers' was a good account.

Besides rearranging his working life, Michael also rearranged the story in his mind. There was no way he was ever going to tell the absolute truth about it. It was an episode in his life that deserved to be fictionalised, with him as the macho stud and Vanessa as the older woman who craved his body.

But not all of it was a lie. The bit about her marrying the other guy was strangely true. Apparently he was a traffic warden who had given Vanessa, or rather Vince, a parking ticket one day. In return, she had given him a lot more than a thirty pound fine to tear the ticket into confetti.

Her traffic warden had obviously been impressed by her/his performance. He had also been unconcerned that her credentials were not entirely bona fide.

Love had indeed found a way. They married in the Netherlands. *Amsterdam,* Michael thought to himself, *is a pretty strange place.*

Spurred on by the shock of his encounter with Vanessa, he had asked Josie to marry him. A wife, he decided, was an unassailable excuse to any woman who might want too much from him.

Josie had said yes very quickly. He had wondered at the time why she had responded so fast. It was almost as though she wanted to get it over with without having to think about it, as if she were trying to blot something else from her mind.

So they had married and from the start Josie had been a very understanding wife, and he had been a very supportive husband.

He had been quite willing to help her financially while she got her career as an artist off the ground.

She in turn had seemed quite willing to turn a blind eye to his sexual adventures, and sexual adventures is all they were – until he had met Crystal.

Soon he would have to come clean, though he would have preferred Josie to want a divorce. That way he could get out on more favourable terms. So he stalled, dithered, and fantasised about Crystal till all hours of the night and early morning. Even at work, he could not get her out of his mind.

Michael's office was in a superb complex of old weathered stone buildings that had once been a collection of cow barns. Even now he could look across open fields to the housing estate beyond.

Grass and yellow flowers – probably dandelions – waved in the breeze across the empty fields. The scene helped relieve his stress when the work load was overpowering or his need to daydream about Crystal was too great.

Big, fluffy clouds were floating across the sky on the morning he first saw the couple walking across the field.

At this distance it was hard to distinguish what age they were or whether they were fair or dark. Instinctively he guessed why they were in the empty field on such a brilliant day.

'Who are you?' he said quietly to himself, and narrowed his eyes.

It was no good. They were too far away to distinguish features.

Glancing briefly down at his desk, he opened a drawer and got out the binoculars that sat there.

They belonged to Cecil, the company bookkeeper who was also a keen naturalist. Cecil used them to scrutinise the skylarks that nestled in the middle of the field and the horde of grey rabbits that inhabited a multi-holed warren beneath a thicket hedge.

The binoculars were powerful enough for Michael to see that the woman had long black hair and a creamy white complexion. From this distance he could not possibly tell what colour her eyes were, but the dark hair was enough to make him catch his breath.

The man appeared to have a beard. He also wore dark glasses and a kerchief around his neck.

Michael frowned at his appearance. There was something familiar about him, yet also something strangely alien. It was almost as though he had come from another time and been put down in this one.

The couple embraced. He saw them kiss and could almost feel the way their bodies pressed against each other. He immediately imagined what Crystal's body would feel like against his. He licked his lips then glanced briefly over his shoulder. There was no one else in the office. Everyone was out at lunch. He could safely go on watching.

He put the binoculars back to his eyes. It gave him a strange sensation to be watching what these two were doing. *Peeping Tom*, he thought to himself, and the thought that he was acting the part of voyeur made his penis harden.

He licked his lips and told himself to concentrate. With the aid of the high-powered lenses, he could see that the young woman's hands were beneath the man's shirt. He sucked in his breath. He could almost feel the man's bare flesh as though it was his own. His stomach muscles tightened as he imagined what the man was feeling. The woman's hands would be soft, gentle, but also demanding as they explored his flesh. Her fingers would be tracing the outline of his muscles. She would be doing it slowly, enticingly. Her touch would be soft, sensual. Each time her fingertips slid slowly over his flesh, shivers of desire would run over the man's skin. Michael trembled as though he were sharing that same skin.

Michael licked his tongue slowly over his bottom lip. His mouth was now extremely dry. Suddenly he had no wish to be alone. He had an urgent wish for a woman to be there in the office with him – preferably Crystal.

But there was no one with him and, in his mind, Michael himself was no longer in the office.

He was out there with them, the girl's fingers following the line of chest hair as it ran down over his sternum, his stomach, and disappeared beneath his waistband. Her pelvis would be jerking against his so that his penis tapped diligently against her mound.

His heart thudded in his chest, in his head, and all over his body.

Lust was taking him over. His blood was boiling in his veins, turbulent as it rushed headlong throughout his body.

'Get on with it,' he demanded quietly.

Before his very eyes, they began doing the things he wanted them to do, the things he would want to do to her, the things he would want her to do to him.

He saw the woman peel the man's shirt down over his brown arms and off over his hands. He saw her kiss his chest and lick the edge of his pectorals. To watch like this made him shiver. It also made him want that woman who looked so succulent and so familiar to him.

The man took hold of the nape of the woman's neck. Her hair tumbled to her waist as she tipped her head back. The man's mouth covered hers. Michael sucked in his bottom lip, then bit it. He could almost taste what that man was tasting. He could almost feel the tip of her tongue entering his own mouth.

As his own lust mounted, Michael's breathing became heavier.

He patted his chest. 'Keep calm, you fool. You're sounding like an obscene phone caller.'

Or a voyeur, he thought again. *A dirty old man in a mac who likes to watch couples doing it in parks – and fields.*

But he was past caring.

'Get on with it,' he grunted through gritted teeth.

The man made swift movements that told him the woman's blouse buttons were being undone.

The thudding of his heart was echoing in his ears. Michael was shocked at his own responses. He wanted to be out there with them! He *was* out there with them!

Something reminiscent of jealousy came to him.

Everything about what they did seemed incredibly familiar. Michael groaned as the woman's breasts bounced free. Even now, as he licked his lips, he could almost taste the hardness of her nipples and the soft pulpiness of her surrounding areolae.

He suddenly wanted this woman himself and again he wondered where he had seen her before. That dark hair reminded him of . . .

Crystal! No! It couldn't be.

He snatched the binoculars away from his eyes and stared wildly at the couple in the field as if he were seeing them for the first time.

It couldn't be! Not Crystal. His lover with another man! No! She wouldn't do that. She wouldn't!

He put the binoculars on the desk and told himself not to panic. But that did no good at all. His heart was still pounding in his chest as though it were trying to escape.

Was it really Crystal? And if so, who was the man with her?

Even though Michael was looking at them now without the field glasses, he could easily see that they were sinking to their knees. It was as though they were melting into the grass. Soon they would be lying out among the greenness. Their clothes would be off and the man's penis would be invading the woman's body. Dandelions would be squashed beneath them, and their juice would smear across their naked backs and limbs.

The thought of it made Michael tremble and swallow hard. He had a terrible urge to get his penis out from his pants and pull on it until the couple in the grass had finally got up and gone home.

But he couldn't do that – could he?

Again he glanced over his shoulder. No one was around yet.

'Damn it. I've got to get rid of this!' he exclaimed, then started to unzip his fly.

Binoculars in one hand, penis in the other, he went close up to the window so that the tip of his naked penis grazed gently against the rough stone wall.

A pair of buttocks rose up and down among the grass. Michael caught his breath. The man was on top of the woman. He just knew it! He could write down what they were doing word for word. Her muscles would be clamped around the man's penis, her back would be arched, her pelvis thudding up and down off the ground in order to meet his incessant thrusts.

Michael was lost in his own lust. The grey stone walls of the office faded around him. He was alone with his penis in his hand – or rather, he was at one with the couple out there in the field and his penis would not be put away until both he and they had come.

Imbued by the essence of sheer lust, the end was not far away. No longer could he keep in either his semen or the sounds in his throat.

'Oh, I'm coming,' he groaned and yet it was not him saying it but the man in the field. Even at this distance and with his eyes narrowed, Michael could tell that the man had finished. His buttocks were tense, his body still, the no-nonsense sign of a climax come and gone.

Michael swallowed when he at last came too. He dropped the field glasses from his eyes and stared down at his hand. It was still clenched around his penis and semen was oozing out from between his fingers.

As quickly as he could, he wiped the stickiness from his hands and tidied himself up.

He took a deep breath, then told himself not to worry about it. What he had just done was perfectly normal. Isn't that what porn videos were all about – people watching other people having sex?

But he knew this was not quite the same. The truth had to be admitted.

It was hard not to stare at the middle of the field even

without the binoculars. Even so, he could not resist looking through the field glasses one last time.

The couple were walking back. The girl's dark hair was again blowing in the wind and, once more Michael was reminded of Crystal.

'Crystal?' He said it quizzically, but there was also fear in his voice now. Much as he still coveted other women, he wanted Crystal most of all. And, anyway, she insisted on him wanting her. It irked him to think she might be dallying with someone else in the same way he dallied with other women.

'Don't do that to me, Crystal,' he said in a cold, thoughtful voice. 'If you cheat on me, I promise I'll kill you.'

His eyes never left the field as he spoke, but because he was using his naked gaze and not the more precise picture provided by the binoculars, he did not see the sly grin that the two people exchanged.

He also did not see the wisp of red hair that blew out from beneath the dark wig. Neither had he seen the scattering of dark moles across the man's back.

Chapter 18

They were sitting in Josie's kitchen, drinking coffee, when Mariana started talking about older men and how stupid they could be.

Crystal was stirring her coffee in a lazy, thoughtful way. She had challenged Michael about the reality of his relationship with Josie. In turn Michael had convinced her that Josie had been exaggerating and, anyway, once he'd taken care of his professional commitments, he would tell Josie exactly where things stood.

Convinced that Josie's tryst with the university lecturer had been pure fiction, Crystal went along with everything Michael said. Poor Josie.

Crystal's eyes travelled to the terracotta figurine of a lounging nude man she had just bought from Josie. She didn't really like it. Buying it from Josie made her feel better.

Josie was listening to Mariana. Her head was tilted to one side. Crystal wondered if she was a bit deaf in one ear.

'Well, I mean,' Mariana was saying. 'Look at that blonde piece parading herself with that bloke the other day. What does she see in that man she can't see in a younger model?'

'Money!' They all said it in unison and laughed.

Josie lifted her coffee to her lips and regarded the older Mariana over its rim. Just as if she were viewing the object for a painting, she took in the high spots and shadows of her friend's hair, the variations in facial tones, the expression, the curve of her eyebrows.

She didn't carry out this exercise with other people like she did with Mariana. There was something about the woman that intrigued her. No matter the angle, Josie constantly had the impression that all she was getting was a two dimensional picture.

Perhaps, she thought, there *was* no other dimension to Mariana, or if there was it was her at fault because she was looking at her with only an artist's eye. She was certain there was more to her friend – just as certain that beneath that controlled, organised persona, there was a darker Mariana – one who had been shaped by her life and experiences, just as they all had.

It was Crystal who restarted the conversation; Crystal, whose persona was more obvious than she could ever know.

'I prefer younger men,' she said with great aplomb at the same time as directing her spoon into the exact middle of her empty coffee mug. 'I have a preference for a firm bottom and some youthful energy. I don't want some bloke over fifty who might not be able to tell the difference between a heart attack and an orgasm!'

'Crystal!' exclaimed Mariana, and grinned as she tutted.

Josie contemplated her clasped hands as she added her own thoughts on the subject. 'I suppose it all depends on what you want from a man. Is it security or virility? A long-lasting and struggling relationship, or a relatively short and comfortable existence?'

Mariana frowned. She looked at Josie and wondered if she knew her as well as she thought she did. 'But you've got a comfortable existence. Are you telling us that Michael only provides security?'

Josie took a deep breath and sat back in her chair. She was aware that Crystal was awaiting her reply with more eagerness than Mariana.

'No, I'm not saying that at all. In fact, Michael has more than enough virility for me. He's even got enough left over for at least two other women. But you are right. I do have security. I needed to have that if I was going to make my mark as an artist. I have to say that without marrying Michael I would never have got to be so successful in the short time that I have.'

'Well!' Mariana slumped back and shook her head. She looked amazed.

Crystal looked shocked. Her mouth was slightly open. There was a new realisation in her eyes now. Her mouth closed into a tighter line than it had before, as though she had made herself some unspoken promise.

Josie ran her fingers through her hair. It was an unconscious gesture. There was an odd smile on her face and a faraway look in her eyes. Then, suddenly, it was gone. She took a deep breath and sat up very straight in her chair. Again she clasped her hands in front of her, but with far more resolve than she had before. Her green eyes seemed brighter and her pale good looks made Crystal's appear a little brash.

Mariana and Crystal were all attention. They could not take their eyes off her. It was as though she were about to deliver them some blistering lecture. What she actually said completely shattered any illusions they might have had about her.

'I don't love Michael at all. I fully admit I used him. I was lonely and upset when we first met. I'd lost contact with the man I loved. He was my first love. The love of my life in fact. But Michael came along and, although I knew of his reputation, I could see he was someone who was going places. We went around a bit at university, then met up again a few years later in London. That's when things became more concrete.'

Mariana rested her chin on one hand. She was a picture of intense interest. 'So he dropped everything and asked you to marry him? I'm amazed.'

'Don't be.' Josie smiled. 'It wasn't quite like that. We

became friends first and foremost. He used to come round and tell me all about his love life. I used to call him the juggler because that's exactly what he used to do. He would juggle his women about so none of them knew that he had more than one lover. I knew about them all and how he felt about them. He confided in me that he was absolutely sure he would never be able to marry and stick to one woman, and yet, because he wanted to get to the top, he needed to be married. There's nothing more likely to impress a board of directors than a man with a stable home life. It doesn't matter that the wife has her own career as opposed to a family. A wife is the emblem of a man's trustworthiness. She's like a medal; something pinned to his chest to advertise the fact that he has made sacrifices.

'Michael could never have married someone who would not accept his infidelities, and I wanted someone who would give me security in order to pursue my career. Call it sponsorship if you like.'

A pin could have dropped when Josie finished talking. The angular lines of Mariana's expertly made-up face had softened slightly. Crystal's more fluid features had done exactly the opposite. There was a pinkness to her cheeks and an odd brightness in her eyes.

'But what about sex?' Mariana interjected. 'I presume you and Michael . . .'

'Of course we do. Or at least, we used to. Both of us have hungers. It's like that, isn't it? Being hungry . . . needing to satisfy it.'

Mariana nodded slowly as the information sank in and she altered her view of Michael's wife.

Crystal stayed mute, swallowed hard as if she had eaten her tongue.

'I'm astounded, Josie. I would never have taken you for the "open marriage" type,' Mariana went on.

Josie raised her eyebrows. There was no doubting the

amusement on her face. 'Then I fooled you all, didn't I? You saw in me the dutiful, though foolish wife. Perhaps because I was always painting figures on canvas or fashioning nudes from lumps of clay, you thought I was sexless or frustrated. But I'm not. I can assure you I am not.'

'Do you talk about . . . I mean . . . does he still confide in you?'

'About his other lovers?' said Josie to Mariana. 'Not so much as he used to. I suppose to some extent he was on a voyage of discovery in his younger days. Now he knows what he wants and where he's going.'

Mariana nodded sagely. 'He wants a change.'

'Yes,' replied Josie. 'He wants a change. He's just taking his time asking me for a divorce. But I won't force the issue. If he wants his latest flame, then it's up to him to push the boat out – not me.'

'You won't be adverse to that happening? I mean, what about your art?' Mariana went on.

'I'm established now. I don't need him any more.'

An empty, echoing silence descended on them. Josie was allowing things to sink in. Mariana was absorbing all this new information, and Crystal was feeling sick.

The clock out in the hallway struck eleven. Its sound drifted out into the kitchen and replaced what conversation had been there.

Crystal was the first to send the pine chair scraping along the floor as she pushed it away from the table. 'Time I was going.' She said it a little nervously, almost as if she were afraid to leave first. 'I've got an aerobics class in town. Mustn't be late for that. My ladies will be expecting me.'

'I didn't know you were still doing that,' Josie remarked.

'She enjoys torturing people,' said Mariana as she helped herself to a biscuit from a dark blue tin. 'You've got to enjoy torturing people if you run an aerobics class. How about another coffee, Josie?'

'Why not?' Josie got up and began to fiddle with the cafetière.

Crystal shifted nervously from one leg to the other as she unzipped her sports bag and quickly embedded the terracotta sculpture between a towel and a grey jersey. 'Then I'll be off. See you at the club?' There was a hunted look in her eyes, a crisp quickness to her movements.

Mariana nodded. 'Fine. Seven?'

'Yes. Yes.'

Crystal's actions were as hurried as her words. Her sports bag bounced energetically against her behind as she marched off down the hallway. She shouted a last goodbye before the front door slammed shut.

Once Crystal was gone and Mariana had used the lavatory, they both sat down again and pulled their freshly filled coffee cups towards them.

'Smells delicious,' said Mariana as she breathed in the aroma of the fresh brew before dunking another biscuit in her mug.

Josie eyed her speculatively. It had never been Mariana's habit to stay long enough for a second cup. Josie recognised curiosity when she saw it.

Small talk over with, Mariana came out with the question she wanted answered.

'So what's Michael like in bed?'

Josie smiled. 'Shouldn't you be asking Crystal?'

'Crystal?' Mariana raised her eyebrows and looked as surprised as she sounded.

'Oh come on, Mariana. I'm not stupid you know.'

'So I see.' Mariana paused and stared at Josie as if she were completely reassessing her character or rearranging her features. 'But why didn't you tell her you know about her and Michael? You could have done.'

Josie shook her head. 'No I couldn't. You see, the

decision has to be Michael's. I will not make the first move to divorce. I'm happy in this house and I want to keep it. That's why the decision has to be Michael's.' Eyes bright with intent, she leaned closer to Mariana and lay her hand over hers. 'But it will come, you know. Do you want to know how I know that?'

Mariana nodded slowly. Her mouth stayed open slightly.

'Because Michael has a guilt complex and Crystal pities me. I'm not stupid, Mariana. I have no intention of ending up in a rented flat and having to go out to earn my living by lecturing to dreadlocked students who want to do their own thing as much as I do. I want the best deal possible and by working on Michael *and* Crystal, I can make damn sure I get it!'

Mariana's expression seemed to have frozen on her face. Her eyes were wide open like the lens of a camera that needs to get in as much light as possible in order to see the subject matter more clearly – and she was certainly doing that. Where was the softly spoken, gentle redhead she thought she knew?

'You little minx! You're a much shrewder bird than you make out aren't you?'

Josie poured more coffee. 'Like you, Mariana, there is much more to me than meets the eye. Now, you tell me what you and Jamie do in bed, and I'll tell you about Michael and me. Is that a deal?'

Josie's look was so direct, so probing, that Mariana had a strong urge to cover her breasts with her hands – as if she were naked. She hesitated before answering. But the challenge in Josie's eyes was too powerful to ignore.

'Alright,' she sighed, her head nodding as if she were submitting to something slightly deviant. 'Alright. But you tell me first.'

Now it was Josie who paused. 'I'll tell you about the first time with Michael.'

'Fine.'

'I had been feeling down, so I went shopping and came back with some new lingerie. I do things like that when I'm fed up. It doesn't cure the problem, but it does take my mind off it.

'That evening I immersed myself in a soapy bath and took a glass of wine in with me.

'Then I got out, did my hair, put on my face . . . almost as if I was going somewhere with someone I wanted to be with. But of course I had nothing arranged. I was home alone and I was dwelling on the past.

'Once I had sprayed a good dose of perfume all over my body, I added more eye shadow and liner around my eyes. I decided my lipstick was too pale, so I covered it with a bright red one.

'After that I put on the new underwear. It was bright red – as red as my lipstick. I put everything on. The cups of the basque barely covered my breasts. I could see my nipples peeping out over the top of them. It did up at the front and nipped in at the waist. The suspenders were made of satin ribbon. I fastened them to some black silk stockings I'd also bought and put on a pair of high-heeled black shoes that I hardly ever wore.

'Once it was all on, I looked at myself in the mirror. I pouted at my reflection, hands on hips, one leg elegantly posed like some high-class whore waiting in a scruffy shop doorway. And that was really what I looked like. Imagine it, me with my auburn hair, green eyes and white flesh, and wearing red. It looked obscene. I looked obscene.

'I drank another glass of wine and laughed at myself. I twirled and pirouetted in front of that mirror and viewed myself in every position possible. I leaned forward so that my breasts almost fell out of their cups. They looked so plump and round and white, my cleavage so deep. I became totally absorbed in what I was doing. It made me laugh at myself.

'I turned my back on the mirror and looked at myself over my shoulder. I was not wearing knickers. My bottom was still bare. My buttocks were two white orbs between the redness of my basque and the blackness of my stockings. Only the strips of satin suspender joined one colour to the other.

'I bent over and opened my legs slightly so I could view my bottom more clearly and wondered how it would appear to some man with money in his pocket and a hard-on to fill me.

'The dark pinkness of my sex peered out from between the curls of my pubic hair. I have very golden pubic hair, so I presented an even more vivid picture than I had before. I looked garish, tartish, ready to do business.

'But it didn't stop there. I had this terrible inclination to debase myself further, to imagine that some paying customer might want more than basic sex. I ran my hands over my behind. Oh, I almost forgot. My fingernails were painted red too. They looked like spots of blood as they ran down the cleft of my behind.

'"You want what?" I said to the mirror. "You want to put it in there?"

'Of course, there was no one there to answer, but I pretended there was. I smiled and told him to go ahead. Then slowly, so very slowly, I pulled apart the cheeks of my behind and shocked myself. The pale mauve of my rear opening seemed to be pulsating, as if I really was expecting some man to push himself into me.

'My heart began to thud like a mad thing. Even though it was only my eyes seeing this brazen act, a blush came to my cheeks.

'It was only when I turned my shocked gaze away, that I saw Michael standing there. His eyes were out on stalks and his mouth was hanging open.

'I stood up slowly. I was as surprised as he was. How was I to know he was going to choose tonight to come round and bend my ear about his latest conquest?

'Like a fool, I hid my sex behind one hand and covered my cleavage with the other. Not that it did a lot of good. There was a mirror behind me. He could still see my bare bottom. Besides that, my nipples were still poking out above my cups, so Michael was still getting a pretty good eyeful!'

Josie paused and took a sip of coffee. Mariana, who was chewing very slowly as she listened, offered Josie the use of the biscuit tin.

Josie shook her head. There was a light of enthusiasm about her, a need to go on.

'As I was saying, there I was looking like a high-class hooker, and there was Michael seeing more of me than he'd ever seen before.

'He muttered something. I can't remember exactly what. I think it went something like, "Josie. You look incredible." I saw his hand shuffling around in his pocket. I knew instinctively that he was searching for money; that he wanted to buy my services!

'I tried to laugh it off at first, but then I thought so what! Why not?

'My hips swayed provocatively as I walked slowly towards him. I stood at his side and ran my hand down over his chest. I asked him what he wanted. What he was willing to pay. I remember seeing his Adam's apple jerk as if he were swallowing it completely. His eyes were staring and had lust in them. Eventually, he managed to find his voice.

'"I want everything," he said. "Everything." So I gave him everything.'

Josie paused and took another sip of coffee.

'Go on,' urged Mariana, her eyes bright with interest. 'Go on, Josie. Tell me what you did.'

'I will. It went something like this. I became what both he and the clothes dictated I should be – a paid whore. I ran my hands down over his hips as I sank to my knees. Slowly, I pulled his penis from his trousers. It was ready for action. It felt warm and smelt of male hormones, enough of them to turn me on.

'I ran my fingers down his stem and poked them through his trouser opening. I felt the softness of his balls. They were like two ripe peaches, but it was his cock that interested me most. I grabbed hold of it with both hands and began to pull on it.

'I heard him moan before his hand again went to his pocket. "A tenner if you suck it," he said, and a ten pound note came floating down to the floor.

'So I did suck it, but first I kissed its shiny end and dipped my tongue into its opening. Then slowly, and so very deliberately, I took his penis into my mouth. I felt the weight of it on my tongue and tasted the maleness of it.

'"I want your breasts out," I heard him say as another tenner floated to the floor. I pulled my breasts from the cups of my basque so that they stood proudly and nakedly on their own.

'"Dip my cock between your breasts," he ordered. Along with the order came more money. I did exactly as he requested.

'The warm head of his penis nestled in my cleavage. He worked it backwards and forwards as if it were my sex he was using.

'"Look at me," he said suddenly.

'I was loath to stop playing with his penis. I liked the warmth it spread across my breasts and I was enjoying the thrills that were running through my body. Besides that, I needed the money he was floating down to the floor. After all, I was a struggling artist.

'I looked up at him. He was holding a wedge of money that must have been something like fifty pounds.

'"It's yours if you let me do everything."

'I told him I would do everything he wanted me to do and be whoever he wanted me to be.

'"Then bend over in front of the mirror," he ordered.

'I did exactly as he said. I bent over facing the mirror. My face was now flushed with the exertion of sucking him. My breasts hung like ripe fruit from a tree.

'He came up behind me and I knew immediately what he was going to do. He had seen me at my most brazen, my most vulnerable. My hands had been holding my buttocks apart when he had appeared. My anus had been open to his gaze. He couldn't wait to have me.

'I wanted to close my eyes, but I couldn't. I wanted to see, to know fully what he was going to do to me. If it was going to happen, then so be it. I wanted my share of pleasure from this experience.

'I heard his trousers drop to his knees. I saw him come up behind me and felt the warmth of his thighs against mine. But the heat of his legs were nothing compared to the heat of the penis that was so urgently pressing against me.

'I couldn't help breathing heavily. I was watching myself, but I might just as well have been watching a movie or reading some arousing passage from an erotic novel. I was out of myself, enjoying sex with Michael for what it was – something to be enjoyed for itself and not as some token of long-lasting love. There was none.

'"First, you whore, I'm going to put it in here," he said to me. "You've already had it in your mouth, but I've paid you for your whole body, and it's your whole body I'm going to use."

'"Do as you please," I told him. "You've bought me."

'He did exactly that. I braced myself as the head of his penis nudged at my behind. At first I felt a degree of pain as he thrust himself into me. But it did not last. Soon I was filled with a glowing warmth – no, not warmth, heat. It was heat.

'The heat of lust and things untried spread swiftly over my body. This man was in me, using me, and I was letting him use me because I had been ready for a man to use me. I had dressed myself for the part and now I was playing that part.

'I felt the roughness of his balls slapping against my flesh as he urged himself into me. I tightened my stomach muscles so that I could more easily take his onslaught and also embrace the intruder that had entered my body.

'At last the full length of his penis was in me and his chest was on my back. I braced myself to take his weight and groaned with pleasure as his hands squeezed my breasts.

'"First this for you, whore," he said against my ear. "I want all your openings. First I had your mouth, now your rear, but I will leave the best till last."

'I cried out, groaned, told him to stop and told him not to stop.

'There were times, as he thrust, that I thought I would burst. It was a strange sensation, but there he was using my behind, and yet his use of it was arousing erotic sensations in the rest of my body.

'A heat of lust and desire was making my sex tingle with anticipation. Soon that too would feel the onslaught of his sexuality, and I wanted that sexuality. I wanted that penis in me.

'He ran his hands down over my belly and, as his penis went on ramming into my behind, his fingers began to play with my clitoris. I stared at my reflection as my breasts began again to swing backwards and forwards like pendulums.

'What a sight I looked. My breath caught in my throat. I thought I would faint away with the sheer eroticism of it all.

'Just when I thought I would have liked it to go on forever, Michael slid out of me. He ordered me to turn round and face him. I did so.

'My bottom stung slightly, but my sex was juicy with longing.

'As Michael played with my breasts, he nudged one leg between mine. His penis followed and ran quickly through my flesh until he found what he was looking for.

'He gripped my behind and thrust deeply into me. My breasts were squashed against his chest. I put my arms around his neck so I could hold onto him better.

'I groaned into his ear. We were doing it standing up and, what's more, we were doing it in front of a mirror.

' "Pretend it's a shop doorway," he said. "Pretend it's a cheap, sordid shop doorway and I'm the tenth customer tonight."

'I wanted to laugh, but didn't. We were like children playing games; mothers and fathers, doctors and nurses. Fact had been replaced by fantasy, a make-believe world with only a tenuous grip on reality.

'I lay my head on his shoulder and closed my eyes. His fantasy had become mine too. I was the whore in the shop doorway, doing this to make a living. I was sordid, I was cheap and I was available.

'The money he had given me earlier lay scattered around my feet like empty crisp bags.

'When I opened my eyes I could see my bottom jerking backwards and forwards with each thrust of Michael's pelvis.

'Because we were still half clothed, we looked more sorded than we might have done if we had been completely undressed.

'There is something more naked about a man with his trousers down at his ankles and his sweater resting around his waist. In fact, he looked even more lewd than I did with my red basque, black stockings, and high-heeled shoes.

'But the scene in the mirror paled into insignificance as my climax started. You know how it is, it starts like a fine tickle in all the feathery bits of flesh around your vagina. Then it escalates until you don't know where you are, but know damn well what you want to be doing.

'"Shameless hussy," I heard Michael say. "Whore! Slut! Tart!" And I knew that I was.

'I was shameless in my desire. Once my orgasm had come and gone, and once Michael had shot himself into me, I was even more shameless as I scrabbled about the floor and got my hands on each and every bank note.

'I was also shameless a few months later after we had discussed everything in detail. We would get married. I accepted what he wanted from me, and he accepted what I wanted. It was a binding contract we were entering into. Both sides would gain from it.'

After swigging back the last of her coffee, Josie threw back her head and laughed. 'I also remember playing the part to the very end. I rolled those bank notes up and stuffed them down my cleavage.' Hair bouncing with confidence, Josie looked pertly at Mariana who had listened in awe-struck silence throughout.

'Well. There you have it. That's my story of how and why I got married to Michael. Now, what's your excuse?'

Mariana's chin was still in her hand. She was staring at Josie as though she were some form of life that had fallen out of the wall. One blink preceded her hand at last falling away from her chin.

'Well! I can hardly believe it. I mean . . . you . . . *you!*'

Josie smiled. There was a world of wisdom in her eyes. 'But that is me. You see, I am an artist. I see things differently. There are a lot more sides to me than most people – except perhaps you, Mariana.'

For the briefest of moments, Mariana froze as though something clockwork inside had run down.

'Me?' she exclaimed and laughed. 'I'm pretty ordinary. I don't think you'll find me very interesting at all.' She laughed again. There was a certain falseness about it. Like her words, it was a lie.

Josie's expression did not alter. Mariana recognised disbelief when she saw it. She also recognised a challenge.

One finger tapped at the handle of her coffee mug as she considered the situation. Eventually, she looked directly into Josie's eyes.

'Can I think about this and tell you later?'

'Not really. You should tell all now, just as you persuaded me to do.'

Mariana got up from her chair.

'I don't know that I want to.'

She gave sure signals that she was off. Her actions were swift and agitated.

Josie remained seated. Her eyes followed Mariana's face. 'You've broken your word, Mariana.'

'I can't help it.'

Josie shrugged. Her green eyes seemed to cloud over. 'Then you have a bigger problem than you think.'

As Mariana drove away from her friend's house, she felt strangely guilty, but also strangely weak.

All her life she had been the strong one, the respected one, the woman who could organise and oversee everything. Josie had burst her bubble. Nothing seemed the same as it had been. Mariana had seen the true woman behind the meek and mild facade that was Josie, and what she saw frightened her.

Chapter 19

Something began and a memory started to fade on the day Mariana went alone to the country club.

She'd left Jamie bound fast as he liked to be and chained tightly to a fixing within his own wardrobe. A few hours of contemplation and he'd be like a cringing boy by the time she got back. In the meantime, she had a few hours to kill and she wanted some time by herself. Today she would use the country-club pool.

With a sweep of her hands, she gathered her hair on top of her head and secured it with a black velvet band. Before sliding her swimming costume up over her naked body, she studied herself in the ranks of shining mirrors that returned her reflection from the wall before her and the one behind.

Her ribs looked good, she thought. No spare flesh and lean enough to exaggerate what breasts she had.

A fine layer of golden hair formed a small triangle beneath her belly. When she moved, the light caught it and made it glisten as though it were wet.

Sighing gently, Mariana ran her hands down over her body as she looked at herself. Eyes lowered, she patted her belly, then looked over her shoulder to view her behind in the mirror opposite. As she did so, she noticed a young woman dressed in a pretty pink swimming costume. She was sitting on one of the wooden benches that ran along the end wall. She was smiling and had glossy black hair and very dark eyes. She was looking in her direction.

Their eyes met. A shiny brown face broke into a wide smile.

'Hello. My name is Sharaz.'

Without a hint of reservation, the girl got up and held out her hand. 'How do you do?' she said, her cheeks glowing and her bright eyes sparkling as she boldly ran her eyes over Mariana's body.

'Mariana. My name's Mariana.' Did she sound surprised? She was. People did not usually make a big effort to speak to her. There was no big sign above her saying she was friendly, and she did not have the jolliest of faces.

A barrier had been breached. The girl's palm was warm and plump against hers. She took comfort from it and gripped it a little longer and a little more firmly than she should have done.

There was only understanding on the face of the girl who had introduced herself as Sharaz. There was no embarrassment, no questioning look. The dark eyes blazed with a certain kind of understanding, a certain kind of affection.

'You have a very trim body. You obviously take great care of it.' Again the dark eyes swept over Mariana's spare frame.

'Yes. Yes, I do.' Don't fight this, Mariana told herself. She felt her face soften and break into a smile. 'Are you coming for a swim?'

White teeth flashed in a honey-brown face. 'Love to. But hadn't you better put your costume on first?'

'Goodness me, yes!'

They tittered like naughty schoolgirls. Mariana pulled on her plain black costume. Sharaz helped her unwind the straps which had twisted over her shoulder.

'There. All straight and better.' She puckered her mouth and kissed Mariana's cheek.

Mariana flushed. An awe-struck look entered her eyes as Sharaz, grinning girlishly from ear to ear, took hold of her hand. 'Are you ready now?' she asked as a daughter might a mother, or a woman a lover.

Mariana, her gaze still fixed on the gleaming countenance of the lovely Sharaz, nodded. 'Yes. I am.'

Hand in hand, they passed through the foot bath and walked out onto the edge of the swimming pool.

It was a Tuesday afternoon, the kids were at school, and those that worked were beavering away wherever they happened to be working.

The pool and its ancillary area echoed to the sound of their voices. One or two older people swam with timorous strokes towards the shallow end. The deep end and the diving stages were virtually empty.

Mariana asked herself why she did not draw her hand away each time Sharaz reached for it. *Because I like it,* she told herself. *I like it. It's affectionate. It's pleasant.*

Self-control, the need to be in charge, the need to make someone suffer for the hurt she had experienced, fell away. This was no Jamie on whom she could take out all her frustrations, all her feelings of injustice. This was someone as dark and attractive as any Ahmed, though, of course, not a man.

Their hips tapped gently against each other as they trod water beneath the overhanging diving stage.

The moment lingered along with their silence. Sharing the same space, the same feelings, their eyes met.

The sheer intensity of her emotions made Mariana's legs weaken in their constant treading. At last, she had to break away.

'Race you!' she shouted, and her long arm curved into a crawl as her head dipped into the water.

A sense of urgency seemed to dictate the pace of their continuous lengths. Up and down, up and down they swam.

Water in her eyes and rushing past her face kept Mariana from seeing Sharaz too clearly. Because of the water and the distance between them, it seemed as if she were viewing her through a mist, and that mist must be agitated to stop it from melting away.

But the moment came when breasts pushed tight against bodices and arms ached from continuous effort.

'Enough for me,' she heard Sharaz shout, and knew she would have to get out of the pool at the same time as she did.

Mariana climbed out of the pool first, water dripping from her hair and her costume; running, converging down her inner thighs. Was that a stirring she felt with the fleshiness of her sex, or was it merely a confluence of excess fluid?

What shivers she was feeling were kept firmly inside.

Smiling, she offered her hand to Sharaz.

Sharaz took it. 'Thank you,' she said. 'I don't know who won but that was a good race. I need to relax now. Will you come for a sauna with me? I think we will be alone in there. I don't think these other people will be joining us.'

Sharaz jerked her head to where the older people were now gathered in a tight little group in the shallowest corner of the pool.

'Neither do I,' returned Mariana.

Swimming costumes were cast to one side and heat clung to their bodies in the privacy of the sauna.

Sharaz bent with her backside towards Mariana as she kicked the sopping wet costume away from her ankles.

Mariana winced and absent-mindedly ran her hand down over her belly. A sudden tingle rushed up from between her legs.

Sharaz straightened and turned around. 'Thank you for coming in here with me,' she said softly as she looked up into the taller woman's face. 'I much appreciate it. Will you let me show my appreciation? Will you let me kiss you?'

Mariana's mouth dropped open as if she were about to

speak. Nothing came out. Her arms hung uselessly at her side, yet she was aware of the most deplorable twitching in her muscles. It occurred to her that a civil war was being fought within her flesh. Part of her body was saying this is not a man. The other half was saying who cares?

The strong side of her, the same side that told her she was apart and above mere men, won the day.

As her lips met those of the delicious Sharaz, her hands gripped the young girl's waist.

It came to her that if there had been a penis between her legs, she would have had an erection by now. There was a certain heaviness in her sex lips as she pressed her hands against Sharaz's back.

The girl's opulent breasts were like cushions against hers. The sharp bones of her pelvis nudged into the plumpness of the dark girl's belly.

Just as if she truly had been born with the same equipment as a man, Mariana began jerking her hips in a constant rhythm against the body of this other woman.

As Sharaz withdrew her lips from those of Mariana, a certain youthful nervousness came to her eyes. 'What if someone comes in?' she asked, her face a picture of wide-eyed innocence.

'Who cares!'

Now I know, thought Mariana, *what it means to want a woman. Now I know what a man feels like.*

Desire was a burning flame within her that made her push Sharaz back onto the lowest bench of the sauna.

The girl melted beneath her, submission quickly replacing her earlier bravado.

'Oh,' she squealed, 'but you are so strong, Mariana. I feel unable to resist you.'

Her voice was high-pitched and she sounded a little frightened. *But it isn't fear that's making her open her legs,* thought Mariana.

All sense of who she was with and where they were

seemed to whirl through her mind, then rush straight out of it again. Mariana was thrusting against Sharaz just as a man might do.

Her golden-crested sex was beating time against the black-haired one of the delectable young woman. This was her, Mariana, lying between the open legs of another woman and they were thrusting against each other for all they were worth.

Mariana braced her arms and raised herself up on her hands. Without interrupting the jerking of her hips, she looked down on the face and breasts of Sharaz.

'Play with them,' Sharaz implored as she pushed her large breasts together.

As though she were doing a press up, Mariana lowered herself onto the young girl, kissed her lips, then rested her weight on her elbows.

With fingers and thumbs, she commenced to play and pull on Sharaz's velvet-soft purple nipples.

'Are you enjoying this?' asked Mariana.

'Oh, yes. Are you?'

Mariana nodded. *You're a fool,* she said to herself. *Of course she's enjoying it. Can't you tell that from her face?*

But of course she could. It was just that Mariana needed absolute confirmation that Sharaz was enjoying this as much as she was. It was like opening a gate on a favourite garden. You needed to know that what you had planted was looked on with as much favour by everyone else as it was by you.

Eddies of sensation were radiating from that little jewel that sat adjacent to frills of pale pink labia. Should this happen? Must it happen? This was another woman, after all!

But I can't stop even if I wanted to, screamed a voice in Mariana's mind. *I just can't stop!*

She closed her eyes and buried her nose in the cloud of thick, dark hair. Peaches came to mind. The girl's hair smelt of fresh peaches. From lower down – somewhere behind her ear – Mariana detected the smell of flowers, a perfume manufactured chiefly from roses.

All these things – the dark eyes of this girl, the tawny skin, the jet black hair, and the aromatic smells of Sharaz's body – ate into Mariana's very soul, and because it got that far, it also infused through her body. In response, her hips jerked that much more fiercely and her clitoris jumped as if it were trying to escape her body.

Their breathing mingled as their arousal soared higher and, between kisses, Sharaz moaned with joy each time Mariana's fingers tweaked and pulled at her rigid nipples.

A climax was forming in Mariana's loins. At least she thought it was. Inner confusion made her frown, but still her pelvis kept up its even tempo and her fingers continued to explore the ample bosoms of the woman beneath her.

The dark eyes she looked into for explanation rolled up into Sharaz's head before closing completely. Her mouth stayed open and let out low groans of ecstasy.

Mariana's eyes remained wide open. This was no dream. This was really happening to her. She caught her breath as Sharaz arched her back so that Mariana's sex hit more fiercely against hers.

A low moan started deep in Mariana's throat and slowly made its way up to her tongue. Amazement in her eyes and a louder, more earthy cry now coming from her mouth, Mariana tensed against the supine body of Sharaz.

She quivered from head to toe, the heat of the sauna causing rivulets of sweat to run from her spine and over her ribs. Her eyes stared as she gasped with unsurpassed delight.

Never in her whole life had she experienced anything like this.

Beneath her, Sharaz shimmered with sweat and the slow tremors of a controlled orgasm.

Once the last shiver of orgasm had fallen away, Sharaz opened her eyes and looked up into those of Mariana. Her mouth parted in a wide grin.

'Wasn't that truly wonderful?'

Mariana paused. She knew what her answer would be, but she also knew she wanted to hold onto the truth of it. She had a need to savour how she was feeling, and she also knew she would very much like to do it again.

'Truly wonderful,' she repeated, her eyes blazing with excitement.

'I think I want you to be my lover,' exclaimed the smiling Sharaz.

Some of the old firmness came back to Mariana's face, though it wasn't quite the same as before. This woman, she decided, needed someone to look after her, not to abuse her. In turn, she herself needed someone to look up to her, to love her for the strong character that she was.

Mariana threw back her head and laughed. 'A lover. What a wonderful word. Not a mistress, a wife, or even a sex object. A lover.' She laughed again. 'I think that's a very good idea.'

The benches within the sauna were wide, and as the sweat continued to run over their naked bodies, Mariana and Sharaz lay full stretch, their arms touching, their fingers entwined.

'Men let me down,' Mariana said at length. Then, in a last ditch attempt to unburden herself, Mariana told her of the event that had shaped her life.

'It was after hearing my mother arguing with Ahmed, my stepfather, that I truly turned against men. Unfortunately, at the same time, I also turned against my mother.

'I heard her saying that Ahmed had become too fond of me, that he preferred having sex with me than with her. I froze where I was. You see, I had been having sex with Ahmed. We used to visit a country villa he owned and, when my mother went outside to lie down on a sunbed and read one of her precious books, he used to take me upstairs and give me sweet drinks. Of course I know now that those drinks were drugged and allowed him to do anything to me he cared to. I used to watch him as though I were watching a dream, as though it wasn't really me lying there naked as he tied my legs and arms to the bed.

'As he kissed my nipples and lay his body flat on me, I could almost believe he was merely a load of heavy blankets pressing me against the mattress.

'But afterwards, of course, there was always the soreness where his penis had been.

'Strangely enough, I was never frightened by anything he did. Perhaps it was the fact that I was in familiar surroundings and my mother was not far away. It wasn't because I was too young to understand, because I did understand. I knew what was happening to me. But I never protested. I never felt any great bitterness until I heard my mother complain that he enjoyed sex more with me than with her.

'That was the turning point. You see, up until then, I had not realised that my mother even knew Ahmed was having relations with me. The knowledge that she did ate into my brain.

'I cried to my real father about what had happened. I tried to tell him and fully expected him to do something about it. I couldn't understand him doing nothing at all. He stared at me with disgust. He called me a liar for saying such things and that I should not tell such childish tales.'

Mariana sobbed and Sharaz kissed her cheek and stroked her arm.

'There, there, my darling. There, there.'

A tear rolled down Mariana's cheek and she sniffed loudly.

'I gradually realised that my father had been embarrassed by what I had told him. Not only did he not want to believe such things about my mother, he also seemed to find it difficult that his daughter could have been having sex with a grown man. The whole thing confused him.

'I was desperate, I was frightened. I shouted at my mother, and she told me that I was only dreaming. But I knew I wasn't. I knew what I'd seen, knew what she said.

'She called the doctor and he put me to bed with a sedative. We were staying at the villa again, and whilst I was in bed, my mother and Ahmed drank loads of wine.

'It was early morning when I woke up. The place was still in darkness, the room slightly blue by virtue of the moonlight that streamed in through the window.

'Feeling thirsty, I got out of bed and made my way out of the room and along the landing.

'I think my mother and Ahmed had quarrelled again because my mother was asleep in the master bedroom and Ahmed was in the bed where he used to have his way with me.

'His bedroom door was open and I stopped when I saw him there. He was naked, I remember, and his bottom looked very bright in the moonlight. The sheets were lying crumpled around his ankles. The straps he used to restrain me with were still there at the head and foot of the bed.

'So I did to him something which he used to do to me. He moaned – almost gratefully – as I pushed him more fully onto his stomach so I could better fasten his wrists and ankles.

'As quickly as I could, I tightened the restraints that would keep him there whilst I took my revenge. I even stuffed his open mouth with his own underpants. He opened his eyes then and struggled once he realised what was happening to him. I was glad no one could hear him yell. How could I take revenge otherwise. One swipe of his body wouldn't be enough to punish him for taking liberties with me.

'Then I looked for something to use on him – something with a sting!'

Sharaz laughed against Mariana's ear. It evoked an immediate response. Mariana just had to cuddle more fervently against her, just had to kiss her cheek and nuzzle her ear as her hand explored the smooth, dark flesh.

'What did you find?' laughed Sharaz.

'A length of rope that was tying the curtains back. I wound some of it around my hand, then, with all my might, I raised it up and brought it down on his behind. His back arched, and his arms pulled against the restraints, but I knew how strong they were. I knew he wouldn't be able to get away.

'Again and again I beat his backside until it was red instead of brown. The more I did it, the more I enjoyed it. Strange that you can achieve an orgasm just from excitement. But that's what I did. Isn't that amazing?'

Sharaz giggled and cuddled closer to Mariana's breast. She closed her lips over it and shut her eyes as she began to suck like some over-sized baby.

'I'll always remember that night,' Mariana went on in a faraway voice, her eyes half closed as she enjoyed the pleasure Sharaz was giving her. 'I enjoyed that orgasm, and I also enjoyed leaving Ahmed quaking and sweating with fright.

'That night altered my life. From then on it suited me to subdue men rather than have sex with them or love them. They had let me down badly – both my father and Ahmed. My father had shut his mind to my problems. He only wanted a pretty daughter to show off to his friends. And Ahmed had abused me and undermined my mother's affinity to me. I never forgave men for that. I swore I would always want to be in control. That's why I married Jamie, but I'll tell you about that some other time.'

Chapter 20

Just as she always did – as though nothing out of the ordinary had happened – Mariana parked her car in the drive, then went in through the back door. With a gentle thud and an accompanying rattle, her keys and bag landed on the kitchen table.

She hummed as she went upstairs and undressed, and she was still humming and thinking of Sharaz as the spray from the shower soaked her hair and her body. As she soaped herself with a moisturising gel, she took deep breaths and her body seemed somehow cleaner, smoother – newer – beneath her hands.

Sweet-smelling lather frothed over her breasts, dripped off her nipples, and ran over her belly. Warm fingers of water ran between her legs.

She stretched her arms above her head and let the water wash the soap away – just like Sharaz had cleansed the past and what she had been from her body.

She turned off the shower and shook the last drops of water from her fingers. All the time she hummed and all the time she smiled.

Dreamily, she wrapped the bulk of a white towel around herself and cuddled it to her as though it were a person surrounding her, holding her close.

She wrapped another towel around her head, then paused as she caught sight of herself in the mirror.

Who was that fresh-faced, almost youthful person she saw there. Her skin was gleaming. Her nose was shiny.

She wrinkled it, then laughed, tossed her head and headed for the stairs.

She got herself a magazine from the drawing room and a drink from the kitchen. Then she sat herself in front of the television, picked up the remote control and flipped from one channel to another until she found a film that looked interesting.

Intermittently sipping her drink, she glanced from magazine to television. Neither held her attention for long. Along with her thoughts, her gaze wandered. What was that Sharaz had said? What was that she had done? Each minute, each second she had spent with the dark young woman was relived and re-analysed in her mind. As she thought about her, she sighed and, as she sighed, the room, the television and the colour-packed magazine seemed to dissolve into a nothingness of existence; the elementary things that are there but not noticed.

A mellowness came upon her. Smiling to herself, she let the magazine fall into her lap, then she folded her arms across her chest and cuddled herself.

Supper was not wanted, but tiredness was descending on her fast. She was eager to get to bed, keen to close her eyes. As she touched herself she would pretend they were not her hands but those of Sharaz.

Yawns were forcibly increased in frequency and intensity. Bed and the possibility of dreams – half truths of reality – beckoned.

She bounced from the sofa and turned off the television, the heating and the lights. She climbed the stairs, her eyes bright with excitement and looking forward to reliving the afternoon all over again.

Still lost in her spell, she used the bathroom, then in the bedroom she took off her white cotton bathrobe and followed the curves of her body with softly caressing fingers.

Thrills of pleasure made her make sweet, soft sounds,

like a cat does when it dreams by a glowing fire.

Cautiously, as if determined to hold the dream, she pulled back the covers on the bed.

She paused, blinked as reality hit her. All hint of dreams and softness left her face. There before her eyes were her black satin pyjamas. Next to them was her husband's more dubious attire.

'Shit!'

Dreams of the delicious Sharaz were temporarily put to one side as she remembered where she had left Jamie. She sprang to where the wardrobe covered one wall and opened the middle door.

'Sorry,' she said, as the wriggling form of her bondage-crazed husband came into view. Silently, she watched him. How ridiculous, she thought. Then she shook her head and ran her fingers through her damp, tousled hair. 'You silly cow!' she said to herself. 'What are you saying sorry for? He can't bloody hear you!'

She reached for the buckles that strapped her husband's wrists together. Her fingers actually touched the cold metal and harsh leather. She paused. A questioning look came to her eyes. She frowned. Did she really want this man beside her in bed tonight as she dreamed of her new love, her new life?

Her hands retreated, and so too did her mind. Still frowning as she asked herself why this had ever started, she stepped back and regarded the man before her.

As he wriggled against his bonds, she covered her mouth with her hand, then moved it as she reminded herself that he could not hear her laughter, though, of course, because she had touched the buckles, he would be aware of her presence.

What went on in his mind, she asked herself, when he was bound up like this? What went on when she was ordering him about or beating his backside? Sexual thoughts?

She began to laugh. There he was, a black leather hood covering his head, his wrists strapped together and bound above him. His ankles were fastened in a similar fashion and, to finish it all off, he wore a leather belt around his waist that had thinner straps coming off of it and diving between his legs. Another strap came from those two and divided around his sex.

Mariana's laugh got louder. Not that Jamie could hear or see. The mask covered his eyes and his ears. He was in a world of his own.

Mariana began to rock backwards and forwards from the waist. Tears ran from her eyes and her shoulders shook with mirth. As she laughed, she tried to speak, but had difficulty doing so. At last it came out.

'You look bloody ridiculous!' she cried. She went on laughing. It only diminished when she at last took a good long look at her husband.

Suddenly she was seeing both him and herself anew. The laughter in her throat bubbled to a halt. She wiped at her damp eyes, then, as her last chuckle turned to a sneer, she shook her head and her expression was full of regret.

'What the hell am I doing with someone like you?'

For the first time that day, the past came back to haunt her. Turkey and Ahmed came to her mind and her sneer changed again. A deep frown creased her brow. A scowl came to her mouth.

'Stuff you, Jamie! Stuff you all!'

Grabbing the wardrobe doors with both hands, she slammed them shut, turned her back and leaned against them.

'That,' she muttered with a powerful sigh, 'is that!'

As she rested her head against the wood, she could hear the muffled wrigglings from within. Normally, Jamie would be in there for two or three hours. That was the time span he preferred. So far he had been in there for seven hours and would now be in there until the morning.

'My choice,' Mariana said with an air of finality. 'Not yours.'

With a final pat for the wardrobe door, Mariana went to bed. In the darkness of the wardrobe Jamie wriggled like a maggot on a hook.

Chapter 21

As though he would really miss her, as though he would kick his heels around an empty house when she was gone, Michael made a big show of kissing Josie goodbye.

It almost made her feel as though she was the most important woman in the world to him, but of course she knew it wasn't true and so did he. But the truth was not a barrier between them, only an unspoken treaty that they each had their lives to live. True they had mutual ground, but their sex lives, their other lives, belonged to them only as individuals and not as a partnership.

She was boarding the train to Penzance where yet another exhibition of her work was being staged and she was likely to be away for a few days. That was the story she had given him and that was the one he had accepted.

It didn't matter that it wasn't the truth and that she was going to stay away from him for four days with her lover. He never questioned her about her relationships and she never went into detail.

Unlike him, of course. He had always fostered a need to unburden himself of the reasons why he had seduced April, taken Emma away for the weekend, or phoned the girl in the florists because she had a pretty face and an even better behind.

Sex with those women usually became infused with fantasy in the retelling. Perhaps that was why he had always talked about them to his wife. That was his need –

---

to talk about his conquests, as if by telling her he was reasserting his own sexuality.

But still he fussed over her as though he would really miss her; as though he was in no hurry to get back to the house, open the wine, and prepare himself for Crystal – the greatest lay of his life.

'Now you have your tickets, darling.' He didn't ask her, he told her 'And you will be sure to phone to let me know you arrived safely.'

'The moment I get there.'

And, the moment she got there, she had indeed phoned him. He made all the usual sounds of endearment, but not once did he ask her for the telephone number of the hotel she was staying at. Neither did he ask her its name and, when she got back, he wouldn't even ask her for details of where the exhibition was. One thing Josie gave him full credit for was that he never enquired about her life.

At the other end of the journey Thomas was waiting for her. Crystal had not asked where he was off to, and neither had she been around when he left. Crystal took advantage of his absences rather than worrying about who he might be with.

Joy lit Josie's face when she spotted her lover. His eyes lit up as he smiled.

Like some couple from a black and white movie, they embraced, kissed, and exuded a warmth from their bodies and faces that needed no shallow words or half-meant platitudes.

'Our usual room?'

Josie did not ask him this until she was sat beside him in the car.

After changing gear, his hand covered hers. 'Yes.'

Their eyes met and, as always something vaguely electrical and spine-tingling swept over them both.

Anticipation glowed on their faces. Thoughts and impressions whirled in each mind whilst those first tense tremblings of erotic sensation ran over their bodies.

Josie was imagining being alone with him again. Not just for a few snatched hours, long enough to make love without having to worry about getting home or about anyone finding out. This was for four days. In that time they could observe the formalities and talk to each other at breakfast, lunch and dinner. So ordinary those meal times, yet each a continuing progression from morning to evening. Each marked a certain facet in an ongoing relationship, the progress of a day.

Breakfast was taken a few hours after the last lovemaking of early morning. Lunch was a meal when mutual understanding and interchange of thoughts would help get them through the day.

The first sparks of licentious intent would begin in late afternoon. The wine and rich food of dinner would be like a form of foreplay, a taste of things to come.

Town buildings, walls and traffic gave way to the winding lanes where high banks of grass and wild flowers hid the land they bounded.

Josie pressed the button that opened the window and breathed in the smell of freshly cut grass and the tang of sopping seaweed.

They left the sea behind them at Penzance as they travelled eastward between the earth banks. Here and there leaning chimneys of crumbling brick poked up at the sky. Within a few miles, the sea was before them again at Falmouth.

When they arrived, a mist lay like white meringue over the calm bay and hid the horizon. It looked as though the world had been set in glue and could not move. The utter stillness was short-lived as a grey shape slid through the whiteness.

Moby Dick, thought Josie, *come to seek vengeance on a latter-day Ahab.*

Without its source being seen, the sound of rigging

rattling against aluminium masts mixed with the wail of a fog horn and the shunting snuffles of struggling tugs.

'What a wonderful scene,' said Josie softly as Thomas took their baggage from the car. 'And a wonderful sound. It's like you might suppose a dolphin makes when it's looking for a mate.'

Thomas put down the luggage, put one arm around her and hugged her close. 'If I practise that sound, will you take notice of me?'

She turned and smiled up at him. 'You mean, will I be your mate?'

He nodded. There was sincerity in his eyes; and gentleness, and all the other things she had always wanted to see in the eyes of a lover.

'You bet!'

He laughed and hugged her tighter so that her head rested on his shoulder and her red hair spread in a silky fan against the navy blue of his jacket.

He shrugged his shoulder against her cheek. 'Come on. Let's find our room and we can be as matey as we like.'

Within the hotel, they walked a maze of corridors and laughed as they followed arrows, got lost, then backtracked.

Footsteps muffled, they trod the narrow passageways which went straight then opened out to places where old clocks, oak chests and ornate chairs gave character to the opulent atmosphere.

Their room was dominated by a huge bay window that seemed to be made of nothing but glass. If merely glanced at, it made the scene appear as if it could be walked into.

Josie walked straight to it. 'What a view!'

'What a view!' repeated Thomas as he came up behind her and rested his hands on her shoulders and kissed the back of her head.

The details of the bay and the moored boats were muted by the covering of sea mist. Above the hill on the other side of the bay, the sun was attempting to pierce the cloak of shifting whiteness.

Still gazing straight ahead, Josie covered one of Thomas's hands with her own. His lips briefly grazed the nape of her neck.

Josie shivered with pleasure. The warmth of Thomas's chest was against her back. She shifted her weight so that she might be closer to him.

'I ordered champagne,' he said softly, and jerked his head to the white cloth that covered the bottle and bucket more efficiently than the mist covered the scene outside.

Josie turned her head away from the window, raised her arms and put them around him. She looked lovingly up into his eyes.

'Let's make love first. Never mind lunch, tea, champagne or dinner. Let me have your body first.' She half closed her eyes as their lips met.

Their embrace and their kiss became more intense. She pulled him more tightly to her and his palms were firmer and hotter against her back as he pulled her close to him.

There were no more words then.

As Josie's long fingers pushed his coat from his shoulders, undid his tie and his shirt, Thomas slid her jersey top away from her skin.

As he slipped his arms out of his jacket and his shirt, he bent his head and kissed the silky softness of her shoulder.

She held her arms tightly to her side as he slid the sleeves of her jersey top down to her wrists and off. Her hands were on the waistband of his trousers when his were on the hook of her bra. They kissed deeply as both were undone.

He sighed as he touched her breasts. It was a long sigh, a sound of undreamed of pleasure. Her breasts were soft skinned but firm fleshed, gentle but responsive. Her nipples thrust unashamedly into the palms of his hands. He tensed as he resisted the urge to sqeeze them.

No, he told himself. *Take it slow. Take it easy. We have four days. There's plenty of time. No need to rush.*

The sound of his zip being undone sliced into his mind.

He moaned appreciatively as her fingers followed the line of crisp dark hair that ran over his stomach and down to his groin.

Cries of pleasure were on his tongue, and yet he did not want her to hear them. He wanted no sound to infiltrate this fusion of senses, this act of sensual love.

His cries were lost in her mouth as his lips met hers and his tongue cruised over her taste buds.

Desire demanded that he did not remain silent. The progress of her fingers would not allow him to.

His penis pulsated as her fingertips touched the base of his stem. A contraction occurred between his legs that made him feel his balls were retreating into his body so that his penis might grow larger.

Her breasts trembled in his hands. He cupped one and brought it to his lips. She mewed above him as his lips kissed her nipple, his tongue licking it as though it were indeed the ambrosia of the gods.

Sucking at each breast in turn, he ran his hands down over her waist and found the fastening that held up her skirt. For a moment his fingers seemed to plait together in their rush to get the job done. He paused long enough to bring them under control then, with a new coolness to his movements, he undid that fastener and slowly began to push it over her hips and down her thighs.

Kissing each inch of her flesh, Thomas slid himself down with the skirt until he was at last facing the thatch of red hair that he remembered so well from the tree house.

Even now as he kissed and licked at her naked sex, he could almost imagine himself back there, her body girlish, naked and dappled by sunlight.

He pulled all her underwear down with her skirt and

smelt her femininity and the freshness of some gentle perfume.

Closing his eyes, he breathed her in, drank the smell of her, the closeness of her and wondered – indeed hoped – that she was as aware of what was happening between them as he was.

While Thomas paid homage to her sex, Josie caressed the hardness of his shoulders, the firm chunkiness of his neck.

With each rush of breath, she tasted the smell of him. With eyes lowered, she gazed at the darkness of his hair, raised her hand, ran her fingers through it.

Just like before, she thought to herself. *I feel the same way about him that I did before.*

As his tongue entered the beginning of her sexual divide, she threw back her head and reached for the hands that caressed her thighs.

Drowning, she thought, *must be like this.* All thoughts, all strength ebbing away as the cool, brilliant green of the sea sucks you into its deep, dark currents. That's what she was doing. Thomas was a deep, dark current sucking at her sex. The sea was her own sensuality and she was slowly drowning in it.

There was a moment, a lull in the wonderful way their bodies moved one against the other as they made their way hand in hand to the bed.

They didn't exactly *walk* to the bed, they just seemed to *go* there, glide there, or even float to where the final consequence of their kisses, their passionate embraces would take place.

Hunger was in her eyes, in her body, and she saw that same hunger reflected in him.

There was no shallowness to that hunger. It was no quick snack, no hastily grabbed bite that was swallowed whole and soon gone.

Shared famine resulted in a need for shared feasting.

That, Josie told herself, *is what we are doing. We are feasting on each other's bodies with our hands, our mouths, and our genitals.*

There were still no words between them, no cries to cease, to give more, to say that this touch was better than that, or to say press here, squeeze harder, or caress more gently.

Their hands and mouths explored all those zones that are said to respond more quickly and more intensely. Their eyes met intermittently and in understanding; unspoken messages that said it all.

Still lying on her side, she raised her leg and folded it over his as his pelvis slid across the bed to butt against hers.

The crispness of his leg hair caressed the softness of her skin as his hardness divided the curling hair of her sex.

She mewed with pleasure; a thin, wavering cry as though she were frightened of this rigid pole that was entering her softness.

Once he was in her, she arched her back as if she wanted his whole body to fuse with hers, not just his penis.

She held him tight against her. She rained kisses upon his face and, between his gasps of growing demand, he heaped kisses back on hers. His hands, his fingers tightly gripped her backside.

Don't leave me behind, she wanted to cry, but didn't. Determination that her orgasm should come at the same time as his made her shift her pelvis more vigorously.

Her clitoris absorbed each thud of his loins. Higher and higher climbed an indescribable accumulation of stimuli, reflexes, tingles of sensation.

As the first hint of climax began to run up from her sex, she pressed her cheek against his, her mouth an inch from his ear.

Now came the time for her to tell him in small, short bursts of words that he was doing the right thing, that his timing was right, his action was right, his body was right.

212

'Oh, no. No, no, no!' she cried. 'Yes. Yes. Give me more. Don't stop. Keep going. Please . . . Oh, plea . . . se!'

She thrust her hips against him. He clenched her bottom so that she stayed impaled on him whilst her clitoris throbbed its steady beat of pleasure throughout her sex.

Like a river it ran through her. Wetness seeped from her vagina and spread over her inner thighs like a film of liquid sugar.

Spasmed muscles held her position, suspended her climax.

Thomas held her tightly against him.

'I can feel you,' he cried suddenly. 'I can feel your body all the way down.'

She breathed a little and, in that short moment, she sensed the tension of the body against hers and felt the pulsing inside her that told her Thomas had come too.

Later they dined, drank the champagne and made love again and again.

Cocooned by their love and the bedding, they lay tightly together, her leg across his.

They'd left the curtains open. The mist had cleared so stars in the sky and lights from the houses across the bay dotted the blackness of night.

The room faced east. Josie found that out in the morning.

From behind the headland opposite, bright sunlight streamed uninterrupted in the hotel bedroom.

Josie woke first, but even though the sun was bright, it was not the first thing to gain her attention.

Dark hair against white pillow, Thomas slept on.

She propped herself up on one elbow to look at him. An overpowering feeling of love came to her. No matter what liaisons she had been involved in over the years, Thomas had been the boy and body she remembered best.

Gently, so as not to wake him, she traced lines across his back from one dark mole to another.

Glossy hair, almost black, curled around the nape of his neck. She touched it gently and smiled as she felt its silkiness against her fingertips.

With the interest of an artist and the affection of a lover, she let her eyes follow the curve of his body beneath the bedclothes.

Again and again she let her gaze drift up and down his sleeping form. There was a terrible need in her to store the way he looked to memory. The moment, too, was precious. That, like his body, must be indelibly marked on her mind.

As if to confirm that all details were correct, she ran her hand down over the sleeping form.

Thomas moved beneath her touch and muttered something unintelligible in his sleep.

Josie smiled. She had no idea what he was murmuring about. She only surmised by the sudden movement of his body – the raising of his hand, his fingers on her, and the undulation of his hips – that she was the subject of this dream. She knew that if he could have spoken clearly, it would have been her name on his lips along with the one word that told her how he felt about her.

Chapter 22

'I want to talk to you, Michael. It's time you told Josie about us, and I don't want any more excuses.'

The no-nonsense tone of Crystal's voice on the other end of the telephone had disappointed Michael.

There he was, looking forward to four days without his wife and with Crystal in his bed, and there she was insisting on him telling Josie that he wanted a divorce. He was glad to put the phone down and just wait for her to come over.

As he had already planned, the wine was on the table, two glasses beside it, and the cork had been relegated to the kitchen bin. His body was honed, perfumed, and ready for action. A sizzling sensation covered his body just as completely as his skin and that old familiar ache was reminding him of what lay between his legs.

Sighing impatiently, Michael poured some wine and drank it quickly as he sat on the settee. He tapped the glass with his fingers as he considered how best to handle the situation.

He glanced at his watch. Ten minutes before Crystal got there. Ten minutes of time. Enough to get the words right.

'But,' he said out loud, 'it isn't going to be easy, Michael old chap. I need a good dose of courage.'

On saying that, he looked at his wineglass. 'That'll do,' he muttered, and downed the lot.

He shook his head as if the wine would go down better

and the words he needed to say might fall easily into place. The wine did go down, but the words did not come. He gave the bottle a steady stare before coming to a snap decision. 'I could do with some more of that,' he said, and poured himself another.

He raised the glass to his lips but did not sip. He set it back on the table. As he stared at the dark, red fluid, he rubbed his hands together. They were damp with sweat and his fingers curled nervously into his palms. He rubbed them on his trousers, then sighed, rested his elbows on his knees, and clenched his hands together.

His eyes continued to stare into the wineglass as if it were a crystal ball and could help him. The wisdom of the glass beckoned and overcame him. His hands flopped down and, before he knew it, he was again swigging at the wine.

By the time Crystal let herself in the back door, there was only half a bottle left.

'Having a party?' Crystal asked, eyebrows raised, one had gripping one hip.

'Sorry.' Michael swayed a trifle as he got to his feet. 'I'm afraid I started without you.'

Crystal flung her car keys onto a chair.

'You can say that again.' Her voice was sharp as scissors.

Michael began to rub his hands together again. Judging by the icy blast in Crystal's voice, their meeting was not going to be that convivial this evening.

Be the old, bluff, breezy Michael, he told himself.

He grinned in a boyish way that he'd been told women couldn't help but fall for. He reached out and opened his arms.

'How about going straight to bed?'

Crystal glared.

'How about you go stuff yourself?'

Michael's boyish expression crumpled.

'Oh, come on, Crys. What's the big deal? I didn't mean to start drinking the wine without you. I just felt a bit lonely, that's all.'

Crystal stood with her hands on her hips. Michael winced and a frown came and went from his face. He hated it when women stood like that. It reminded him of Supergirl, or Catwoman, or some other dominant, female super-hero. Dominant women were something he thought he could well do without.

Her eyes were glaring – like a cat, he thought.

'The big deal, Michael,' snarled Crystal, 'is that you've been deceiving me. Deceiving, Michael! "I can't tell her yet," whined Crystal in a voice that was supposed to mimic his. "I can't hurt her. She'd be lost without me. She'd be devastated if she knew I'd been having an affair with you." Bullshit, Michael. Utter bullshit! You and Josie have an open marriage and, before you deny it, it was Josie who told me about it!'

Crystal's face was now bright red.

Michael shoved his hands in his pockets, glanced at her, then steadied his gaze on the safer subject of the wine bottle. He shrugged. 'Is that all?'

Crystal's cheeks turned redder.

'All? What do you mean, all? In effect, my dear Michael, this means that we have not really been having an affair.'

Michael frowned and, with his mouth open, he looked at her anew. This was not at all what he had expected her to say. 'It's all over, get lost, or drop dead,' were the phrases that had come to mind.

But she's a woman, he told himself. Women have got a quirky kind of logic. He shook his head in disbelief. 'Sorry? I don't understand. What's the big deal about that?'

'The big deal is, my dear Michael, that you've been lying to me.'

Michael shook his head emphatically. Now it was his eyes that were blazing. 'No, no, no! I haven't been lying about anything. I just didn't tell you the truth. It's personal business. Mine . . .and Josie's.'

'Personal!' Crystal's voice seemed to hit the ceiling and echo off the walls. 'Personal! You little shit. What the hell do you think we are if we're not personal? Never mind Michael and Josie, what about Michael and Crystal?'

'I never . . .' Michael spread out his arms, palms upwards, as he tried to explain.

Crystal cut him dead. 'Don't give me your waffle, Michael. I'm not Josie – though neither is Josie. She's no shrinking violet from what she's told me about her sexual adventures.'

'I never said—'

'No. I know,' interrupted Crystal. 'You never said she was hot stuff, and you never told me the two of you had a special arrangement. But that's not the point. The point is, Michael, there should be no problem whatsoever in you asking for a divorce. So why the delay?'

Crystal set her jaw firm and folded her arms across her chest.

Michael swallowed nervously and stared. Where was the hot little cutie whose hips went up and down like a yo yo when his cock was in her? Who was this harridan that had replaced her?

He shrugged pathetically as he tried to find the right words.

'I . . . uh . . .' The words didn't come. He shook his head, then attempted to explain. 'All that didn't matter, Crystal. You see, whatever it was and whatever it wasn't, my relationship with Josie has always been a partnership in the true sense. We both understood entirely why we were getting married. I needed a wife for my career, and she needed someone to bring home the bread while she pursued her art. We both had needs to fill, and we filled them.'

He sighed heavily then, with sad eyes, he looked at her and shook his head in a mournful, regretful way.

'We pursued our careers, and I pursued other women. That was the way it was.'

'And Josie knew about these other women?'

Michael nodded. 'Yes. I had a need to have other women. One woman would never have been enough for me. I used to tell Josie all about them, right down to how we made love and how many times we had it. If we were in the mood for each other after I'd finished telling her, we'd make love ourselves, but it didn't happen very often. That wasn't really the point of the exercise. Josie was a good listener, you see. I liked telling her all about my women and my problems.'

As Crystal listened, her hard expression began to change and the stiffness of her shoulders began to quiver. Her voice started to shake before turning to a sniffle. 'You mean . . . you mean . . . you told her all about what we used to do together? All of it?'

'Only about the others. Not us.' Michael reached out to touch her. Crystal hit his hand away.

'Don't touch me!'

'Crystal . . . please. That was the problem, you see. I just couldn't find the words to tell her about you. I never ever mentioned to her that I was having an affair with you. You were the only one I couldn't tell her about. You were different, and I couldn't explain why you were different. That's why it was so hard to tell her. It wasn't just another seduction I was talking about. It was you and I knew I felt something for you that I'd never felt for another woman.'

Crystal stared at him through her tears. Her face looked a bit blotchy as she began to shake her head. 'I don't believe you.'

'Please, Crystal.' Again he reached out to touch her.

She glanced at his hand as though in two minds to hit it off again; or as though it belonged to some alien being, someone she did not really know and didn't want to know.

But she didn't hit it away. Instead, trembling with a fever that was directly linked to her contact with him, she let him hold her closer and closer, his arms gradually drawing her against his chest.

Sobbing softly, she lay her hot cheek against his shoulder. His fingers caressed her hair and the warmth of his breath was soft against her ear.

'You see, Crys,' he said with a light chuckle. 'You and me are two of a kind. We were made for each other, and that's what's so bloody frightening!'

She raised her head. Her blue eyes looked at him through a wet mist of tears. 'You're a bastard, Michael.'

He grinned. 'And you're a right cow, Crystal.'

She sniffed as she smiled. 'Do you still want to go to bed?'

He shook his head. 'No. Not bed. Let's be a bit more adventurous about this. Let's go out into the garden. It's a lovely night. The neighbours won't see.'

He stepped back from her before offering his hand. It was as if he were giving her that space not only to decide for herself whether to go out into the garden with him, but also to re-evaluate whether she wanted to be with him at all.

Eyes dry, confidence returned to Crystal's seductive features. Here she was again, the old Crystal who could have any man she wanted but, at this moment in time – or perhaps longer – she only wanted the man she was with.

'We . . .ll,' she said in a voice as slow as the smile that spread across her face, 'I'm not really the outdoor type, but for you I might make an exception.'

She kicked off her shoes and bent her head to one side as he kissed her.

One arm round her waist, and the other higher so that his hand rested on the nape of her neck, he held her close.

'Clothes off in here,' he said softly.

He was quick in removing his white shirt and black chinos. Once he was down to underpants, Michael touched the thick contour of his penis that pushed against the front of his shorts. It swelled perceptibly against the fabric that restrained it.

'I'm being strangled,' he said with a laugh, and pulled his underpants off in one sweeping gesture, then stood with his hands on his hips, penis upstanding.

Crystal, who was undressing as slowly and provocatively as possible, stared wide-eyed at Michael's glorious appendage which rose so rigid and so splendid from its copious head of hair. She could almost smell its warmth and could certainly see its longing.

'Oh, baby,' cooed Crystal. 'Is that all for me?'

Smiling, Michael nodded and pivoted his hips so that his weapon swung from side to side.

'All yours, Crystal, honey.'

Purple bra, suspender belt and stockings were all that were left adorning Crystal's voluptuous figure. Her breasts trembled as she reached for his penis. Her tongue ran over her dry lips, her eyes opened wide as she regarded Michael's superb erection.

'That's cool!' Michael gasped as her fingers wound tightly around his penis. The veins in his neck became more prominent as he threw back his head and closed his eyes. 'That is so incredibly cool!' His voice was thick with desire.

'So's the garden,' breathed Crystal before her bright red lips gained contact with his mouth.

When they parted, she still had hold of his penis. As she backed away from him, she pulled him along by it as though it were some fleshy, but rigid handle.

'Oh, boy!' Michael's voice was like a broken groan.

Penis gripped tightly in her hand, Crystal walked slowly backwards in the direction of the door to the garden.

'You'll stretch it,' Michael protested, his steps short and quick as he went with her.

'What a good idea!

'OK. Stretch it if you must, but don't pull it off.'

Crystal laughed.

Step by step she walked backwards, pulling Michael with her.

At last they were outside, but still Crystal did not stop. No matter who might have been watching from neighbouring windows, by the time they got to the lawn there was no way they were going to resist their natural urges.

Michael, his penis throbbing in the palm of Crystal's hand, pulled her to him. The warm, firm roundness of her luscious breasts pressed against his chest. He raised his hands and felt the undercurve of each breast. Her skin was like silk and was enticing in itself. He wanted to feel more of her, so he followed the line of her ribs round to her spine, then felt and heard her skin passing beneath his palms as his hands travelled down to her buttocks.

The feel of her thighs were against his as she began to pull on his cock. His pelvis picked up the tempo and began to nudge gently against her.

He murmured against her hair, then cupped her face in his hands. He kissed her. He sucked on her lips until the taste of her lipstick was all gone and only natural sweetness remained.

Their bodies writhed one against the other, cloaked in passion and in darkness.

The heat of their own desire protected them against the night breeze which might otherwise have cooled their flesh.

Michael moaned with grateful pleasure as his weapon pulsated within Crystal's grasp.

There was a tenseness in his belly, a fine-tuned gathering of sensations and liquid energy somewhere deep in his groin.

He knew what was happening to him, knew that the thick vein that ran up the back of his penis was pulsating in her hand. Normally narrow and folded unto itself, it would now be expanding, throbbing as it ran with the heat of his blood. Even now he could feel the first moistness seep from its opening and tremble like a dewdrop on its sensitive tip.

As though she too knew at what stage he was at, Crystal stopped pulling on him. Warm palms brushed against his inner thighs as her hands went between his legs and cupped his balls.

He cried a long, blank cry, before he found the right words. 'That's good,' he cried out. 'That is so good!'

His cries ignited the woman who did these things to him.

Crystal became the flame of passion that had made him see her in a different light to his other women. Her hands were all over him, her mouth kissed at his chest and the tightly packed muscles that ran from beneath them and down to his groin.

Her whole body seemed to undulate as the desire to please and to be pleased swept through her blood and brought colour to her cheeks and a panting, animal breathlessness to her luscious lips.

Like him, her body too was secreting an initial moistness, a taster, a preliminary to what would eventually come.

She rubbed her thighs one against the other, felt the touch of soft flesh on the crispness of pubic hair. There was an ache in her clitoris and a tightening of her stomach. It was as if the muscles of her womb were preparing themselves for Michael's intrusion, just as her clitoris was aching for orgasm.

A tension came to Michael's shoulders and a tautness came to the small of his back as Crystal's mouth progressed downwards to where his penis throbbed and hardened with blood and desire.

A breeze blew Michael's hair across his face and into his mouth. It did nothing to muffle his cry of pleasure as Crystal's yearning mouth covered his hot, burning rod.

'Don't stop,' he breathed, but Crystal did not hear him. Her mouth was working fast as if she were afraid that what she had in it might melt away and leave her hungry.

This was her way of pushing Michael over the brink, of proving to him once and for always that she was the woman for him and that it was well worthwhile giving up everything for her. Her mouth was working as determinedly as her mind.

Michael was falling. Crystal could not look into his mind but, if she had been able to, she would have seen that she was sucking his resistance as well as his semen from his body.

There had been nothing, no one to match Crystal ever before and, as the hot vein that ran up the back of his penis became more swollen with fluid, Michael promised himself that he would divorce Josie no matter what.

Damn the house, he thought to himself as he thrust his pelvis towards Crystal's mouth. Let Josie have the house. It was probably what she wanted anyway now she was established as an artist.

'Have it,' he cried out. 'Have it!'

And in the new enlightenment of his mind, he meant for him to have Crystal, Josie to have the house, but also for Crystal to receive his semen which was now spurting into her mouth.

Once the pumping of his organ had ceased, she withdrew her warm lips from his penis, tilted her head back and looked up at him. As she did so, he caressed her hair with his hands and thought of how soft it was and how bright the blue of her eyes.

As she smiled up at him, she licked away a droplet of white fluid from the corner of her mouth.

'Now me,' she said to him, her eyes as bright as a child who thinks Christmas and birthdays have all come together.

Slowly, she rose up and, as she did so, she ran her hands up over his thighs, his waist and his arms until her hands were resting on his shoulders.

In the aftermath of his climax, a great softness, a great feeling of wellbeing came over him. He stood there so relaxed, so full of satisfied warmth.

He enjoyed her caresses and tasted himself on her lips before he lay her down on the damp grass.

For a moment, he studied her as she lay there. Supporting himself on one arm, he ran his free hand over each breast and then her belly.

His mouth hung open slightly and his eyes gleamed as he followed the progress of his hand and wondered why her skin still seemed to have a warm glow despite a white moon and a star-spangled sky.

'You look beautiful,' he told her. In his mind he thought of her not just as sexy, but as sex itself. 'You are a very sexy woman,' he said at last, but didn't add what he really felt.

Crystal arched her back. Her hips lifted from the damp grass. Michael gazed at her pubic hair. As she held her pelvis high, he touched her hair and ran his fingers through it.

She was like a witch, a spell he could not escape.

'What are you waiting for?'

Michael shook his head. He pushed his finger between her sex lips and felt the warm, glistening fluid that was swiftly covering her inner flesh.

He pushed his finger into her vagina, then, all resistance gone, he gasped with delight.

He retrieved his finger from her willing portal and took a firm hold of her hips.

Above him, Crystal writhed on the grass and stretched her arms far above her head.

Bending his head, Michael kissed her nipples, her belly and the soft skin of her inner thighs.

Then slowly, patiently, as though he wanted to hear her moaning forever, he ran his tongue up each thigh, then opened her lips and sucked on the small flower of delight that nestled so secretively there.

He felt it jerk on his tongue, a small, hard nub of pure sensuality. A warm wetness transferred from her flesh to his chin, his nose and his mouth.

This was her arousal he was drinking. This was her sexuality spreading over his tongue and trickling into his throat.

Head digging into the soft, sweet-smelling grass, Crystal arched her back and the noises she made were like small shudders of delight.

Michael continued to lap at the juices that were part of her arousal and part of her sex. The tip of his tongue was like a small penis as it flicked delicately at the frills of her labia and probed more determinedly into her welcoming vagina.

'Do it there,' she cried, and reached for his head, grasping handfuls of hair and pushing him to where she wanted him to be. 'That's it! Put your tongue there! Lick me there!'

For a moment Michael thought he would suffocate. Crystal's hands were like vices either side of his head. At the same time as she held his mouth to her sex, she jerked herself upwards, her sex dividing over his nose. Her clitoris was like a piece of gravel on his tongue, her labia like warm jelly against his chin.

Faster and faster she jerked her hips and louder and louder came her cries.

'Oh, I'm coming. I'm coming!' She shouted the same words again and again, higher and higher, until they were like a thin scream coming from her throat. One last jerk of her hips and her sex against Michael's mouth, and it was at last over.

'Oh, baby,' gasped a breathless Michael as she smothered him with kisses. 'You almost suffocated me. I thought I would never breathe again. What a girl you are!'

His vision was slightly bleary as he fought to catch his breath. But Crystal's kisses felt good upon his face, and her breasts were warm against his flesh.

Almost as if they might give him some support, he grabbed hold of them before sinking back onto the grass.

'What a woman! What a beautiful bosom!'

Crystal's hair swept the grass as she threw back her head and laughed.

'Are you exhausted, honey? Am I too much for you?'

He groaned in reply.

'Never mind, Michael honey. We'll lay here a while, and then we'll get back inside and start all over again. Won't that be nice?'

'Huh, huh.' It was all he had the strength to say. His chest was still heaving as his breathing slowly went back to normal.

Crystal plonked an affectionate kiss on his nose. Her lips still tasted of penis.

'I don't mind it outside,' Crystal said in a matter-of-fact voice. 'But, like I told you before, I never was the outdoor type.'

Michael's eyes snapped open. Something about that saying jolted a memory of two people making love in a field near his office.

He took a deep breath. 'What did you say?'

'I said I'm not really the outdoor type. I did this only for you, Michael.'

'Crystal, have you ever made love in an open field?'

Long black hair fell over his chest and hid Crystal's breasts from view as she looked lovingly into his face. Then she frowned and looked thoughtful.

'We ... ll ... let me see now ...' She shook her head. 'No. I don't think so. Why do you ask?'

Is she lying, Michael asked himself? He decided she wasn't.

'No matter.' He reached for her, covered her breasts with his hands and, using them in the same way she had used his penis, he pulled her down to him.

Chapter 23

Crystal was getting petrol when she saw Jamie. At first she pretended not to notice him, but had to say 'Hi' when he came strolling up to her.

'Been to the country club?' she asked him brightly.

He shook his head. Crystal glanced over his shoulder to his car. It looked packed to the gunnels with suitcases and cardboard boxes.

Her eyes flitted between the nozzle she had stuffed in her petrol tank and the flickering numbers that were telling her she was close to filling it up. The memory of an afternoon in a hotel bedroom was still in her mind.

'I'm off,' said Jamie abruptly.

Crystal took the pressure off the petrol pump and, with a puzzled expression, glanced – but only glanced – up into his face.

'Off where?'

'I've been offered a job with Egyptian Oil. I've decided to take it.'

'Good for you. I always did like a man with a spirit of adventure.'

Without even the hint of a blush, she managed to grin at him.

Jamie tood a deep breath and stood up very straight. 'I think so. I don't think a workout at the country club, some changing-room storytelling, and a detached house complete with wife will ever be enough for me.'

Crystal stopped grinning. Her mouth fell open at the implication of what he was saying.

'Do you mean that Mariana's not going with you?'

'Absolutely not.'

Jamie's eyes did not meet hers.

'Are you two splitting up?'

'I think that would be best. I'm not really what she wants, and she no longer wants to be what I want. Besides, I think she's found her own brand of happiness.'

Crystal gaped then took a deep breath before she spoke. 'If that's the case, I'll have to go round and see . . .'

'No! No, don't do that. She's not there, you see. She's gone away . . . with a friend . . . a few months I think. We decided it would be best that way . . . for everyone.'

Jamie's mouth altered shape. It might have been a smile or it might just as easily been a grimace.

Crystal thought how pink his complexion was against the whiteness of his shirt. She stared at him, wondered if he was hurting inside and just not showing it.

Without really meaning to, without even really wanting to, she reached out and touched his arm.

'Jamie . . .'

He started.

She quickly withdrew her fingers.

'Jamie . . . look, if there's anything I can do . . .'

Without a sign of any body language whatsoever, Jamie stared her straight in the eye. 'Nothing. I told you. I know what I want. You should know it too.'

His grin was very wide. He winked.

'You should know exactly what I like and what I want.'

Crystal went pink. She stammered before she could find any word to speak. 'I'm not quite sure . . . I don't think I . . . damn it . . . I . . .'

'Don't get embarrassed, Crys. I quite understand that it's not something you usually do. But you had a reason for doing what you did that afternoon. You were angry with men and you were taking your anger out on me. I quite understand that. I understand it a lot better than I used to, you see, because my wife obliged me for the same reasons. The trouble was, I hadn't realised it. I took it for granted that she liked it too. She didn't, but I've only just found it out. No problem. We each have our own Achilles heel. No sweat.'

'No sweat,' repeated Crystal in a small voice, her mouth too dry to say anything loud.

Jamie took hold of her shoulders, leaned forward and kissed her on the cheek.

'Take care, Crystal baby.' He winked. 'Take care of yourself – and Michael.'

She stared at his broad back as he went. The petrol nozzle was still in her hands. She was not aware that her fingers were stroking the long length of silver metal. Her mind was not switched on to such a mundane matter. In her mind she was again in the humid closeness of a hotel bedroom and a man's broad bottom was growing pink because of her.

She didn't bother to fill the tank completely. Her movements became suddenly agitated. She glanced at her watch as she pushed the nozzle back into its rest. Her feet flew aross the forecourt, her fingers fumbled for her charge card.

She grabbed and paid for a can of Diet Coke before she rushed out of the service-station shop and back to her car.

One hand on the wheel, she drank her Coke, her eyes bright with thought as she considered how fast she could get the news to Michael – or even Thomas.

Thomas.

She hadn't thought about her husband for a few days, not since he'd gone away on that business trip. He was due back today and she hoped he was at home now.

The moment she arrived, she rushed into the house and

out into the conservatory where Thomas was standing dressed in only his dressing gown. It occurred to her that it was a strange time of day to be wearing a blue silk dressing gown.

'You'll never guess what,' Crystal blurted. 'Jamie's left Mariana . . .'

Her rush of words stopped abruptly the moment she realised that Thomas was not alone.

'Josie! I didn't know you were here.' She forced a smile, then noticed that Thomas and Josie were both holding wineglasses; white wine with bubbles floating around the top. Champagne!

'I was just passing. I wondered if you fancied working out.'

Josie spoke softly and smiled that calm, infuriating smile of hers.

For a moment, Crystal was taken in by it, lulled into feeling that Josie was exactly as she used to be – or rather, as she had thought her to be. Then she remembered the truth.

'That's what you say! In fact, I was on the way to the country club when I saw Jamie. I thought you would have already been there.'

There was no doubting now the exchange of looks between her husband and Josie.

A cold feeling flowed over her. She grimaced, a thing she hated doing because lines have a habit of ingraining themselves in features. But they were hard to dispel, bearing in mind their cause. No one had done this to her before. No one had played the same games with her husband that she played with theirs.

But Josie looked pretty serious. She was frowning as she put her glass of champagne down on the table before walking over to Crystal.

'Are you sure he said that?'

Crystal nodded. 'Yes. That was exactly what he said.'

Josie shook her head. 'I'm not so sure he was telling the truth.'

Crystal frowned. 'What makes you say that?'

Now it was Thomas who stepped forward. 'Josie was just telling me she'd called in to see Mariana before coming here.'

'And she said nothing?' Crystal found that incredulous and her voice echoed that view.

Josie shook her head. Worry lines creased her brow and her lips were turned downwards.

'Nothing at all. She was laughing when I called in to see her. Alex was there and they were having coffee. She offered me some too, though I did get the impression she wanted me to leave, but not because of any specific problem. I just got the impression that she and her father-in-law wanted to be alone.'

Crystal frowned and shook her head. 'I find that hard to believe. He sounded so adamant that she had gone away with a friend and that their split up would be amicable.'

'Like ours?' voiced Thomas.

Crystal blushed. Here was Thomas actually talking about the one thing that she really wanted.

'I don't now what you—'

She stopped herself. Why lie? Why pussyfoot around?

'Yes!' she exclaimed firmly. 'Yes! Just like us. An amicable arrangement!'

A glow came to Crystal's features. Suddenly, her cards were spread out on the table. There it all was for her husband and Michael's wife to see.

She took a deep breath as though a great lump had suddenly been plucked from her breast. She couldn't help smiling, couldn't help feeling proud of herself. She had done it, but the strange thing was that neither Josie nor Thomas looked in the least bit surprised.

What happened next amazed her.

Josie and Thomas moved closer together and put their

arms around each other. Josie smiled up into Thomas's face.

'The truth is out at last,' Josie exclaimed. Thomas hugged her closer and kissed the top of her head.

'I didn't know . . .' Crystal's mouth hung open. 'You and Thomas?'

Josie smiled her enigmatic smile, glanced at Crystal, then gazed again into the eyes of Thomas, the man who was now holding her more tightly to his body.

'Thomas was my first love,' Josie explained. 'Every other man I ever went to bed with had to match up to him. That first time is the criteria against which every other lover has to measure up to. Don't you think so?'

Crystal stared at the deep green eyes that looked so boldly at her. Her mouth opened and closed like a goldfish. It was hard to put what she was feeling into words. Faith in the power of her own seductive skills had made her oblivious to that of others. Now she was seeing things a little more clearly.

'I never knew,' she said quietly.

Thomas shook his head and smiled a little sadly. 'You never did see what was under your nose, Crys.'

'No.' Crystal shook her head. 'No. Perhaps I didn't.'

A calmness seemed to hang over all three of them. There was a sense of suspended time around them, as though each were suddenly contemplating exactly why none of them had spoken about this before.

But there it was, this calm, just waiting for someone to pierce it and get things into motion.

It was Josie who broke the spell.

She looked up lovingly into Thomas's eyes. He looked back down at her. Some unspoken message seemed to flash between them.

As they both looked at Crystal, they held out their arms to her. Both were smiling.

'Don't look so worried, Crystal,' said Josie.

'Come on, Crys,' Thomas added, jerking his head to indicate he wished her to join them.

Crystal stared. Was this her husband doing this? The man to whom she had never been faithful?

And Josie. Her friend? Josie whose friendship she had abused by having an affair with her husband.

Suddenly, everything seemed so unreal.

I'm sleepwalking, she told herself. *I must be sleepwalking.*

But she couldn't be. She could hear her footfall on the solid tiled floor as she walked towards them, she could feel the warm softness of their arms as they folded her to them.

'This is the way it should be,' said Josie, and kissed her cheek.

'Free up, Crys,' added Thomas, and kissed the other.

Relaxation did come to Crystal. Along with it came other feelings aroused by the fact that both Josie and Thomas's bodies were close to hers.

Why now? she asked herself. *Why now?*

Thomas had never made her feel that responsive before, yet now, here he was with another woman, and Crystal could feel her nipples hardening and a curling, folding sensation between her legs.

Suddenly, she didn't want just to be hugged by them, she wanted more. Much more.

They all began kissing each other. There was an incredible feeling in doing this, thought Crystal, as though all flesh was her flesh, and her flesh was theirs.

It was as though there was no Thomas, no Josie, and no Crystal, but only one tremendous, primeval force that once unleashed was unstoppable.

That force was now taking the three of them, moulding them together as lips kissed and hands caressed.

Crystal was aware of Thomas's silk dressing gown falling open and his penis folding it apart as he erected.

Half dizzy with ecstasy, she ran her hand down over his stomach until her fingertips met the hardness of his penis. It felt warm, it felt so much more beguiling than it had ever felt before.

Her fingers also touched those of Josie's. She too was exploring the rod of firm flesh. Briefly, their fingers touched, entwined in silent understanding, then went on their way to clasp the hot penis in the tightness of their hands.

Their hands no longer worked as of two separate women. They were now one and the same, both fired with the same desire to explore this man's body, to give him pleasure and, in return, to give themselves pleasure.

Crystal continued to grasp his penis, to jerk her hand up and down it and to feel the throb of his vein as his climax drew nearer.

As she did this, Josie stroked his balls, her fingers playing over his flesh as though she were playing a refined tune on some fantastic instrument.

Josie smiled provocatively and her dark green eyes met the blue ones of her husband's lover.

'Are you going to go down and suck him, or shall I?'

Crystal looked at her with amazement. Was she dreaming? *No,* she told herself. *No, you are not.*

She felt Josie's hand on her breast, felt her fingers undo the buttons of her crisp, white blouse.

No, she was not dreaming.

In fact, no dream could make her breast feel so warm as it came naked out of her blouse. No dream could make her nipple as hard as Josie's fingers were making it.

Crystal swallowed hard. She had a need in her to reciprocate Josie's actions.

She reached out and pulled Josie's tee shirt from her body so that her round, firm breasts bounced free.

Eyes filled with the pink and white perfection of them, Crystal reached out and touched one of her friend's nipples. Her other hand maintained a firm pull on Thomas's penis.

'Well?' asked Josie, eyebrows raised. 'Are you going to suck your husband, or shall I?'

Suddenly a fire of sheer lust, and an overwhelming need to see Thomas being sucked by someone else, came over Crystal.

'You,' she said softly.

Josie smiled.

'I hoped you might say that.'

'No,' said Thomas suddenly. 'No,' he repeated. 'I want Crystal to do it, and at the same time I want her to play with your sex.'

They both looked directly at Crystal. So aroused was she that Crystal did not protest. The whole idea was lustful, sordid even. But she couldn't help that. She wanted to do this, wanted to pleasure both as they'd never been pleasured before.

'Alright,' she said throatily. 'I'll do it.'

With that, she sank to her knees.

Thomas's penis was already near her face.

Keeping her eyes on Josie's trim white legs as she raised her skirt, Crystal took her husband's penis into her mouth and began to suck on him.

As she sucked, she stroked Josie's thighs. Josie pulled down her own knickers. A thatch of golden hair came into view. *She's right,* Crystal said to herself, *it does glisten as though it's wet.*

Immediately it came into view, her fingers reached out to touch Josie's pubic hair. It was crisp to the touch. Still sucking vigorously on Thomas's penis, she ran her fingers through the nest of hair, then pushed it into the first inch of Josie's divide.

There was a slickness there, a wet juicy slipperiness as Josie's sexual juices seeped throughout her sex and over Crystal's fingers.

Crystal closed her eyes. The smell of sex, the feel of sex was enough to inflame her ardour and make her want more of her husband's prick in her mouth, more of his mistress's juices pouring over her fingers.

This is lewd, she thought to herself. *Here I am giving my husband and his mistress pleasure, and yet I do not feel abused. Instead I feel as if I am adding an extra flavour to their relationship.*

But in that one moment, there was nothing of Thomas except for this part of him she had in her mouth. His smell was in her head and the coarseness of his pubic hair enveloped her nose. Above her, Josie and Thomas were kissing each other, lost in their love, lost in their lust.

Josie's hands were stroking Thomas's chest muscles and tangling her fingers in his light smattering of chest hair.

In return, Thomas was playing with Josie's breasts, squeezing her nipples and cupping her flesh.

There was a need in Crystal that she had never felt before. A need to give others an orgasm when she herself was getting nothing.

She would show them! An odd thought to enter her head. Why would she want to show them? Why would she want to add another dimension to their affair?

She didn't know! She didn't know and she didn't care! That was the truth of it.

She was riding an extraordinary wave of control, of sex, and of personal urgency.

The urgency was the need to make both of them come, to be their puppet master and have them orgasm because of her and not because of them.

The penis in her mouth began secreting the first of its juices.

The female sex that was warm and moist beneath her fingertips, began to tense, to tremble a shivering, shimmering effect.

But there would be more, she told herself, there would be more she could give them.

In order to do so, her tongue flicked delicately into the eyelet of Thomas's penis.

Simultaneously, she pushed her finger into Josie's vagina and consistently tapped her thumb against her clitoris.

Josie's clitoris hardened and spasmed beneath her touch. Glowing with satisfaction, Crystal added greater zeal to her ministrations until neither could resist the need to orgasm, to tremble beneath the terrible touch of Crystal's fingers.

They showered afterwards, all three of them together.

As though it was the most normal thing in the world, Thomas made coffee and they sat around the table and drank it together.

There was a silence at first and eyes seemed shy to meet eyes.

Josie, who Crystal now thought of as the boldest of their group, was the first to speak.

'We need to talk more. Think what might have been avoided if we'd all got together round the table from the very beginning.'

'True,' said Thomas and flashed a look across at Crystal. 'But it's not too late. We can still salvage something out of our various relationships. I mean, do we all want to end up like Mariana and Jamie?'

'No,' said Crystal and shook her head.

Josie frowned and put her coffee mug down on the table.

'Talking about Jamie and Mariana, what do you think about it? I mean, it does seem a bit incredulous that Mariana made no mention of Jamie leaving when I saw her at home with her father-in-law.'

Thomas frowned. 'That worries me.'

Both women looked to him for further enlightenment.

'I mean,' Thomas went on, 'Mariana would have said. Can we take it that she said nothing because Alex was there? Surely not. Alex was always close to them.'

'Especially to Mariana,' said Josie. 'She always did like the father figure. I think her own father kept her at a distance even though she adored him.'

'Or perhaps she adored him too much,' added Crystal, and the eyes of her husband and his mistress were immediately directed at her.

'Why do you say that?' It was Josie who asked her.

'Well you know,' said Crystal, directing her words at Josie. 'You were there when she talked about the Turk and the way her father pushed her away from him – as though she were trying to seduce him or something. Remember?'

Suddenly, Josie's eyes were staring. There was fear in her look.

'You don't think that . . .'

Thomas was first up from the table. 'There's only one way to find out the truth of this. I'll get dressed. Lets get over there and sort this out. Phone Michael. Tell him about it. See if he knows anything more than we do.'

It was Crystal who sprang to her feet to phone her lover.

Josie sat silently, eyes wide, mouth open, and complexion as pale as snow. It never had been of any consequence that Michael was having an affair with her friend, so it certainly was not going to matter now they all knew where they were at.

'He'll meet us over there,' said Crystal as she put the phone down.

Josie nodded.

Thomas had returned. He was dressed in cream slacks, navy sweater and sneakers. His dark eyebrows met above his nose and there was a look of anxiety in his eyes.

'I'll drive,' he said quickly, and no one argued.

240

Josie sat alongside Thomas and Crystal sat in the back seat.

They drove silently for a while, each engrossed in their own thoughts.

Josie thought how strong Thomas's fingers looked on the wheel. She had an intense impulse to touch them, to caress them and speak naughty words to him as to where he might put them later. On this occasion she would control her urges. First Mariana. Just to make sure. To make sure of what was ... She didn't know. None of them knew.

Thomas knew his knuckles were turning white, knew he was driving too fast. Every muscle in his body seemed to have turned to iron, though he couldn't quite work out why. After all, they were only going over to Jamie's place to check things out ... Or was this rigidity a simple reaction in the aftermath of the sex game with Josie and Crystal, his lover and his wife.

Crystal was staring out of the car window. She was thinking of the country club and how they had all first got together; her and Thomas. Michael and Josie, and Mariana and Jamie. Perhaps that was the problem, the catalyst. They had all met, they had all become friends. That moment had been the one to change them all, to alter the format of their relationships. It was almost as though they had each taken off their clothes and lain them aside to reveal their true selves; just as if they had entered a changing room. That's what their meeting had been, a changing room.

Her thoughts dissipated as they swung behind the bank of dark trees that hid Jamie and Mariana's house from the road.

The outside security light came on as they swung into the gravel patch between the garage and the side door of the house.

A soft blue light was shining out through the glass of the door.

Thomas was the first to reach it. He knocked. Crystal
rang the bell and Josie went round to the front window to
peer in.

'No one at home,' said Josie.

Crystal got down on her knees and opened the letter
box.

'There's a light on inside and . . . oh, my God!'

'What is it?'

Thomas pushed her away and dropped to his knees to
take her place.

The sound of running footsteps heralded Josie rushing
breathlessly back to them.

'Thomas!'

'I know!' he shouted. 'I know. This place is a mess. It
looks as though a bomb's hit it.'

'We have to call the police. We *do* have to call the
police, don't we?'

Crystal sounded frantic – and confused.

A sort of relief came to her, and also a kind of apathetic
femininity as she ran into Michael's arms. He looked
highly embarrassed as she threw her arms round his neck.

'It's alright, Michael. They know. They don't mind. It's
alright.'

He looked a little relieved, but not much. 'What's all
this about?' he asked as he restrained Crystal from plast-
ering him with kisses.

'Jamie's left Mariana,' Crystal explained, 'but Josie saw
Mariana earlier with Alex, her father-in-law, and she
made no mention of Jamie leaving. Now we've found that
the place is in a mess – as though there's been a fight or
something. We're going to have to call the police.'

'No we're not,' corrected Thomas. 'We're going to
break in and make sure everything's alright before we
make ourselves look like fools and cause unnecessary
problems for Mariana and Jamie. If they are off to try and
construct new lives for themselves, the last thing they are

going to need is the police nosing into their affairs. Can I borrow your jacket, Michael?'

Michael, without looking Thomas in the eye, took off his jacket and handed it to his friend.

Thomas wrapped it around his hand before punching it through the door.

The sound of shattering glass sounded like a bomb going off to those standing next to it, and Crystal almost shrieked.

'You'll have all the neighbours round to find out what's going on!'

'They're too far away,' muttered Thomas as he put his hand through the broken glass and turned the handle from the inside.

Soundlessly, the door opened. Their footsteps were less quiet as they trod over the broken glass and made their way into the matrimonial home of Mariana and Jamie – now parted.

'It wasn't like this when I was here earlier,' murmured Josie, hardly daring to raise her voice much above the minimum.

There was a table lamp lying on its side on the floor. It was lit.

'Security light,' explained Thomas. 'Jamie had a few of them wired up to a timing device. Good system.'

'We'll check the bedrooms,' said Josie, and jerked her head at Crystal to follow her.

Michael followed Thomas around the ground-floor rooms. He never spoke. It was for Thomas to speak or act. For Thomas to warn him off his wife or turn round and bury his fist in Michael's face. That's what Michael was expecting.

Any time, he thought to himself. *Any time he's going to spin round and break my jaw. This is all a farce, this business with Mariana and Jamie. All just a farce.*

Like Thomas, Michael stood open-mouthed when they

opened the door on one certain room at the back of the house.

'Good grief!' he exclaimed at last.

Thomas walked forward into the room. Almost with a trace of reverence, he touched the leather straps that had once bound the wrists of either Mariana or Jamie. Jamie, he decided when he saw the high leather boots and red velvet basque hung on a hanger in the corner.

'I don't think we should say too much about this room,' said Michael. 'It doesn't seem right.'

Their wives came up behind them. 'There's more of this stuff up in the wardrobe,' Josie explained.

Crystal stared. 'So this was what he meant. Jamie said something about thinking Mariana liked the same things he liked, but she didn't. Everything had changed. That's why he said he was going to work for that Egyptian oil firm. By the sound of it he reckoned he could get what he wanted out there.'

Thomas picked up some kind of iron chastity belt that had a hole at the front. He poked his finger through it. 'Too big for a finger,' said ruefully, a little sadly. 'This, I presume, was for our friend Jamie to wear. His penis and his balls were meant to be trapped through here, I should imagine.'

Crystal had hung back by the door. She crossed her arms over her chest as she looked around the room and shivered. 'So that's all there is to find. A load of kinky torture gear.'

'Sad,' said Thomas. 'Though interesting. But it doesn't explain anything. Still, we should be grateful for small mercies. There's no blood here and no dead bodies.'

'Is that what we've been looking for?' asked Michael. 'Blood and bodies? Whose bodies?'

It was his wife who put him in the picture. Josie who explained things. 'Michael, listen. Jamie said that Mariana had gone away with a friend. But I was with her this morning. She was here with Alex and made no mention of going away. We were suspicious.'

Michael shrugged and looked awkward. 'I still don't see why we're here.'

'Michael's right.' It was Thomas. 'Why don't we go over to ask Jamie's father if he knows any more than we do? We'll fix the door first. There must be some hardboard or something in the tool shed or garage.'

'Right,' said Michael. 'I'll see what I can find.'

Each of them glanced a last time around the room where Jamie had indulged in his sexual fantasies and Mariana had obliged – for whatever reason.

The headlights of a car suddenly brightened the semi-darkness.

'Mariana!' Crystal ran out along the passageway. The others followed.

Crystal stopped short at the front door.

'Who are you?' they heard her say.

'I'm Sharaz. What are you doing here? Why have you broken the glass?'

It was Thomas who explained.

Once he'd finished, Sharaz burst out laughing.

Her dark eyes flashed in the fall of light that came out of the doorway.

'Are you her lover?' Josie asked.

Sharaz stopped laughing. 'I thought I was, but I'm afraid that, like poor old Jamie, I was superseded.'

They all stared silently at her as they awaited an explanation.

Sharaz laughed again and shook her head. 'There was a Turk she remembered. I believe he took her virginity. She may have told you about him. I was a substitute for that man. But he wasn't the most important man in her life.'

'Her father,' said Josie suddenly. 'Her father was the most important man in her life!'

Sharaz nodded. 'Yes.'

Crystal frowned. 'So where is she? Why the mess in here? Did she have a fight with someone?'

Josie was shaking her head emphatically. She grabbed hold of Crystal's shoulder in an effort to add emphasis to her understanding and explanation of the situation.

'She's with Alex – Jamie's father. He's the father she wanted – in whatever way she wants him. That's what Sharaz is saying. Am I right?'

She turned to Sharaz. The girl nodded. 'Yes. That's it exactly. I've just come here to tidy up for her. She went a bit scatty when she found out that Jamie was going at last. I'm not her lover any more, but I'm still her friend.'

They stood aside to let Sharaz in. Silence hung over them as they watched her disappear down the passageway. Another change had happened and each of them was letting it sink in.

Chapter 24

After leaving the house where the glass in the back door had been broken and the contents were scattered over the floor, the four of them made their way to the country club.

'So how do we see the way forward?' asked Thomas once he'd set the drinks out on the table.

Michael hummed and hawed and made an effort to clear his throat. 'Well, Crystal and I thought—'

'About a divorce,' interrupted Crystal.

'Just like that?' said Thomas. 'You and Michael moving in together, and me and Josie doing the same.'

Michael nodded. 'Yes. Yes. That's right.'

Crystal covered his hand with hers. Blinking a trifle nervously, he glanced at her and smiled before staring back at his drink.

Josie had been sitting quietly.

'What's the point?' she said suddenly.

They all looked at her.

She sat up straight and brushed her hair back from her eyes.

'What's the point? Does it matter where each of us live? Does it matter if one of us lives with one, and one with the other? Who's to say we can't interchange? You must admit, Crystal, that was a pretty good threesome we had.'

Josie looked directly at her friend. Crystal blushed and Michael frowned because he had no idea what anyone was talking about.

'In fact,' Josie added, 'why can't we make it a foursome

on occasions? Just think of how exciting that would be.'

Michael stared.

Crystal still blushed.

A slow smile spread over Thomas's face. Suddenly, he burst out laughing.

'You didn't mean it?' Michael sounded confused.

'Of course she means it!' Thomas shook his head in disbelief. 'Don't you see? She's right. Josie is absolutely right. Just think of the fun we can have. Sometimes Josie can be with me, and sometimes with you – especially useful in your business career. And the same with Crystal. Sometimes with you and sometimes with me.'

'And other times, all four of us can share a house, a room, a bed,' added Josie, her eyes shining with enthusiasm. 'Come on. What do you think?'

Michael, so masculine, so quick to boast of his conquests and outstanding virility, stammered as he fought to find the right words.

Crystal, who had made a career out of being vivacious, sexual and highly desirable, licked at the dryness of her lips and felt a sudden moistness seeping between her legs.

Michael looked at Crystal, and Crystal fluttered her eyelashes as the rationality of the situation became more clear.

'Let's do it!' Crystal's face was suddenly a picture of sexual intent. 'Just imagine how it could be. Oh, Michael! You cannot believe how incredible it was with both Thomas and Josie. Really it was!'

Michael stared. 'You did it with both of them?'

Eyes bright, Crystal nodded. 'Yes. Both of them.'

Michael gulped. 'Yes!' he exclaimed at last. 'Yes! Why not!' And he began to laugh.

Adult Fiction for Lovers from Headline LIAISON